OUR SPACE, OUR PLACE

*Women in the Worlds of
Science Fiction Television*

Sherry Ginn

Illustrations by Louise S. Napier

D1528253

University Press of America,® Inc.
Lanham · Boulder · New York · Toronto · Oxford

Copyright © 2005 by
University Press of America,® Inc.
4501 Forbes Boulevard
Suite 200
Lanham, Maryland 20706
UPA Acquisitions Department (301) 459-3366

PO Box 317
Oxford
OX2 9RU, UK

Library of Congress Control Number: 2005924775
ISBN 0-7618-3215-7 (paperback : alk. ppr.)

For daddy,

Freddie I. Ginn (1929 – 2004)

Love always

Contents

List of Tables

List of Illustrations

Preface

The seed for this book was planted when I saw a copy of *STARLOG* magazine with Tracy Scoggins and Jeri Ryan on the cover under the title "Babes in Spaceland."[1] While both are beautiful women, the characters they portrayed were more than that, or at least they were supposed to be.[2] Since I was looking for a topic for my next SEWSA[3] conference and since I watched the programs in which both of these actors appeared, I thought "bingo!" The rest is history. I presented a paper on women in sci fi TV that year and have continued the trend (Ginn, 2000; 2002a; 2002b; 2004). The papers were well received and invariably someone would come up to me afterwards and say, somewhat guiltily, that they too liked science fiction, as if it were a social disease. As I did more research about women as depicted in science fiction, I discovered that colleagues used science fiction novels as supplementary texts in their women's studies and psychology courses. I am quite well known now around campus as the professor who shows movies in class, so I adopted the tactic of using science fiction stories and novels in my classes as well.[4]

What I most love about science fiction is the variety found in the storylines; I contend that science fiction allows the most creativity of any genre currently on television. The characters exhibit a variety of personality characteristics ranging from altruistic to zealous. Some are good and some are evil. While I do not particularly like the terms, because of the history associated with them, some of these women[5] are what would be considered traditionally feminine and some are more masculine. Luckily, not many of them are so stereotypical. Gone are the days of the 1950s movies in which women went into space: they might have been scientists of one type or the other but usually only served the coffee.[6] We rarely observed them doing anything more scientific than boiling water. Such is not the case in the new science fiction. As Claudia Black, who plays Officer Aeryn Sun on *Farscape*, explained: "To be someone of my age and to be confident is a blessing that has come with time, and the women that have come before me in television and real life. I don't think Aeryn would have been possible without archetype roles like Xena. Science fiction is a genre where strong women survive."[7] I second that sentiment and would add the word "thrive" as well.

I believe part of the reason is the current crop of writers, directors, producers, actors, and of course, fans. These women have come a long way from the time when writers such as Dorothy Fontana had to hide their gender behind initials when publishing their stories, since as everyone knew women did not like or read sci fi![8] Today's professionals and fans were exposed to ground-breaking science fiction, such as *Star Trek® The Original Series*, which showcased Gene Roddenberry's vision of the future, where all humans were equal and good. During a time of civil unrest, the Enterprise's crew was racially and sexually integrated, and children watching this program, such as myself, could envision a future far removed from the memory of nuclear terror and race riots. Female characters became more common and less stereotypical into the 1970s, culminating in the butt-kicking Ripley in *Alien* and its sequels.[9] People currently involved with science fiction television grew up during the turbulent 1960s or later. They learned the lessons that their mothers and sisters taught them about women's rights and human rights, and these lessons are reflected in much of science fiction today. If the Women's Movement was about giving women the choice to be whoever or whatever they wanted, then the current crop of science fiction reflects that right, as will be discussed in detail in the coming chapters.

The purpose of this book is to examine the female characters as portrayed in four popular science fiction television programs of the past few decades. I will discuss the programs in approximate chronological order. First I will discuss Dr. and Special Agent Dana Scully of *The X-Files*. Then I will present information on all of the women on *Babylon 5*, while concentrating on the 2 major characters, Ambassador Delenn and Commander Susan Ivanova. Next I will discuss all of the women on *Farscape*, concentrating on Officer Aeryn Sun. Finally I will discuss all of the women on Gene Roddenberry's *Andromeda*, Captain Beka Valentine, Trance Gemini, and Rommie. In addition, I will discuss the women found on the 5 *Star Trek®* programs of the last (almost) 40 years; however, the discussion of these will not be as detailed as the other 4 primarily because so much has already been written about *Star Trek®*.

I will first summarize the storyline and introduce the characters for each program. Then I will discuss the female characters in terms of their roles within the program, their relationships with the other characters, and their involvement in the quest for a personal identity. To do this I will present information on the characters' history as well as information on their relationships with other characters, using episodes from each series and published interviews with the actors to illustrate their understanding of their characters. I will discuss each woman with respect to her relationship with other characters in the series and, more importantly, with us. I will also discuss ways in which women's search for identity is illustrated by these characters. As Cioffi (1985) states, "Women, are, at this time, engaged in a massive search for themselves. Perhaps this is why fantasy and science fiction have emerged as such a dominant voice for feminist thought; it may be the way to find us" (p. 92). Each of the programs I have chosen to discuss in this book has, at its core, the search for self. If science fiction has been noted for providing a backdrop against which adolescent boys can achieve a sense of masculinity (Sheen, 1991), it is no less a background for adolescent girls and women to explore their identity and find a space and a place to call their own.

§

Several comments are in order here. First, I apologize to any author whose work I have not cited in text or used as a reference. I first conceived this project in 1999. I have been searching the literature for sources since that date. Because I am an academician, I mostly use peer-reviewed sources. That means someone with expertise in the field reviewed the paper in question before publication. It is a humbling experience and most people hate it, but acknowledge that the resulting paper is better than the original. The other reason we subject ourselves to peer-review is convention (it's always been done that way!) and to protect the public from fraudulent science, plagiarism, etc., and usually it works. However, just perusing the Bibliography will inform you that I did not always use such references. Nevertheless, I have tried to find everything written on the issue of women and/in science fiction. And, there's the rub. If you have published a paper in a non-peer-reviewed source AND it was not indexed in one of the many databases available via my library AND you did not use the words "women and/in science fiction" somewhere in the article, then I did not find it. I am very sorry. Please send me a copy.

Second, you will notice that I use both in-text references as well as footnotes. Psychologists use in-text references in their scholarly work and only list references that are actually used when writing. My students do not seem to be able to grasp this concept, at least in the beginning, since a reference list and a Bibliography are two different things. A Bibliography contains all sources whether cited in text or not. Thus my Bibliography contains all of the sources that I read in preparation for writing this book. It contains books on the topics of women and science fiction, identity development, feminism, criticism, and the programs discussed herein. It also contains peer-reviewed journal articles, book chapters, book reviews, and articles from the popular press. It does not contain everything ever written on the topics above. It would be hundreds of pages long if so! Nor does it contain everything I read. Footnotes are included throughout each chapter when additional information about a topic is warranted. Websites are only listed in text and not in the Bibliography.

Third, I am prejudiced. There, I said it! As a scientist and a psychologist I was taught to be an objective observer of human behavior. In my other research I am. But this book was written more as a labor of love for the subject matter. I hope it will become clear why I chose this subject, why I chose to write this book, and why I chose these programs. Be forewarned however that much as I love the programs I am discussing here, I will be critical. I will not be a cheerleader, and I will state my opinion. After all, it's my book.

Last, I will enjoy myself in this endeavor and try not to put you or myself to sleep. That means that I am writing this book as if you and I were sitting at the local watering hole discussing these programs and these ideas. That means hopefully none of that academic writing that can put you to sleep faster than the best sleeping pill on the market. I am not trying to insult your intelligence here, but I am writing this book for everyone to enjoy, as much for the fan of sci fi who does not have a PhD in literature or psychology or popular culture as for the one who does. So if this book sounds "folksy," it was meant to.

No project of this scope or magnitude occurs in a vacuum, and this one was certainly no exception. I am indebted to all of the people who attended presentations I have given on this topic and the comments and helpful suggestions that they have made. Furthermore, I would like to thank all of my colleagues who discussed the programs and characters that are profiled in this book. Specifically I would like to thank Drs.

Marion Eppler, a Trekker from way back, John Lutz, who introduced me to *Babylon 5*, and Marie Farr, who made me rethink Delenn, all of East Carolina University. My sister, Bonnie Harper, is an X-Phile; we had great fun discussing the "monster-of-the-week" episodes, and we both liked Doggett much more than Mulder. Colleagues at Wingate University who were especially helpful were: Drs. Greg Bell, Brian Odom, Aaron Culley, and Wyndom Whynot, all victims of sci-fi-itis. I also had great discussions with Dr. Matt DeForrest, of Johnson C. Smith University. Several colleagues provided valuable assistance by reading and critiquing specific chapters.[10] Each is noted in the particular chapter. Finally I would like to thank my husband, Larry Williamson, for encouraging me in everything I do and for keeping me laughing.

This book is dedicated to my father, who died while I was writing it. While not a fan of sci fi, he watched *Star Trek®* with me every week during the 1960s. He helped me find my own identity because he always encouraged me to be the best I could be. He supported me in everything I ever did. He was my cheerleader and my hero. I cannot even begin to tell you how much I miss him.

Notes

1. Cover feature: Babes in Spaceland. *STARLOG: The Science Fiction Universe* (1998, April). This issue contains interviews by Ian Spelling with Jeri Ryan, "The Lady Borg" (pp. 27 – 31) and Tracy Scoggins, "Captain Courageous" (pp. 41 - 43).

2. Unfortunately things have not changed very much. *Starburst* published a *Star Trek* Special (No. 45) with a cover "The Babes of Trek." Later, Ian Atkins presented an article entitled "SF Babes," with the tag "Post-Feminist Irony," in *Starburst Yearbook 2000*, Special No. 46, pp. 28 – 39. A recent issue (2004, April) of *Sci Fi, the Official Magazine of the Sci Fi Channel* contained an article, with pictures, of the "25 sexiest women in sci fi."

3. SEWSA stands for the Southeastern Women's Studies Association. We have meetings annually at a college or university located in our region (AL, MS, GA, FL, SC, NC, VA, TN). References for the papers to which I refer can be found in the Bibliography. For those of you who are not academics a word of explanation is necessary. Most people in academia specialize within their fields. So, for example, although I am a psychologist, I am actually an experimental psychologist, whose specialization is in behavioral neuroscience (how the central nervous system directs behavior). But I have other interests as well (obviously). I attend meetings every year with people who share my interests.

At these meetings, we learn about what people at other institutions are doing in their fields. It is usually great fun—we see old friends, meet new ones, get ideas for new projects, form collaborations, lament society, sightsee in new places, and eat lots of good food. It is an opportunity to present our work and get feedback and criticism.

4. I use a variety of movies in my classes, depending upon which class I am teaching at the time. So for example, in my cognitive psychology class, I show *Momento* (2000; Writer/Director Christopher Nolan; available from Columbia Tristar). Lips (1990) used novels by Ursula K. Le Guin and Marge Piercy in her classes. I have used those as well as Mary Shelley's *Frankenstein*. See also Cooper, 1977, for more resources.

5. For lack of a better word, I will use the terms woman/women to refer to the female characters on these television programs. While I realize that women are humans and the characters I am discussing are not necessarily women, since they are not human, I do not want to constantly type "female characters" nor do I want to keep using the term female, since the American Psychological Association's guidelines state that the word female is to be used an adjective and not as a noun. *The Oxford Desk Dictionary* also lists female as an adjective. So I am aware, for example, that Aeryn is not a woman but a female Sebacean; however, I will revert to using the term woman for simplicity's sake. I recognize the frustration inherent in the fact that English does not have genderless pronouns and other ways to refer to women and men, as many women before me have noted (see for example, Le Guin, 1976).

6. One example is *The Angry Red Planet* (1959), directed by Ib Melchior. A woman scientist is a member of the crew on a spaceship bound for Mars. She does occasionally look in the microscope, but mostly she is there to serve the men.

7. Sloan, J. (2001, April). Inside their minds: Starbytes. *Starburst Special*, No. 47, 13 - 17.

8. But, not too far. Dorothy Fontana still uses the initials D. C. And, one of psychologist Alice B. Sheldon's pseudonyms is James Tiptree, Jr.; the other is Raccoona Sheldon.

9. Ridley Scott directed *Alien* (1979). To date there have been 3 sequels: *Aliens, Alien 3*, and *Alien Resurrection*. All 4 films starred Sigourney Weaver as Ripley.

10. I am grateful to my friend and colleague, Dr. Brooke McLaughlin, Department of English, Wingate University, for her helpful comments on this section.

Chapter 1: *Psychology and Women*

Psychology is defined as the scientific study of behavior and mental processes, and 5 perspectives have been developed to explain the origin of both (a more complete description of each perspective can be found in Tavris and Wade, 2002).[1] Your personality is reflected in both: you are who you are, having thought of and about whom you are from a very early age. Those thoughts then manifest themselves in your actions. Whether you have ever taken an academic course in psychology is not the issue, as a human being you have acted as a "naïve scientist and psychologist" throughout your life as you attempted to figure out why others act the way that they do. We all want explanations for others behavior, but we also want explanations for our own as well. Before I discuss the specific issues about the psychology of women as presented in the sci fi TV of the last decade or so, I will briefly introduce you to the beliefs that psychologists have about the underlying causes of behavior and mental processes. Then I will specifically discuss these perspectives with respect to gender and identity.

Why do you act that way?

The Biological Perspective. Psychologists who attempt to explain behavior and mental processes from this perspective reduce both activities to biology. They believe that our behavior and mental activity are products of the working of our brains: the mind is what the brain does. Thus, all human activity can be reduced to the biochemical transmission of information within our nervous system. And, the working of our nervous system is predicated on our genetic heritage. We inherit the blueprint of our very existence from our parents. The genes contained within our cells are composed of DNA that in turn codes the proteins that compose our teeth, skin, hair, nails, nerves, etc. Abnormalities in the genetic blueprint may translate into abnormal behavior or abnormal mental processes.

Belief in the biological perspective has both positive and negative consequences. Belief that there are biological abnormalities as a cause of abnormal behavior presupposes that if one can only find the cause of the abnormality then one can also find the cure. When this view gained popularity in the mid-18th century, the mentally ill finally gained advocates for treatment rather than imprisonment. However, reducing behavior to biology inevitably led many people to search for biological differences between the sexes and races in order to demonstrate the "superiority" of the white man and perpetuate discrimination, imperialism, and capitalism.

The Behavioristic Perspective. The behavioral revolution occurred in psychology in 1913 with the publication of John B. Watson's *Psychology as the Behaviorist Sees it.* Watson was greatly excited by the work being conducted by Ivan Pavlov and his students in Russia. Pavlov had demonstrated that behavior could be learned through association and that learning could occur without conscious awareness. In Pavlov's classical experiment dogs were conditioned to salivate to the sound of a tuning fork that signaled the arrival of food. Simply pairing the sound of the tuning fork with the food in close temporal contiguity resulted in the establishment of a conditioned salivary response to the sound of the tuning fork alone. One hundred years of research have since shown that neutral events in the environment can become conditioned to innately reinforcing stimuli through a simple process of timing. Pavlovian conditioning can explain why certain perfumes "turn us on" and others repulse us. It can explain why we are afraid of dark, enclosed places or furry puppies. It can explain why drug and food addictions are so difficult to cure.

BF Skinner, one of the most prominent 20th-century American psychologists, demonstrated the importance of rewarding behavior. Skinner referred to this process as positive reinforcement and discovered that behaviors that are reinforced on intermittent schedules of reinforcement are highly resistant to extinction. In other words, actions in which organisms engage that are occasionally reinforced are difficult to extinguish. The parent who only occasionally praises their child for hard work will find that the child only occasionally works hard. While psychologists do not believe in the value of punishment in attempting to change behavior, partial punishment is nevertheless a very real phenomenon. So, the child that is occasionally punished for swearing will quickly learn when to swear, when friends reinforce him or her, and when not to swear, when mom or dad is around to punish. This is referred to as stimulus discrimination and is a very important part of the learning process. Skinner referred to operant conditioning as the ABCs of behavior: antecedents lead to behavior, which has consequences.

Many psychologists however were not completely comfortable trying to explain human behavior, or even the behavior of other animals, without mentioning the organism itself as an active participant in the process. Albert Bandura proposed that organisms could also learn by observing the behavior of others and the consequences of that behavior. Observing a powerful and attractive model engaging in behavior that is reinforced makes us want to engage in that same activity so that we can reap the same rewards. Bandura was quite aware that both prosocial and antisocial behavior could be modeled. Those who protest against sexually explicit lyrics in music or violence on television certainly believe that behavior can be modeled.

The Cognitive Perspective. Bandura's theory was proposed several years before the beginning of the so-called cognitive revolution in psychology, which occurred in the 1970s. Nevertheless, Bandura's theory had a distinctive cognitive "feel" to it. That is, Bandura was aware that people could be consciously aware of their observations of others and *think* about the consequences of their actions. The cognitive revolution signaled that it was okay to study what went on between the organism's ears. Thus, cognitive psychologists viewed human beings as active in the construction of themselves. We can act in certain ways, observe how those actions affect others, and then consciously decide to discard or keep that action. So, if I am ridiculed for spiking my hair and dying it purple, I will quickly wash and return to normal. However, if I am praised for such actions, then I will proudly wear my hair in purple spikes.

Cognitive psychologists are particularly interested in how thought develops and note the ways in which children and adolescents' thought processes differ from those of adults. The ways in which adults think is more logical than that of children. Furthermore, cognitive psychologists study the components of thought and how these components interact to produce complex behavior. Finally the cognitive perspective emphasizes the role that memory plays in producing our perceptions of the world, which in turn guide our behavior. Clinical psychologists who practice from a cognitive perspective believe that faulty thought processes underlie mental illness and psychopathology.

The Sociocultural Perspective. The newest perspective in psychology reflects the importance of social and cultural factors when attempting to explain behavior. It only took psychology about 100 years to admit that the experiences of women and men might be different from each other. This perspective would state that sex and gender are two different but linked terms. Sex is defined biologically: you are male or female depending upon which sex chromosomes you possess and gender refers to the psychological perspective you have of being male or female. Sociocultural psychologists believe that you learn your gender; it is a product of the environment in which you are raised, in other words gender is socially and culturally constructed. Thus, we hope that if we can change our cultural expectations about what constitutes male or female, we can change people's attitudes and behaviors of what it means to be male or female. For example, some people believe that the sex hormones women release monthly result in irrational behavior, which has long been considered pathological, and for this reason, women cannot hold positions of authority. After all, if a woman were President and she had PMS, she might get so irrational and pissed off, that she would nuke Miami. Rarely, if ever, does anyone mention the daily fluctuations in male sex hormones, which reach their highest level in the early morning. So if our male President woke up with a painful erection from his too-high testosterone and didn't have time to relieve himself, might he not also nuke Miami? Of course not! {But I did read of one wit who suggested that peace treaties should never be negotiated in the early morning since all of the men at the bargaining table would be at their most hostile.}

Sociocultural psychologists would also be interested in examining how other people influence your behavior, positively and negatively. Thus, social psychologists would study group dynamics and how group pressure produces compliance and conformity as well as deindividuation and groupthink. They would be interested in examining violence and aggression and how the social group in which one is raised affects the development and expression of both. As you can see sociocultural psychologists believe that many of the behaviors in which men and women engage are socially, rather than biologically, constructed.

The Psychodynamic Perspective. Actually the psychodynamic perspective predates the others and was conceived by Sigmund Freud. Basically, Freud believed forces of which you were unaware govern your behavior, and these forces lie within a part of the personality called the unconscious. Consciousness itself is composed of 3 parts: the conscious (that of which you are aware), the preconscious (that of which you could become aware if necessary), and the unconscious. Although you are unaware of the forces operating within your unconscious, these instincts and drives attempt to "escape" into awareness, via slips-of-the-tongue and dreams. Furthermore, Freud believed that the consciousness contains 3 components. The id contains primitive sexual and aggressive energy; you are born with an id. The ego develops as you are socialized to behave in accordance with the demands of society. If the id seeks self-gratification, the ego arises in order to aide the id in its desires. Finally the superego develops as you are taught the difference between "right" and "wrong." So, I might crave a hot fudge sundae tonight. It is my ego's job to find me some place open selling hot fudge sundaes and figure out if I have the money to buy it. But, it is my superego's job to chant, "a moment on the lips is a lifetime on the hips." Another colorful picture illustrating the interaction of these 3 components is a person with a demon and an angel sitting on each shoulder, trying to tell him or her what to do. The ego and superego develop via socialization by parents and because it is a painful process, most of us are quite messed up by the time we are adults. Because of the heavy burden laid on parents by Freudian theory and its emphasis on sexual energy as a motivating force, several theorists throughout the 20th century have modified Freud's theory. In addition, Freud's theory was also not very complimentary to women, as discussed in more detail below.

Tell me about yourself

Personality itself refers to the relatively enduring traits and dispositions that characterize a person; it is the distinctive character of a person and some synonyms for it include: nature, temperament, disposition, persona, and identity (*Oxford Desk Dictionary and Thesaurus*, 1997). Some psychologists believe that personality is fairly stable across the lifespan of the individual, whereas others believe that it is not. First let me briefly[2] introduce you to the prevailing theories that have been proposed to explain how the personality develops, concentrating on two specific aspects of the self: gender and identity. The two are intricately interwoven in our society, with children being gendered even before birth, which, in turn, shapes societal expectations of the child as soon as that gender is published, and that shapes the child, etc.

Each of the perspectives previously introduced attempts to explain how the personality develops. Thus, the biological perspective states that we are *born with* our personalities and there are data to support this argument. Babies are born with a particular temperament that apparently colors how they interact with their caregivers and vice versa. That is, some babies are born more easy-going and relaxed than others. Not surprisingly these infants elicit more affection from their parents. Unfortunately, some babies are not as easy-going. They are considered to be difficult and hard to warm-up. They do not like to be held and cry in response. Not surprisingly, parents report more dissatisfaction with such infants. After all, if you believe that your child will love you unconditionally, as so many people erroneously believe, and it cries every time you pick it up, then you are going to be quite upset.

However, just because a baby is born with a particular disposition does not necessarily mean that it will stay that way. The behavioristic perspective states that the *environment shapes development* and thus even a difficult baby can learn to show affection for its parents. And, even easy-going babies raised in the wrong environment may grow up to be hostile and mean adults. Furthermore, because parents control their children's environments to a great extent when the child is young, parents shape their children's behavior. To use the oft-used argument, children who are raised in abusive homes may exhibit abusive behaviors when they themselves are parents,[3] that is, they are exhibiting a learned behavior. But not all abused children grow up to be abusive parents. Some of these children make conscious decisions not to be abusive parents. They remember what it was like, they think about how they did not like it, they think about the terror and the danger, they think about how unhappy they were in such an environment, and they make the decision to be better parents than their own. In other words, they have used their own *cognitive abilities* to alter their lives. Thus examination of our own attitudes and behaviors can lead us to counter the *socialization pressure* effected by our parents, our biology, and our culture.

Let me give you a personal example. I am southern, born and bred. I lived in the same city from the time I was 2 weeks old until I left for graduate school at 25, and I have only ever lived in the South. I love the South, even the bad parts. I remember white-only and colored-only drinking fountains and restrooms. I remember once when I asked to go swimming and was told we couldn't swim in the river anymore. Years later I realized that we couldn't swim in the river anymore because of integration: we would have had to swim with Black people. As I grew older I began to read more and think more until I realized that racism was wrong, not just socially but morally as well. I overcame the racism that I had been taught by the society in which I lived; my attitudes changed and so did my behavior. I grew beyond the social norms of my culture, which thankfully are very different now in the New South.

Thus I can examine the influences of the behavioristic, the cognitive, and the sociocultural perspectives on my own behavior with respect to racism (and all of the other –isms as well). Most of these – isms, such as racism, ageism, and sexism, are predicated on biology. That is, some are taught that biology is destiny. So, the sociocultural prejudice against Blacks in America rests upon the biological assumption that Blacks are inferior to Whites. And the same argument is used for discriminating against women: that women are biologically inferior to men. Both arguments neglect to account for the fact that a woman or person of color might be exposed from birth to an environment hostile to their development.

Is that a boy or a girl?

The issue of gender pervades this book: after all, it is about women and sci fi television. So first, let me introduce you to the issue of sex and gender with respect to psychology and feminism (I will discuss feminism in the next chapter). Sex is the term we use to distinguish people on the basis of their chromosomal pattern. Men carry the XY pattern and women carry the XX pattern.[4] A series of complex interactions, involving the sex chromosomes (X and Y) and the sex hormones (the androgens and estrogens), beginning at the 3rd week prenatal and culminating around the 12th week prenatal, determines whether a child will be born male or female. Usually all goes well and the child is born with external genitalia that match his or her chromosomes, with the appropriate internal genitalia as well. Based upon the appearance of the external genitalia the child is proclaimed a boy or a girl, and enters into a world where all aspects of its life will be gendered. Given that we can now determine the child's sex well before birth, we can also gender the child prior to its entry into our world.

Gender is the term we use to refer to the psychological experience of being male or female in our world. Since gender is considered to be socially and culturally constructed, gender role expectations vary depending upon the culture in which a child is born. Our society is much less rigid in its gender role expectations than it once was. I have certainly seen many changes in my lifetime. Nevertheless men and women are still constrained to act in ways that are appropriate for their gender and are considered abnormal if they do not. For example, girls can still be "tomboys," but boys can never be "sissies."

And that leads me to the ways in which women have been defined throughout history, as the anti-man. Men have been considered the normative standard since the beginnings of written history and the tradition of defining women in terms of men continues even to this day, much to the dismay of women. Glancing through medical, law, religious, literary, and other books throughout the ages will give you an idea of the contempt with which women have been held throughout history. Even though women have been relegated to the home and deemed only worthy of bearing and rearing children, they were vilified for being silly, unintelligent, talkative, untrustworthy, wanton, (keep filling in the blanks with demeaning and insulting adjectives). It makes you wonder why men would have trusted their children to women!

Unfortunately psychology was no different and psychologists have spent inordinate amounts of time, money and energy attempting to show that women are inferior to men and thus not worthy of having jobs or careers, satisfactory sex lives, choice in whether to have children or not, the right to vote, the right to make their own decisions regarding finances, medical treatment, etc. A look at all 4 editions of the *Diagnostic and Statistical Manual*, prepared by the American Psychiatric Association, will show you that more and more diagnoses related to women have been added with each additional revision. So, did you know that if you have any of the following symptoms, irritability, tension, headache, difficulty concentrating, and loss of interest in activities, within the last 30 days and you are a woman who still menstruates, that you might "suffer" from premenstrual dysphoric disorder (PMDD)? Even though men are just as likely as women to report these symptoms, if women report them, then they can be diagnosed as suffering from PMDD.[5]

There are many, many negative stereotypes about women. Stereotypes refer to thoughts and cognitive reactions that do not necessarily correspond with reality (Matlin, 1996). Thus gender stereotypes are organized sets of beliefs about the characteristics of women and men (p. 30). A negative stereotype may lead to a negative attitude, which is the definition of prejudice, and that in turn may lead to discrimination, which involves negative actions toward women or men. So the stereotype that women are physically weak leads to the attitude that women cannot handle certain jobs, which then keeps them from being hired. Examining the many stereotypes about women will quickly make you realize that these descriptors are mostly negative. If you then compare female stereotypes with male stereotypes you will find that they are frequently mirror images, with the male characteristic being positively valued, or considered normal, and the female characteristic being negatively valued, or abnormal. Examples of the negative descriptors about women are: gentle, kind, emotional, weak, loud, dreamy, modest, gullible, fickle, nervous, talkative. So how do we become gendered? Just consider each of the perspectives previously mentioned. The biological perspective would say that sex and gender are synonymous. That is, you are born either female or male and both sex and gender are biologically determined. If women are weak it is because they were born that way—their chromosomes have dictated how their bodies will develop and since female chromosomes are different from males' then women must be different from men. Plus, female brains are hardwired differently from male brains and that also affects the ways in which the two sexes act. What this perspective leaves out is that environment can modify biology. It also leaves out the fact that the overlap in abilities between women and men is much bigger than the difference in ability. For example, the average IQ is 100. Some men have IQs higher than 100 and some have IQs lower than 100. The same is true for women. Nevertheless the majority of people score around 100, with only a few people scoring at the extremes of intellectual ability and the people scoring at the extremes are just as likely to be female as male. And, the same holds true for every characteristic you can think of, and yes that goes for strength and speed as well.[6]

Environmental influences on gender are very pervasive and sometimes very insidious. Nevertheless, our environments shape who we are. As mentioned before, our parents control our environments, especially when we are very young. Parents may reward a child for engaging in gender-stereotypical ways, or they may reward their child for engaging in gender-neutral ways. What parents will quickly learn is that even when they attempt to teach their children that gender does not matter, they will find the children themselves perpetuating gender stereotypes, leaving the parent shaking their head and wondering where the child learned such rubbish. Well, just look at how gendered our media are! Women's magazines are filled with advertisements for beauty products and diet-aides. Men's magazines are filled with half-naked or naked women in sexually provocative poses. Music videos are increasingly sexist, with female characters posed in positions of subordination to the male characters. Television commercials show women worrying about cleaning the house, dieting, or debating feminine hygiene products. Men are doing things (more about this later). Newspapers devote more column space to writing about men, except on the women's or family pages. The list goes on and on. Thus, children are exposed to our culture with its gendered messages. They are reinforced for acting in gender-appropriate ways. They learn their lessons well, or they suffer ridicule, or worse. Some gradually learn that they can change those gendered perceptions and prejudices; some do not. Some are able to define themselves beyond their gender. That is, some are able to go beyond gender and develop identities that encompass all of their personality traits, not just the ones related to their sex.

Who are you? What do you want?

So for many people the key to life is determining who they are, what they want, where are they going, and what it all means. Psychologists also study this desire to know who we are, this drive to construct a self, a persona, an essence. Part of the difficulty lies in simply defining these terms, as each definition uses the terms themselves: thus, self is defined as persona and persona is defined as identity! Nevertheless psychologists have attempted to explain how we define our self, our persona, and our essence and how we come to know who we are, if we ever do that is. As before we can discuss the development of identity in terms of psychological perspectives on how human beings develop their behavior and mental processes.

Thus, the biological perspective would attempt to state that we are born with a sense of self. But we know that that is not true. Children really do not develop a sense of self until they are about 18 months of age. Not surprisingly this is also around the time that they begin to use language and especially to signify "I." Furthermore, if identity were biologically constructed, we should not have to continually think about it. However, this perspective would emphasize the importance of biology in defining our gender identity. But doesn't biology interact with our social environment and our reinforcement histories to influence our gender? Since we know that the answer to that question is yes, then it stands to reason that our identity, beyond our gender, also develops as social and cultural forces interact with reinforcers we have received throughout our lives from those important to us, in conjunction with the beliefs that we develop about our identity. I believe that any attempt to explain identity formation by excluding any of the perspectives will be incomplete. All are necessary for an adequate explanation of identity formation. Nevertheless, I wish to discuss some of the psychodynamic theories that have been proposed to explain identity formation. You will notice that they do have many features in common with the other perspectives, even though in some respects they predate some of the perspectives proposed in the latter portion of the 20th century.

Psychoanalytic theory. Freud's theory of personality development was as controversial as the other parts of his theory when first proposed in the late 19th century. Freud proposed that the personality developed in a series of stages, 4 to be exact. The first stage is referred to as the oral stage and lasts through the first year or so of life. In this stage, in which the id predominates, the child's pleasure centers on the mouth. Children certainly take nourishment through the mouth, but they also use their mouths to explore and to aggress. Anyone who has ever been around babies will note how quickly objects enter their mouths, and also how quick they are to bite.

The second stage, lasting from approximately 18 months to 3 years, is referred to as the anal stage and pleasure centers on the anus. Children at this stage of life begin toilet training, learning how to control their bodily functions. Relaxing and contracting the bowel and bladder sphincters yield pleasurable sensations and the child enjoys these sensations. And yet, the child quickly learns how important these functions are to the parents, receiving praise or punishment depending upon the outcome of elimination. They also quickly learn that they can control these functions and use them as punishers of their parents. Any parent who has anxiously awaited their child's bowel movements, only to have the child finally comply after entering church, or the movie, or the restaurant, etc. will understand what I mean.

But, it is the third stage that is the most controversial of Freud's stages. This stage is referred to as the phallic stage and it lasts from about 3 to 5 years. The two controversial aspects of the stage are the Oedipal complex with its castration anxiety, experienced by male children, and the Electra complex with its penis envy, experienced by female children. The Oedipal complex occurs when male children desire to possess their mothers and eliminate their fathers from competition. However, fathers are much bigger than little children and are not about to relinquish their wives to their children. The little boy experiences anxiety as he realizes that his father could hurt him badly and one method by which the father could harm the child would be to castrate him. Thus, if the little boy lost his source of masculinity, his mother would not want him. The little boy is quite aware of how important a penis is and realizes that the only way to keep his intact is to renounce his mother and identify with this father. In effect the little boy learns that "if you can't beat 'em, join 'em." As he identifies with his father, he incorporates personality characteristics possessed by his father and other male figures into his own personality. His superego, or conscience, develops as his identification with his father proceeds.

Young girls on the other hand wish to eliminate their mothers and possess their fathers. Yes, this may manifest in seductive behavior toward the father (but is no excuse for child sexual abuse). Actually the reason that girls want their fathers is because daddy has what they don't, a penis. They reject their mothers because mom does not possess that all-important penis. But, the young girl must eventually come to terms with the fact that she can never possess a penis, she is a woman, and must identify with her mother, always desirous of possessing the male organ. Because her anxiety over not possessing a penis is never fully resolved, women's superego does not develop as well as does a man's. Thus according to Freud, women are not as moral as are men. And, now you can see why Freud is not very well liked by a lot of psychologists and feminists. (Following the phallic stage, children undergo a latency period in which their sexual and aggressive energies are dormant. When they reach puberty, they enter into the genital stage in which sexual energy focuses on the sex organs and the child becomes a sexual being.)

Freud certainly revolutionized the way that psychology, neurology, and psychiatry perceived personality development. His influence has survived well over 100 years and many Freudian terms have entered into the modern vernacular: id, ego, penis envy, and Oedipal complex to name a few. So pervasive is Freudian theory, that any psychologist will tell you that one of the first questions they are asked by new acquaintances who learn they are psychologists is "Are you analyzing me?" (The answer is no. Although I usually say, "Not unless you are a rat."). Freud had many disciples, but he also generated a great deal of criticism. Not surprisingly much of this criticism centers on his views concerning sexual energy, the libido, infantile sexuality and those views on women. One of his critics was the Danish-born theorist Erik Erikson, whose theory, while sexist (Erikson, 1964), was much more positive than Freud's and proposed that personality development continued throughout the lifespan.

Psychosocial theory. Erikson (1950, 1968, 1974, 1980, and 1982) proposed that development of the personality proceeded through a series of 8 stages, with each stage occurring in response to the social demands placed upon the individual by his or her environment. The individual must resolve a conflict occurring in response to environmental demands. Resolution of the conflict leads to growth and psychic development. That is, resolving the conflict at any particular stage compels the individual toward growth and failure to resolve the conflict results in failure to develop. Each of Erikson's stages is a time of increased vulnerability but also a time of challenge and potential, representing a turning point in our lives. The first stage, which Erikson labeled trust vs. mistrust, confronts the individual during the first year of life. The infant must come to trust that his or her caregivers will fulfill his or her needs for food, warmth, comfort, and love. Feelings of physical comfort coupled with a minimal amount of fear about the future sets the stage for the lifelong expectation that the world will be a good place in which to live. When the child fails to have its needs met, he or she will come to mistrust not only his or her caregivers, but also others in his or her social environment as well.

The second stage arises during the second and third years of the child's life with the first demands for autonomy. By this stage the child is learning to walk and talk, and the parents now demand that the child toilet-train. Successful resolution of this stage of autonomy vs. self-doubt leads the child to begin life independently of the parents.

During the third stage, named initiative vs. guilt, the child becomes even more independent and begins interacting with its world, primarily through fantasy and play. These activities serve the purpose of preparing the child for the roles that it will play as an adult. Behavior becomes active and purposeful within an ever-widening social environment. In addition the child assumes greater and greater responsibility for his or her body, toys, pets, and behavior. Erikson cautioned parents to allow the child freedom to pursue play; the child must learn how to interact with other people. If the child's attempts to master its environment are denied, anxiety and guilt may develop. However, Erikson believed that such learned guilt was easily relieved whenever the child experienced a sense of accomplishment.

Erikson called the fourth stage industry vs. inferiority. Children begin formal education during this stage and come into contact with people, other than the parents. These new people begin to exert influence over the child. The industrious child will learn to master the rigors of school while also learning to deal with more and more people within its social environment. Children should be directing all of their energy during this period of development toward mastering their own intellectual skills. Erikson cautioned parents, saying that a child must be allowed to develop at his or her own pace as he or she learns about the world.

During adolescence the child confronts the question "Who am I and why am I here?" The heart of the fifth stage of development, identity vs. role-confusion, is the identity crisis. The adolescent must confront the roles that he or she has played in his or her life thus far and synthesize these roles into a cohesive identity. Adolescents must be allowed to explore new and different roles or a different path in a former role. Failure to synthesize an identity leads to the inability to find direction in life and pursue a meaningful future. Following identity development the adolescent enters young adulthood, in which the overwhelming social pressure is to find a mate. Increasingly intimate relationships with friends and the drive toward marriage and procreation characterize the young adult stage of intimacy vs. isolation. Thus, young adulthood is a period of childbearing and childrearing.

Middle adulthood, named generativity vs. stagnation, is characterized by launching the children into the world. The individual's children are now entering into their own 4th or 5th stages of development and the middle-aged individual may now feel a need to "give-back" to the world. The person becomes concerned with future generations; this concern may manifest itself in charitable work. However, the primary task of this stage is helping younger generations of people develop useful and productive lives. Finally, the individual enters old age, the stage of integrity vs. despair. The individual must look back upon his or her life and be satisfied. They should have developed a positive outlook throughout the previous 7 stages. If they have done so, then reflection on their life will show a life well spent. Not every decision was a wise one and life may not have turned out exactly as one wanted; however, failure to look back upon one's life with satisfaction yields despair.

Erikson's theory of psychosocial development should be modified suggests several researchers (Archer, 1992; Gilligan, 1992; Rogers, 1987; Patterson, Sochting, & Marcia, 1992; Rossan, 1987). For example, whereas Erikson proposed that identity decisions are made in the 3 principle domains of vocation, ideology, and family, Archer notes that a wealth of research data suggests that this list should be expanded to include vocational plans, avocation, religious beliefs, sex-role orientation, political ideologies, sexuality, values, friendship, dating, marriage, ethnicity, and family and career prioritizing (Archer, p. 34). While Erikson acknowledged that identity issues surface and resurface during each stage of development, some propose that women's identity formation revolves around intrapersonal areas of life. That is, women are socialized to pursue intimate relationships and these relationships are more important concerns for female adolescents than is the development of an identity. Indeed Rogers (1987) found care and concern for others was related to the development of a sense of self; the development of intimate bonds with other people predated identity development in young women.

Another Personal Story

After working for a couple of years, I entered college when I was 21. I went straight from college to graduate school and then right into a postdoc. I tell my students that I went to school longer than they have been born—all total, somewhere between 14 and 15 years of post-secondary education. I taught my first class, as a grad student, in 1981. After I completed my postdoc I began to learn more about the academic field of women's studies, being thrilled to learn about issues important to me as well as learning about women's history, literature, psychology, etc. Part of this learning process was an awareness that women's studies gave name to things I had experienced throughout my life, like sexism and sexual harassment, and the knowledge that not only was I not abnormal, I wasn't even alone. Now don't get me wrong, I have never felt like I was inferior to anyone; when I was younger my peers said I was stuck up. What they thought was stuck up was loneliness, but that is a different story.

The time in my life to which I am now referring is my mid-30s. I found it very difficult to get a job in my field without completing 2 or 3 other postdocs. This I was unwilling to do; I wanted to teach, but teaching jobs were very hard to get in the early 1990s. I became very depressed. I also became increasingly allergic to the animals that I had studied for 15 years. Now consider my plight. I am no longer a student—the identity that had defined me from the time I was 21 until I was 35. And, I was fast losing my identity as a psychologist, a neuroscientist to be exact. I found myself at the ripe age of 35 reinventing myself and it was not easy. I did eventually get a job, although the less said about that the better. Eventually I obtained the job that I have now, which I love very much. Throughout these last 14 years I have had to confront many things about myself, learn about myself: who I am and where I am going. It has not been easy and sometimes it has been downright painful. But I have finally reached a state where I can truthfully say that I am comfortable in my own skin. I have been studying issues related to identity formation in women, off and on, for the last 5 years. I am by no means an expert, but what I have read leads me to believe that the psychological changes which I have undergone over the last decade or so are characteristic of many women of my generation. Let me qualify that. I am white, Protestant, middle-class, middle-aged woman who grew up during the Women's Movement. I believe that my experiences are similar to other women of my ethnic group, social class, and age. Women of other ethnicities, social classes, religions, and ages may undergo this process differently than me. I believe that Erikson's basic theorizing about identity formation is correct, but I believe that for women the process comes later in life. Or, perhaps it resurfaces later in life for women. Certainly I remember being consumed by thoughts of men, wanting one of my own very badly when I was a teenager. But, men became less important later. That's easy for me to say now since I consider that I have found a prince.

As I evaluate the specific television programs in this book, I will be discussing the characters' search for an identity, something that defines who they are on the psychological level. I will not just discuss them in gender terms, although that is certainly important since I am talking about women here. But, I want to define these women as human beings. Thus, I will attempt to explore how these women are portrayed beyond being merely women. I happen to think that femaleness is a part of my identity, but it is not all of my identity.

Gender Schema Theory and Androgyny

One theory about women, gender and identity that I have not mentioned yet is gender schema theory proposed by Sandra Bem (1993). Basically Bem states that one way in which children organize their worlds is through the lens of gender. Gender is a schema that guides perception of self, others, and objects in the child's environment. As children learn about what it means to be male or female in their society they will construct their world according to the characteristics and traits particular to their sex. This will be both a passive and an active process. Children are reinforced for acting in a gendered fashion, but are also cognitively aware of their actions and how others notice those actions.

Look back at the characteristics that define maleness and femaleness in our society and notice that they are what we refer to as bipolar or opposites. For example, you cannot be high in femininity and high in masculinity. You cannot be passive and aggressive, weak and strong. However, trying to characterize yourself or your friends using a traditional gender measure in psychology may lead you to despair as you realize that you are not one or the other. You may actually possess some characteristics that are traditionally considered to be masculine and some that are traditionally considered to be feminine. I am quite assertive, but not overly aggressive, for example. I also do not like children and would never consider myself weak, not even physically. In other words, I possess a combination of both masculine and feminine traits. In the early 1970s, Sandra Bem and others proposed that the people who possessed both masculine and feminine characteristics should be referred to as androgynous. However, the term androgyny did not "catch on" probably because it sounded more like a person who was sexless or genderless, rather than a person who combined both masculine and feminine personality traits and used them as the situation warranted. In other words, being tender to children but being tough at work, or, not being passive when in a dangerous situation. You get the idea.

Nevertheless, today psychologists propose an approach more correctly referred to as blended androgyny. Such a view proposes that men and women combine traditionally masculine and feminine traits within their personalities, a blending of polar opposites. Thus you do not have to be either passive or aggressive, but rather may exhibit a combination of the two. Such a person would not let others "walk all over them," but they wouldn't climb over the "dead bodies" to get ahead in the world either. Instead they would work hard but stand up for their rights if they felt that their rights on their job were being violated. They would not go out of their way to start a fight, but would defend themselves if necessary. They would not be overly concerned with being thin and fashionable, but would be concerned with their physical health and appearance. Once again, I think that you get the idea. It is my contention that the female characters I will discuss in this book reflect the concept of blended androgyny.

Before I begin discussing each of the particular female characters and their search for a personal identity in a place all their own, I wish to introduce you to the different types of feminism. Part of the reason that there are so many strong, independent, and capable women on TV these days, is because of the influence of feminism: women demanded the rights that men had experienced for centuries. The freedom experienced by the early feminists, and their daughters and students, resonates in each of the following series' stories and characters. I will not try to trace the feministic theories influencing the people involved in these programs; that would take a lot more space than I have available. Nevertheless, I think that after reading this chapter, with its brief introduction to the psychology of women, and the next chapter, with its brief introduction to feminism, you will better understand and appreciate these women of science fiction TV.

Notes

1. I have been using this textbook in my general psychology classes for quite some time. I like the way that the wealth of information is presented by perspective and believe that it just makes sense to teach the information that way. Both authors, Carol Tavris and Carole Wade, are feminists, which I greatly appreciate. There are a number of good general psychology textbooks, some are written at the introductory level and some are written for more advanced students. I would suggest contacting the psychology department of your local university for more information. Note that I am writing this chapter using 20 years worth of experience. As such, I have not cited specific references to each perspective as to do so would increase the length of this book by several dozen pages. I am thus using the Tavris and Wade book as a secondary source. If you would like more information about anything in this chapter having to do with the psychological perspectives, then have your library order a copy of this book, visit the web site at www.prenhall.com/tavris, or contact me and I will be able to point you to the specific references for a particular topic.

2. The interested reader should know that entire textbooks, with hundreds of pages, are devoted to personality theory. I even taught an 11-week class on personality theory many years ago. A look through the psychology section at your local bookstore or library will give you lots of options, although I recommend that you head to the library. At the very least, get an introductory psychology textbook since they are more likely to summarize each of the major theories in a nonbiased fashion.

3. Note that I did not say that abused children become abusive parents. It is true that when studying abusive parents we all too often find that they were victims of child abuse. Nevertheless, many abused children do not abuse their own children. And, that is one of the reasons that I chose psychology as a career: to search for the answers to such riddles.

4. Sometimes a child is born with a chromosomal pattern different from what is considered normal. Chromosomal patterns such as X0, XXY, XYY have been observed. In general, children born XO, called Turner's syndrome, are female, but typically of below normal intelligence. Men with the XYY pattern were reported to be super-aggressive, but since the population studied consisted of prison inmates, it remains to be seen if such behavior would be observed in a sample of men living in a non-prison setting.

5. I am not saying that you will be so diagnosed, but you could be. Why should a perfectly normal biological function, menstruation, lead to diagnoses of mental illness? I am well aware that some women suffer serious physical symptoms when they are menstruating but hopefully they will not be told that

"it is all in their heads" as a friend of mine once was. Women who experience serious symptoms should seek medical help and demand their physicians treat their complaints seriously and exhaust all medical reasons (e.g., fibroids, cysts, etc.) before even suggesting that menstruation is making women crazy. It's men who don't take us seriously who are driving us crazy.

6. There have been quite a number of good books written critiquing the theories concerning the so-called biological differences between women and men. I highly recommend Bleier, Fausto-Sterling, and Tavris. I also highly recommend Caplan and Caplan for a general overview of the bias in research on sex and gender (see Bibliography for the specific references).

Chapter 2: *Women in the Worlds of Science Fiction*

There are plenty of images of women in science fiction.
There are hardly any women.[1]

A Personal Story

This book is about science fiction on television, specifically about science fiction television as presented during the last few decades, although I will also discuss all 5 *Star Trek®* series and they span almost 40 years. For the sake of this book I am defining sci fi as per Weedman (1985): "actions and events that have not yet occurred within the realm of human experience but conceivably might" (p. 6). I will not talk about fantasy; that is, the genre that presents actions and events that cannot occur because they are beyond the realm of reality, for example, stories that involve fairies, elves, goblins, magic, and the like.

My friend Chrissie first introduced me to science fiction in written form. She was a great reader of sci fi when we were in high school. She also wrote a sci fi story for our English class that I remember 30-some odd years later as being absolutely wonderful. I believe that she continued with sci fi as her choice of genre reading, whereas my choice has always been mysteries. Nevertheless, my interest in sci fi goes back a long way, even before *Star Trek®* first burst on the television screen in 1966. I fondly recall watching sci fi and monster movies (actually sci fi monster movies are even better), when I was a little girl, and I continue to watch those to this day. It's for me, and people like me, that movies like *Alien*, *Predator*, *Alien vs. Predator* and all of their cousins are made![2]

I eventually went off to college and graduate school, earning my PhD in General-Experimental Psychology with a major in physiological psychology in 1988. I pursued more education with a post-doctoral position in an anatomy department at a university in my home state of NC. I taught for a number of years at the local community college and the university in my adopted town. I will not go into details, but suffice it to say that I have had a few unpleasant experiences over the years. It was while I was teaching that I discovered the academic discipline of women's studies. I began to take classes in women's studies. I began reading in the field. I began talking to other women about their experiences inside and out of academia, and I began to attend meetings. I know this sounds somewhat silly but I learned there were names for some of my life experiences. Like many women I became angry, although that has changed, for the most part, over the years.

Now, I proudly use the "f" word and proclaim myself to be a feminist. Before you close the book and refuse to read on, let me tell you what a feminist is. A feminist is someone who believes that women and men should be considered equal, socially, economically, and legally. A feminist, to quote Matlin (1996), "is a person whose beliefs, values, and attitudes reflect a high regard for women as human beings" (p. 5). Feminists do not hate men; some of us are married to them. Feminists can even be men for that matter. This book will be written from a feminist perspective, because everything I do, I do from that perspective.

The Personal is Political

Before I begin a discussion of feminist theory, I need to digress for just a moment and discuss the word theory. My students quake when they hear the word theory and sometimes I cannot blame them since the word has connotations for the general public of something overly wordy, esoteric and pedantic. Most people don't understand why theories are important: they are useful as guides to research. The scientific enterprise is predicated on observation. As a psychologist I observe behavior in any number of ways and in a number of settings, the primary ones being the field and the laboratory. That is, psychologists observe the behavior of humans and other organisms in the natural habitat or in the highly controlled atmosphere of the laboratory. Both of these settings are important and much information can be gained from research in these settings. We collect data in our field research and our laboratory experiments in a number of ways. These include direct observation of behavior with or without our research participants' knowledge; interviews or surveys of our participants' attitudes and opinions; psychological tests of general knowledge, mental state, traits, etc.; and, carefully controlled experiments of participants' reactions to variables. Usually we collect the data ourselves, but sometimes we make use of data collected by others that are stored in archives. These are written, oral, or visual records of the participants' behavior, attitudes, and opinions, sometimes even in their own words. The scientific enterprise is a public endeavor as well as being self-correcting because the peer-review process serves as a means of disseminating information to the general public only after careful review by a scientist's peers. As data about psychological phenomena are placed into the public record the conclusions drawn from empirical data are available for other researchers to use. As more and more data are collected, certain facts and trends about psychological phenomena emerge. In an attempt to make sense of these facts and to make them more manageable we look to see how these facts fit together coherently and simply. When we are able to unify certain facts because of the ways in which they address certain phenomena, then we develop a theory. Thus a theory is simply a way of explaining related facts. We can then use theories as a guide to look for other facts that support the theory or we can look for facts that do not support the theory. Either way our goal is to look for the reasons underlying human (and animal) behavior. Once we have learned why organisms act the way that they do, then we can attempt to control the causes of the behavior in question. For example, if we know why certain abused children will grow up and abuse their children, then we can intervene and stop the cycle of child abuse.

At the heart of all feminist theories is the need to determine WHY women are so denigrated by men. Why are women considered to be inferior to men? Why are women perceived as the anti-man? Why are women denied the right to choose what to do with their bodies and their lives? Why are women considered to be "the second sex?" A number of theories have been proposed to account for the ways in which women are treated in contemporary society. It should come as no surprise that these theories are as varied as women themselves and all theories are written from the perspectives of the women who conceive them. These authors thus set their theories within the domain of their own lives, focusing upon those issues that they deem to be most important to women. In preparation for writing this section I read a summary of feminist theory written by Tong (1989)[3] and I highly recommend it. It is written in an easily understood fashion, which is good considering that some feminist theories are quite complicated. Frankly, some of these theories seem to be written for the academic community, becoming so theoretical as to be beyond comprehension (and remember that I have about 24 years of education!). Theories of why women are treated the way that they are need to explain the issues to women in such a way as to resonate with every woman's life, not just a woman attempting to obtain a promotion within the highly sexist world of academia.

Liberal feminism places feminism firmly within the bounds of political liberalism. Such feminists believe that women should be given equal access with men to educational and vocational opportunities. They believe that legal barriers to women's rights must be destroyed, but they also believe that such destruction should come within the system via political activism. In addition, liberal feminists recognize that sex and gender are not synonymous, and that traditional gender roles are stultifying for men as well as women. Thus, liberal feminists would advocate that men and women become more androgynous. This view was condemned by other feminists who argued that liberal feminism was too White and too middle-class, that is, it was too exclusive of women who differed from the founding mothers of the Women's Movement. We owe liberal feminists many laws that now protect women and their rights, although the job is far from done.

One criticism leveled at liberal feminism came from women who believed that women's oppression could only be been seen through the lens of class. Women who espouse this position are called Marxist feminists. They believe that women have been suppressed by a capitalist society that places value on what we do rather than on who we are. Because men are needed to work in a capitalistic society, women are needed within the home to ensure that men are able to work outside of the home. However, even women working within their own homes began increasingly to undervalue women's work. Women came to be seen as consumers rather than as workers. Marxist feminists believe that women's work should be valued, as is men's, and that one way to place value on such work is to socialize it. As Tong notes, once people realize "just how difficult domestic work is, society will no longer have grounds for the oppression of women as parasitic people of inferior value" (p. 54). Nevertheless liberation of women will only come when capitalism is completely destroyed. We owe these women our gratitude for reminding men of the jobs that women do for them as well as for their charge to liberal feminists to note the effects of class structure on women's lives.

Whereas liberal feminists place the oppression of women within the legal system and Marxist feminists place it within the structure of capitalism, many radical feminists center the oppression of women on their bodies. These feminists look to ways in which men have attempted to control women's bodies throughout history, by controlling female sexuality and reproduction. That is, men increasingly defined women in ways that either sexualized or desexualized their bodies. Radical feminists argue that women have the right to use their bodies as they see fit: to be sexual or not and to mother or not. Indeed one group of radical feminists states that women will only be free once they refuse heterosexuality and embrace Lesbianism. Others state that women should refuse to bear children, remaining childless, or instead embrace the new reproductive technologies that would free women of this biological burden. While some radical feminists are indeed quite radical we owe a great deal to such women for pointing out the myriad ways in which women have been sexualized in our society, from pornography and rape to sexual harassment and domestic violence.

The last type of feminism I will discuss is psychoanalytic feminism, which attempted to seat feminist theory within the structure of Freudian theory. Freud argued that girls experience "penis envy," and never completely resolve the conflicts arising during the phallic stage of development (as if the very name of this stage didn't exclude girls from consideration!). Because the little girl can never have a penis, she compensates by desiring children. Traditional Freudian theory thus insults women in three ways. First, girls develop penis envy. Second, girls never completely resolve their Oedipal-Electra complexes and thus never completely develop a conscience. Third, women's ability to bear children, instead of being celebrated, is seen as a way to compensate for not having a penis. Psychoanalytic feminists however repudiate the concept of penis envy, instead framing the young girl's conflict within the frame of power differentials. That is, a girl even at such a young age can see that male children are valued more than is she, even by her own mother. Some psychoanalytic feminists (e.g., Chodorow, 1978) place greater emphasis on the pre-Oedipal stage of development than they do the Oedipal stage. Thus they note the bonding that occurs between mother and child early during the child's development and state that even at such a young age the boy-mother connection is different from the girl-mother connection. Girls never completely separate from the connection of women because it is the first connection they made when young. This connection is non-sexual and continuous with mother, leading to the development of an identity in terms of relationships. Unlike the girl child, the boy child's connection with his mother is sexual, but not continuous with mother. The boy child must separate from mother and develop an identity that recognizes the power and prestige of men. Psychoanalytic feminist theories emphasize the interconnections between women as well as women's desire for love and children, even at the expense of a job or career, and we owe them much for this.

Each of the theories that I have briefly mentioned attempts to explain women in terms of women rather than explain women in terms of men. Each theory has its critics: not all theories resonate or relate to all women. Personally I believe that they all have validity and welcome the day when a theory combining the best of all possible theories is developed (although I'm not holding my breath). But each of these theories gives us a framework in which to explore women's lives in the 21st century. I believe that no matter which theory personally resonates with you, all of these theories have helped women define their lives in contemporary society and each has given us the **choice** to do so. We can explore our lives in terms of these theories and make choices about which "fits" best within our own personal philosophy about how the world operates. Each also causes us to think deeply and acknowledge how some of us may be more privileged that others; certainly I recognize that I am a middle-class, white woman. The use of these theories as the means of expression has empowered women's voices in ways never before seen in history. Many of these theories have found expression in science fiction as written by and about women during the last 30-odd years.

Frankenstein starts it all

Mary Shelley's novel *Frankenstein* (1818, 1831) is generally considered the first example of the genre we now call science fiction. Thus, Mary Shelley, the daughter of one of the first feminists,[4] could rightfully be called the Mother of science fiction, which is odd considering that her novel is pretty much devoid of female characters. Only four women populate the novel. Mrs. Walton serves as the recipient of the Frankenstein story: Victor tells his story to Walton who in turns tells his sister in a series of letters. We actually never see Mrs. Walton or learn anything of her; she is simply an expository device. Justine Moritz, a servant of the family Frankenstein, stands accused of young William Frankenstein's murder and is executed for the crime. The

Creature, seeking revenge against Victor, murdered William and Victor knew it but did nothing to help Justine. Caroline Frankenstein, Victor's mother, dies after nursing her ward, Elizabeth Lavenza. Caroline's role in the novel is merely to show a mother in selfless relation to her husband and children. Finally, Elizabeth Lavenza was Victor's childhood companion, "given" to him by his parents, and eventually his fiancée. The Creature kills her on her wedding night. Many scholars have commented on the lack of women in *Frankenstein*; considering the ways in which women were treated in Mary's time, their exclusion served to illustrate the anti-femaleness of 19th century science and society. And women were pretty much excluded from science fiction from the time of Mary Shelley until the 1960s and 1970s.

Many scholars have discussed the lack of women in science fiction and to review them all is beyond the scope of this paper; a number of these works can be found in the Bibliography (see for example, Sargent, 1974 but for a different perspective see Rabkin, 1981). The majority of the criticism centers on the under-representation or sexual exploitation of women in the so-called Golden Age of science fiction, the 1930s and 1940s. Women in the early days of sci fi were virtually nonexistent. If presented at all, they were depicted in the traditional stereotypical roles of wife, mother, and homemaker. Women beyond these roles were evil, stupid, childlike, or a combination of these. For the predominately male audience, women were presented as toys, threats, or enigmas (Sanders, 1981). If women were presented in any role other than wife, mother, and homemaker at the beginning of the story (such as scientist), by the end of the story she had fallen safely in love with the hero and realized that fulfilling her natural role as wife, mother, and homemaker was all that mattered. Rabkin (1981) however points out that sci fi written with these characterizations was merely a reflection of the prevailing culture, not that that makes it right. Understandably, women were not satisfied with such characterizations, although to hear people tell it, women did not read science fiction in any case, so what did it matter? Well, it mattered plenty. Women did read science fiction then, just as they read it now (Bainbridge, 1982). We go to see sci fi films and we watch sci fi TV. We read sci fi stories, and we write them too.

As a matter of fact women had always written sci fi stories, even in the Golden Age; some used initials or pseudonyms to disguise their gender (Monk, 1980; Sargent, 1977; Weinkauf, 1977) and some did not bother. The 1960s saw more women entering into the field, and more of them using their own names, sans initials (Sargent, 1996). Science fic-

tion began to reflect the social changes occurring during that time: the
Civil Rights Movement, the Women's Movement, the Vietnam War
and the Peace Movement. As the US entered the space race and actually put a man on the moon, it appeared almost as if science[5] fact was
outpacing science fiction. And, more writers, female especially, became interested in exploring psychological and sociological aspects of
the imagined future. Women authors during the two decades from 1960
to 1980 increasingly wrote novels exploring utopian societies, especially those in which women were valued as women. Gender role expectations were reversed in some of this fiction, nonexistent in others,
and increasingly different from the traditional gender roles espoused by
American society post-World War II (Friend, 1972; Sanders, 1977;
Vaughn, 1991). Indeed, science fiction became increasingly feminist in
the latter part of the 20th century and continues to be so today, notwith-
standing the Conservative Backlash (Faludi, 1991), which would have
women renounce their desires for careers and embrace their instinctive
drive for children—but only if they are middle-class.

Nevertheless, while set in the future science fiction is written in the
present, and that present is reflected in what is written (Green & Lefanu, 1985). Written science fiction thus puts into words what cannot
be put into words (Le Guin, 1979; Shaw, 2000) and I would argue that
science fiction television puts into images what cannot be imagined.
Shaw (2000) writes that science fiction serves to distance the reader
from her present, thereby increasing her awareness, especially her critical awareness of that present. Such a philosophy resided at the heart of
Roddenberry's use of *Star Trek* to illustrate problems afflicting 20th
century American society. Such a strategy is no less important today.
Indeed, it may be more important today given the increasing hostility
and polarization of contemporary society and not just in the US.

The Conservative Backlash

But, in some ways, science fiction became more sexist. As women
demanded equal rights and, particularly as women gained reproductive
freedom, this new found sexuality awakened terror in men. No longer
menaced by the big-eyed space alien, her virginity assured by the arrival of Our Hero, women now threatened to sexually overpower the
male characters. Not for nothing has society restricted female sexuality
throughout the ages, sometimes in hideous ways. Unfortunately, the
increasing sexual freedom of the 1960s and beyond has in some cases

led to more and more violent, almost pornographic sci fi (Rabkin, 1981). Whereas roles for women in sci fi became less traditional and stereotypical, they became increasingly sexualized, particularly in film and television. But, if sci fi rendered its female characters in stereotypes, it did the same for the male characters as well. Male characters were expected to be macho, sexually promiscuous or asexual (depending on the decade), strong and silent, and always confident. Nevertheless, they were still the stars, even many times in stories written by women.

On the other hand, sci fi was accused of neglecting human relationships and emotional involvement (Ketterer, 1974), characteristics believed to be more attractive to female fans than male. Ketterer argued however that the nature of sci fi causes us to lose sight of humans as we contemplate the sheer awe and wonder of events described and depicted within the genre. I understand his point here but wonder if he expects that these events will occur in a vacuum, where people, male or female, are not found. Those of us who have lived in the nuclear age and remember the astounding scientific discoveries of the latter half of the 20th century (I was born in 1955) can marvel at the pace with which science has progressed. We can only guess at what achievements will be made in the years to come and hope that these achievements do not come at the expense of the population of Planet Earth. Relationships I would argue make a fine background, or foreground for that matter, in sci fi. Certainly relationships, particularly romantic ones, reflect mainstream, contemporary life in America and most Western European countries. For that reason, homosexual relationships are usually not depicted in sci fi television programs, with one notable exception being *Babylon 5*. I will discuss interpersonal and romantic relationships in more detail in the chapters on each of the various sci fi programs.

Sex is a different story. Women and men in contemporary society are bombarded with messages about sex: how to attract members of the opposite (or same) sex, how to be sexy, how to not be too sexy, when to be sexy, how not to be smelly since that is not sexy, what to wear to be sexy, etc. Men and women are also taught that each sex has different expectations about sex. That is, women are taught to be monogamous and look to a man for the fulfillment of her role in life and the development of her identity. Men define the female identity. Men on the other hand are not taught to be monogamous, but to rather "sow their wild oats." They are taught that their careers and jobs provide fulfillment in life. The more recent trend in the Sex Wars involves teaching young men and women that communication problems abound in their relationships because men and women essentially come from different planets (I cannot bear to write about this much longer). Women are taught that they are "talking" creatures. They show their love and affection by talking to the men who stereotypically are not listening because they have been taught to show their love and affection for women by doing manly stuff, like changing the oil in the car. In sci fi the men are roaming around the galaxy doing stuff, like pulverizing aliens and exploring brave new worlds. Women, if invited along for the ride, are distracting him by asking endless questions, nattering on about nothing important. Much sci fi was written using these stereotypes (trust me, scientists from the 17th century until the present day have attempted to prove female inferiority by examining their skulls for differences in the language areas—do not even get me started on this shoddy science). Sex in sci fi, if present at all, was not very pretty, usually involving rape. It still does for that matter; however, more male and female writers are choosing to examine sexual and nonsexual relationships in their stories (Mumford, 1985) in ways that are natural to the story, rather than being contrived for the prurient entertainment of the reader. The same can be said for sci fi film and I will discuss sex in the chapters that follow.

Images of Women in Sci Fi

Cornillon (1972) stated that women in literature fall into one of 4 categories: heroine, invisible, hero, or feminist aesthetic. In her essay on women in science fiction, Susan Wood (1978-1979) discussed the images of women in science fiction, which include the heroine, the alien, and the hero. The woman as heroine is a stereotypical woman and many women in science fiction fall within that category, particularly in the sci fi films of the 1950s and some of the television programs of the 1960s, such as *Lost in Space*. The invisible woman, or the alien, concerns the ways in which women are perceived as the Other— the thing against which Our Hero tests himself (Russ, 1995). Whereas Wood believes that all of these images are degrading, Cornillon views the woman as Hero as a new portrayal of woman. Here the woman is portrayed as a whole woman, one who is "discovering [her] wholeness, ...seeking and finding other metaphors for existence than men, or martyrdom, or selflessness, or intrinsic worthlessness" (Cornillon, p. xi). She further states that such women are "working, being political, creating, . . . living in relationships with other women, . . . being alive, adventuresome, self-determining, growing, making significant choices, questioning and finding viable answers and solutions—of being, in other words, human beings" (ibid, p. xi).

Barr (1987) believes that contemporary speculative fiction (which includes sci fi) addresses 3 broad themes: community, heroism, and sexuality/reproduction. These themes do often overlap and this will be seen quite often in the analysis of the programs that follow. Furthermore Barr considers that whenever women form communities or act as heroes or take charge of their own sexuality and reproduction, they become alien, especially to the patriarchal society in which they (and we) live. Such women are behaving in ways that are alien to the concept of femininity, which, as stated previously, limits female development and identity. Reading feminist science fiction thus allows women to unlock "patriarchy's often hidden agendas" (Barr, 1993, p. 4), to deconstruct the patriarchal narrative that defines and confines us in narrow ways (Cranny-Francis, 1990). I believe that watching sci fi cinema and television allows us to do the same. Certainly, the women that I choose to discuss in the following chapters allow us to examine women as heroic characters navigating worlds that are sometimes familiar and sometimes alien to us.

Fortunately, heroic women are the new women in science fiction and embrace values reflective of the Civil Rights and Women's Movements with their demands for the inherent rightness of equality. Such women are increasingly visible in the science fiction television and cinema of the latter half of the 20th century and beginning of the 21st. That is not to say that there are no examples of sexism in the current crop of science fiction. Certainly there are as has been lamented by many a male and female fan. Sex sells and women in the sci fi of today may be brainy or tough, but they also have to be beautiful in order to attract the young, male viewers that advertisers believe wield vast amounts of money in America. Certainly literate print sci fi is centuries ahead of its cinematic counterpart (no pun intended). Thus, while cutting age sci fi of the 1960s and 1970s, like *Twilight Zone* and *Star Trek® The Original Series*, could present wonderfully written allegories on racism, sexism, the Cold War, Vietnam, social classism, etc., today's sci fi depends largely on special effects: the bigger the BOOM, the better the movie even if the plot is ridiculous, the actors can't act, and the director looked like he was on vacation during filming. Writing these words during the winter of 2004 when there are very few literate sci fi shows still on the air and the majority of network fare revolves around so-called "reality," it is easy to understand Biersdorfer's (2000) lament about how sci fi television has not lived up to its promise. And yet, as Pamela Sargent (1974)[6] noted, "Science fiction at its best could be seen as superior to the culture around it in its attitudes toward human rights, despite the crudities which can be found in sf" (p. lxi)). Furthermore she said, "Science fiction opens the mind. Even the worst sf, with its old-fashioned adventure and stereotypical characters can sometimes serve this purpose. . . . It also provides the reader with some understanding of the immensity of our universe" (p. lix).

Whetmore (1981) challenged us to address not only the television programs themselves, but the relationships that develop between the audience and the characters. We all to often dismiss the content of the program and neglect the incredible power that television has over the viewer. After all, said Whetmore, "commercials depicting women as mindless housewives in search of a male to tell them what detergent to use may have done more to stir the collective conscience of women than anything else" (p. 160). Young people of today gain much of their information from television and as much as we do not like that we must recognize that this is so. The television audience does not live in a political vacuum. Rather the audience has predetermined social and political values and, for today's young people, those values are most certainly being shaped by television. That is why it is important for us to note the content of the television programs that people in our society are watching. Science fiction programming can thus be very educational, when it is done well. Quoting Sargent (1974):

> Science fiction can provide women with possible scenarios for their own future development. . . . Only SF and fantasy can show us women in entirely new or strange surroundings. It can explore what we might become if and when the present restrictions on our lives vanish, or show us new problems and restrictions that might arise (p. ix).

Notes

1. Joanna Russ (1972). Russ is a relentless critic of male-dominated sci fi and she has written extensively on the problem. Russ also writes sci fi stories and novels under her name, notably *The Female Man* (see the Bibliography).
2. My husband deplores my taste in movies; imagine this coming from a man who watches wrestling on TV (thank goodness, he watches it for its comedic

value and does not think it is "real"). He watches much more television than I do; most of what I watch is science fiction and he watches a lot of that with me. Since he is an intelligent man and I value his opinion, I can watch his reactions to such programs and use him as a sounding board.

3. I have not included specific references to every theory here because once again it would simply increase the length of the book without necessarily adding information. Some references to feminist theory are located in the Bibliography, but I recommend beginning with Tong and then using her reference list for further explorations of feminist theory. I also highly recommend Kolmar and Bartkowski's (2005) reader as it contains historical and contemporary texts by a large number of women.

4. Mary Wollstonecraft, author of *A Vindication of the Rights of Women* (1792).

5. I won't go into a long discussion here, but I do agree with Jung (1978) when he noted the spiritual distress of the general public and their tendency to look to the paranormal and the extraordinary to give meaning to their lives. He was writing this at a time when it appeared as if science and psychology had rendered all things normal. I would add known as well. While sci fi may be fantastic, certain elements of it have found their way into the consciousness of contemporary society, most notably UFOs and alien visitors. Such beliefs found their greatest expression in *The X-Files*, which is why that program is contained in this book.

6. Pamela Sargent (1974). Sargent is also a critic of male-dominated sci fi. She has written extensively on the problem. Furthermore, she has collected much short fiction by women authors in several well-edited volumes and has written her own fiction too (see the Bibliography).

Scully views the body

Chapter 3: *The X-Files*[TM]

The periodical database for *The X-Files* is quite extensive, although the academic periodical database is not. The program once had a magazine[1] devoted to all things that X Philes, as fans call themselves, might consider important about the show, and *The X-Files* fan club is apparently still functioning. Many of the episodes were novelized for young adult readers and several stand-alone novels, written by some of today's best science fiction authors, were published. *The X-Files* and its actors won several awards when it was produced. The series has been released in syndication; check your local TV listing to determine if it is screened in your market. I am not trying to advertise for the Sci Fi Channel here, but they are screening this series at the present time (winter 2004). The official website has apparently been removed from the web.

I will discuss *The X-Files* for all 9 seasons that it was on the air. The last two seasons saw minimal involvement on the part of Mulder and the final season saw minimal involvement on the part of Scully. Two new characters were introduced, Special Agents John Doggett and Monica Reyes. While I liked both of those characters very much and wish that the program could have continued with a focus on them, it was not to be. I will not discuss these characters.

I will first briefly summarize the 9-year storyline of *The X-Files*. Then I will discuss Scully in terms of her relationship with Mulder (as focus of the series). Next I will discuss the character of Scully, first presenting information on her history, and then presenting information on her relationships with family and co-workers, using various episodes from the 9 seasons to illustrate her character. I will discuss both of these, the storylines and her character, with respect to Scully's relationship with Mulder and, more importantly, with us.

Scully and Mulder's Excellent Adventure[2]

It is hard to imagine that anyone on this planet has not heard of *The X-Files*, but for those who have not, I will provide a summary of the program. Special Agent Fox Mulder (played by David Duchovny) has willingly chosen to investigate cases for which there appear to be no logical explanations. He and Scully will "work to uncover the truth behind unsolved cases that defy normal investigation – cases the government has buried or ignored, labeling them 'X-Files'."[3] Mulder is driven by his own personal demon—his sister's abduction when he was 12 and she was 8. He believes that aliens abducted her. He is Oxford-educated with a degree in psychology and was once considered to be the star of the Violent Crimes Section of the FBI.

Special Agent Dana Scully (played by Gillian Anderson) is a medical doctor recruited from medical school to work at the FBI. Her specialty is forensics and she taught at the FBI's training facility at Quantico, VA before being assigned to the X-Files. Her assignment to the X-Files is to work with Mulder and ensure that his investigations do not stretch too far into the incredulous. In the *Pilot* episode, Section Chief Blevins asks Scully if she has ever heard of an "unassigned project outside of the bureau mainstream." He then tells Scully "we want you to assist Mulder on these X-Files. You will write field reports on your activities along with your observations on the validity of the work." When Scully asks, "Am I to understand that you want me to debunk the X-Files?" Blevins replies, "We trust you will make the proper scientific analysis." Mulder believes that Scully has been sent to spy on him.[4]

During their 7 years together,[5] Mulder and Scully's investigations fall into two categories: mythology/history and "monster of the week," also referred to as the stand-alone episodes (Delasara, 2000). The mythology/history episodes are those that center on the alien invasion scenario. At the core of this epic storyline is the fact that aliens are in fact present on Earth and have indeed been here for millions of years in the form of a virus. Members of our government know that the aliens are here and are collaborating with the aliens in their efforts to create an alien-human hybrid that will serve as slave labor once the aliens' colonization is complete. Unknown to the aliens, the collaborators are secretly developing a vaccine that will stop the alien virus from destroying humankind. The collaborators each gave a child (or other family member) as hostage to the aliens and Bill Mulder gave his daughter Samantha, for which his wife never forgave him.[6] Fox Mulder's quest, and thus the center of the entire program, was to determine what happened to his sister and expose the conspiracy surrounding our government's collaboration with the aliens. The episodes that furthered this plot were referred to as the 'mythology' episodes. They also gave us background information on both Mulder and Scully; hence, they were also referred to as histories. Personally I find these episodes to be tedious and unbelievable because I am not a fan of conspiracy theories. I believe the old adage "Three people can keep a secret only if two of them are dead." I simply find it hard to believe that the numbers of people needed to maintain such a plot could actually keep quiet about it, even with family members as hostages. I do however like the "monster of the week" episodes. These episodes do not necessarily give us any new information about Mulder or Scully's past lives; however, they do allow us to explore and examine the agents' relationship with each other, as well as each agent *in toto*.

Dana Scully does not believe in aliens, or at least not in the beginning. I think of Scully as Mulder's Watson. Given that analogy then, Holmes' famous comment regarding implausible events readily pertains to Mulder and Scully. Holmes said "When you have eliminated the impossible, whatever remains, however improbable, must be the truth."[7] Scully's function within *The X-Files* universe is to be Mulder's foil. He looks at the heart of every case and sees beyond the facts to the improbable that must be true, whereas Scully's job is to look at the facts and counter his nonscientific explanations with her own rational ones. Upon their first meeting, discussing the murder of a young woman in Oregon, Mulder tells Scully ". . . when convention and science offer us no answers, might we not turn to the fantastic as a plausibility?" To which Scully passionately replies:

> The girl obviously died of something. If it was natural causes it's plausible that there was something missed in the postmortem. If she was murdered, it's plausible there was a sloppy investigation. What I find fantastic is any notion that there are answers beyond the realm of science. The answers are there, you just have to know where to look (*Pilot*, 1X79[8]).

They thus make the perfect crime-fighting couple albeit with reversed gender roles, a plot device developed by series creator Chris Carter, who wanted to flip the gender roles in the series, with the man as the believer, the intuiter, and the woman as the skeptic.[3] So, Mulder is the dreamer and the romantic whereas Scully is the ever-practical, hard-nosed scientist. They complement each other; they are companions, twins, and fellows.[9, 10] As Mulder tells Scully in *The X-Files*[11] motion picture, "You made me whole." That was not necessarily a job that she wanted, at least in the beginning.

Scully's History and Mythology

Nine seasons of *The X-Files* have taught us much about Scully. She is one of 4 children, having two brothers and one sister, Melissa, who was murdered when she was mistaken for Scully. Scully's father was a career Naval officer whose death from a heart attack resulted in one of Scully's first paranormal experiences—her father's ghost appeared to her upon his death (*Beyond the Sea*, 1X12). Scully adored her father; she called him Ahab and he affectionately called her Starbuck (from their favorite book *Moby Dick*). Scully has no life outside of the FBI beyond season 1. That is, after the first year of production we no longer see Scully in social situations, with the exception of a Christmas celebration that figures prominently in 2 episodes that further her own abduction arc. To explain Gillian Anderson's real life pregnancy during season 2, a former FBI agent named Duane Barry who claims to be an alien abductee, kidnaps Scully. Duane Barry abducts Scully believing that, by offering the aliens a replacement, he will be spared further experimentation (*Duane Barry*, 2X05). Scully mysteriously returns with no memory of what happened to her (*One Breath*, 2X08). We subsequently learn that her ova were harvested and that at least one child was produced from that harvest. Scully learns of the child during another paranormal encounter: Melissa, her murdered sister, phones Scully at their brother's home one Christmas to tell Scully that the child is in danger (*Christmas Carol*, 5X05). The child will die and we will see a distraught Scully, one who is fully cognizant of the choices that she has made with respect to life and career (*Emily*, 5X07), a topic that will be explored in more detail below. We observe Scully as she deals with her inexplicable, inoperable, and incurable cancer (*Momento Mori*, 4X15) and her miraculous recovery (*Redux I*, 5X02 & *Redux II*, 5X03), all tied to the removal and re-insertion of a metallic chip of unknown origin. Finally we observe Scully give birth to the miracle baby, William, a son she never thought she would bear given that her ova were supposedly harvested (*Existence*, 8X21). Thus as Mulder learns his sister's fate and the truth behind the alien abductions, Scully's own X-File becomes thicker and thicker. By the end of the series' nine-year run,

Scully comes to believe that the implausible is not only plausible but possible as well.

Scully: On the Job and at Home

Like all of the women discussed in this book, Scully is a complex character. Analysis of literary figures by modern scholars relies upon the author's presentation of the character through the words on the printed page. We can learn how the character acts in the situations in which the author places her and we can learn about the character's reactions to those situations by reading the words given to the character by the author. But, unless the character recurs in future text we only have one body of work in which to understand her. When analyzing Scully we have 9 years worth of situations in which to observe her reactions to her life, the changes that have occurred, the situations she has confronted, and the decisions that she has made.

Scully is fully cognizant of the fact that she is a woman working in a non-traditional setting. Even in 2004 the FBI is predominately male-oriented. Whereas the FBI specifically recruited Scully, the fact is that they wanted her because she was a medical doctor and thus perfect for forensic analysis of crime scene evidence. Her scientific background led to her assignment on the X-Files, but she is definitely a minority among field investigators. In the episode *Soft Light* (2X23) a former student, Detective Kelly Ryan, asks Scully for help solving a case. Detective Ryan is under a great deal of pressure to prove that she is just as capable as her male colleagues when it comes to investigating and solving crimes. Scully explains this to Mulder noting that she understands exactly how Ryan feels. Scully also feels pressure from those who do not understand why she is working with Mulder. Her Academy classmate, Special Agent Tom Colton, wants her help with a case that will advance his career (*Squeeze*, 1X02). At lunch, he talks about what their classmates are saying about her work with Mulder and calls her Mrs. Spooky (Mulder's nickname at the FBI is Spooky). Colton recognizes that there are aspects of his case that are a little unusual and may be typical of an X-File; however, he cannot bring himself to acknowledge this or directly ask Mulder for help. He appeals to Scully, but gets quite angry when Mulder does begin helping, with his usual brand of intuition. Colton and Scully have a heated exchange when he says that he will get her reassigned from the X-Files and Scully tells him that she can take care of herself. When Colton asks, "Whose side are you on?" Scully tartly replies, "The victim's." Colton's jealousy of Mulder and

Scully almost gets Scully killed. Although it is never stated, Colton probably did not make the fast track after that.

As stated earlier we see no evidence of Scully's personal life. Gillian Anderson commented that Scully's too busy[12] in an interview with *TV Guide*, and Chris Carter has no interest in what the agents do on their time off.[13] That is not to say, however, that Scully is unaware that she has no personal life. Several episodes serve to illustrate this. In her off time Scully does what many of us do, maintenance activities, such as washing her dog and cleaning her gun (*War of the Coprophages*, 3X12). Scully, at least, has family that she visits; her relationship with her mother appears to be quite healthy, unlike Mulder's relationship with his. In the episode *Shadows* (1X05), Mulder asks Scully if she believes in an afterlife and Scully replies "I'd settle for a life in this one." Likewise in *Dreamland I* (6X04), Mulder and Scully are off once again investigating a lead. As they drive through the desert, Scully looks out of the window, clearly not interested in whatever Mulder is saying. When he pauses she says:

> Mulder, it's the dim hope of finding that proof that's kept us in this car—or one very much like it—more nights than I care to remember. Driving hundreds, if not thousands of miles, through neighborhoods and cities and towns, where people are buying homes, and playing with their kids and their dogs. In short, living their lives. While we just keep driving. Don't you ever just want to stop? Get out of the damn car? Settle down and live something approaching a normal life?

For Mulder however this is his life and even though he does not admit it, he wants Scully to share it with him. He wants to share it with her so badly that he is willing to do just about anything. One Christmas Eve, he calls her to meet him at a reputed haunted house (*How the Ghosts Stole Christmas*, 6X08). Scully does drive out to meet him, but refuses to stake out the place with him. She tells Mulder that she has presents to wrap and places to be. Mulder, of course, has no one with whom to celebrate the holiday. He resorts to stealing her car keys to keep her with him and force her into following him into the house. As they encounter the ghosts, a man and a woman who completed a murder-suicide pact years before, they are forced to confront their lives and their relationship. The episode ends with Mulder sitting forlornly on his sofa watching "A Christmas Carol." Scully arrives, telling him that she cannot sleep, wanting to discuss what the ghosts told them about their loneliness and motivations for being partners. They exchange gifts; the first time they had ever done so. Their relationship changed from that point and continued to evolve throughout season 6.

I want to backtrack however and discuss several programs that deal with Mulder and Scully's professional relationship. Two very humorous episodes allowed us to observe the agents' interactions with each other, but also *theirs or others perceptions* of their interactions with each other. *Jose Chung's From Outer Space* (3X20) was part of the mythology arc. Mulder and Scully had investigated the disappearance of two teenagers along with a couple of Air Force pilots. Along the way they discover an "alien" spaceship that had apparently crashed, but was in reality a top-secret US prototype. The alien body found in the wreckage was actually a pilot dressed up like an alien. We never really figure out what is going on in the episode, because it is all told in interviews with the people involved by a writer named Jose Chung. He is writing a new type of book, nonfiction science fiction, and he characterizes Mulder as being a "ticking time bomb of insanity." Scully he calls a dear lady and clearly feels sorry for her, having such a dubious partner.

Even better is the episode *Bad Blood* (5X12), where Mulder and Scully confront a town of vampires. Mulder kills one of the vampires by staking it in the heart. Mulder and Scully are called back to Washington to explain why Mulder killed the boy, whom no one believes is a vampire since his fangs were so obviously fake. However, when the stake is removed from the boy's chest, he rises and leaves the morgue. Mulder and Scully are called back to Texas to investigate. This episode is told in flashbacks as first we get Scully's version of events and then Mulder's. Each is complimentary to him or her and not especially complimentary to the other. For example, the sheriff of the town is very handsome. In Mulder's version of events, Scully acts giddy and silly around the sheriff, whom Mulder claims is not very attractive since he has buckteeth (he does not!). Scully characterizes Mulder as flying off half-cocked throughout the entire episode, whereas his version of events presents her as a bitchy whiner. Clearly the thought that they might go to prison for killing the young boy in such a gruesome fashion did not bring out the best in them or their relationship in this episode!

It was rare for Mulder or Scully to investigate a case alone; however, it has happened on a few occasions, for example, when one or the other actually took time off from work. Two episodes that showcase Scully without Mulder are *Never Again* (4X13) and *Chinga* (5X10). Not surprisingly it is Mulder who has the most difficult time letting Scully go. *Never Again* is best left for later. In *Chinga* Scully rents a convertible and drives to Maine for the weekend. While there she en-counters a town where decidedly odd things are happening. An autistic girl's doll is forcing people that anger the child to kill themselves. Her mother is trying to keep the child happy so that the doll does not "waken." Scully solves the problem by roasting the doll in the micro-wave. The back-story of this episode concerns Mulder's attempts to be involved in the case via those ubiquitous cell phones. Scully refuses to "play along" and repeatedly hangs up or refuses to answer the phone at all. Moreover, she won't tell him about the case after she returns.

The episode *Never Again* opens with an apparently depressed Scully angry with Mulder for the way he is treating her. Mulder has been ordered to either go on vacation or forfeit 8 weeks of pay. He decides that he will actually comply with the edict. Scully is in no mood for Mulder's hyperactivity and asks him first why she has no desk in their office. When Mulder gives Scully information on a case that he wants her to follow-up while he is away and she is less than enthusiastic, he makes a comment on her refusal and she testily replies "Refusing an assignment? You make it sound like you're my supe-rior." She does go to Philadelphia on the case and while there meets a young man, Ed Jerse, having a rather unusual relationship with his new tattoo—it is talking to him and telling him to do quite antisocial things. It seems that the dye used in the tattoo is an ergot alkaloid that is induc-ing hallucinations, or is it? During the encounter with Ed, Scully also gets a tattoo and appears to develop quite a relationship with the young man. Scully is hospitalized as a result of the ergot poisoning and when she returns to work, Mulder tries to make amends, but does not know how. As a matter of fact, I think Scully nailed it on the head. Mulder says, "All this because I didn't get you a desk?" Scully looks at him for a long time and then says, "Not everything is about you, Mulder. This is my life." In the very next episode she discovers that she has inoperable cancer.

Learning that her prognosis is terminal changes Scully in many ways, forcing her to confront personal demons, such as the deaths of her father and sister, and reflect upon the decisions that she made, such as joining the FBI rather than practicing medicine. Mulder, convinced that her cancer is related to her abduction, races to find answers that may lead to successful treatment. Along the way he must make a deal with the Cigarette-Smoking Man to save Scully's life, thus compromis-ing his own beliefs and values. Scully has become what she was sup-posed to study and refute: an X-File. While Mulder's quest is to solve the mystery of his sister's disappearance, he is determined that he will save Scully. This time he is not a young boy, who could only watch helplessly as his sister was abducted. This time he would make a difference. He does succeed in saving Scully, but the storyline itself continued the unfortunate story arc of Scully as victim.[14]

Scully and Mulder's Relationship

Chris Carter had always stated that Mulder and Scully would not be romantically involved. Oh, there would be sexual tension, but the focus of the program was to be on the story. However, as time progressed it became increasingly clear that a relationship had developed, one that was increasingly romantic, albeit platonic. While the relationship clearly developed over the course of years, the episodes of the 6th season really brought it into focus. In *The Rain King* (6X07), Mulder and Scully fly to the Midwest to investigate a man who can reportedly cause rain. We learn through the course of the episode that the rainmaker is actually a man named Holman Hardt who is in love with a coworker, Sheila Fontaine. She is unaware that he loves her. This episode is filled with humorous quips. For example, Holman asks Mulder for dating advice and Scully is so incredulous that she cannot speak, finally asking Mulder "When was the last time you went out on a date?" Both Holman and Sheila are incredulous that Mulder and Scully are not romantically involved. Holman even mentions the way that Mulder looks at Scully, to which Mulder replies that he is perfectly happy with his relationship with Scully. When Sheila finally learns that Holman loves her, she and Scully share a few private moments in the ladies' room. Sheila does not know what to think about Holman's love for her. She never thought of him that way, to which Scully says:

> Well, it seems to me that the best relationships, the ones that last, are frequently the ones that are rooted in friendship. You know, one day you look at a person and see something more than the night before—like a switch has been flicked somewhere. And the person who was just a friend is suddenly the only person you can imagine yourself with.

Another great example of the evolution and changing dynamics of their relationship is shown in The *Unnatural* (6X20). Mulder is looking through old newspaper articles. Scully brings him another bound volume and then stands up to look longingly out of their window.

"Mulder, it is such a gorgeous day outside," says Scully. "Did you ever entertain the idea of trying to find life on this planet?" He is actually looking at some rather unusual baseball statistics and upon further exploration discovers that one summer in Roswell, New Mexico an alien had assumed the countenance of a Negro man in order to play baseball. At the end of the episode, Mulder calls Scully down to the ballpark and gives her lessons on how to hit a baseball. The scene is playful but provocative in the way Mulder holds Scully and places his hands on her.

Scully has a strange encounter with an obsessed writer in the episode *Milagro* (6X18). The writer, Phillip Padgett, is so obsessed with Scully that he moves into the apartment next door to Mulder; none were available in Scully's apartment building. He is writing a book about a serial killer. This is how he will meet Scully—she will investigate the killings. The things that he writes about Scully are eerily reproduced in her life and she finds herself acting in ways that are uncharacteristic; for example, she actually goes into Padgett's apartment and into his bedroom even though she would never really do such a thing. Mulder is sure that Padgett is linked to a series of grisly murders, in which the victims' hearts are torn out of their chests, with no visible means of exit. Padgett believes that he loves Scully. He says: "In my book I'd written that Agent Scully falls in love. But that's obviously impossible. Agent Scully is already in love." In the end, Padgett saves her life by throwing the book into the fire, thus destroying his protagonist, the murderer.

Mulder and Scully's relationship does become sexual, at least for one night in *All Things* (7X17), written and directed by Gillian Anderson. In this episode we see Scully confront her past as she tries to determine if she has made the correct decisions—to leave medicine and join the FBI and to leave a man who was falling in love with her and planning to divorce his wife so that they could marry. As Scully visits Dr. Waterston in his hospital room, he asks her what she wants. She replies: "I want everything I should want at this time in my life. Maybe I want the life I didn't choose." Later when Scully discusses the revelations that have occurred to her, she tells Mulder "I once considered spending my whole life with this man. What I would've missed." The dialog between the two continues:

> Mulder: I don't think you could know. I mean, how many different lives would we be leading if we made different choices? We don't know.

Scully: What if there was only one choice? And all the
other ones were wrong. And there were signs along the
way to pay attention to. . . ."
Mulder: All the choices would then lead to this very moment. One wrong turn and we wouldn't be sitting here together.

At that moment Scully falls asleep and Mulder gently covers her with a
blanket. At some point after that, she joins him in his bed. And, surprising all of us, her most of all, is Scully's pregnancy. After all, Scully
supposedly has no ova. In an effort to keep us guessing, we learn in
Season 8 that Scully had asked Mulder to donate sperm (*Per Manum*,
8X08) in the hopes that she could conceive via *in vitro* fertilization.
However, at the end of this episode we learn that the procedure was
unsuccessful. We are still unclear if (Fox William) Mulder is the biological father of baby William, but consider the significance of the
baby's name: he is named for the fathers, Mulder's, Scully's, his own?
We can surmise that he is Mulder's child. Perhaps Scully's most heart-
breaking moment is when she places William for adoption in order to
protect him from those who believe that he is the savior of the new race
of humans: the alien-human hybrid.

Whereas Scully's relationship with Mulder changes during the 6th
season, beginning a romance that clearly does not conform to traditional notions of romantic relationships, Scully confronts many events
that change her, in many ways making her stronger and in many ways
serving to reinforce traditional gender stereotypes. For example, she
battles cancer and survives. She learns that she has a biological child of
whom she knows nothing and watches that child die. Mulder discovers
the lengths to which the Syndicate has gone to use Scully in their
schemes to create the alien-human hybrid, and he tries to keep the information from her, ostensibly to protect her. However, he only succeeds in angering her, providing another example of a man determining
what do with a woman's body. And yet, Scully realizes that Mulder is
her soul mate. She attempts *in vitro* fertilization with Mulder as the
donor, but the attempt fails. Mulder is abducted and Scully discovers
that she is pregnant. Mulder is found, buried, and resurrected only to
abandon her and the child in an attempt to save his own life. After
Mulder's abduction Scully gains a new partner, whom she does not
trust, much as Mulder did not trust her in the beginning.

Scully: Life and Death

The episodes that showcase Scully's cancer allow us to explore Scully's take on her life as well as her relationship with Mulder in more detail. Scully is diagnosed with a nasopharyngeal tumor in *Momento Mori* (4X15). We learn more about her attitude toward life and her feelings about her work in this episode as Scully records her observations in a diary she writes for Mulder:

> I feel these words as if their meaning were being lifted from me, knowing that you will read them and share my burden as I have come to trust no other. That you should know my heart, look into it, finding there the memory and experience that belong to you, that are you, is a comfort to me now as I feel the tethers loose and the prospects darken for the continuance of a journey that began not long ago, and which began again with a faith shaken and strengthened by your convictions. If not for which I might never have been so strong now as I cross to face you and look at you incomplete, hoping that you will forgive me for not making the rest of the journey with you.

The poignancy of these words stresses the love that Scully has for Mulder. As Carter states: "It's absolutely plain that they love each other—in their own way. And it's the best kind of love. It's unconditional. It's not based on a physical attraction, but on a shared passion for life and for their quest."[15]

Mulder believes that Scully's cancer is the result of whatever happened to her during her abduction, because a number of women who were abducted contracted the same type of cancer as Scully and later died. As Mulder tries to find answers to the puzzle and, in doing so, find a cure, he discovers a secret laboratory facility using the abducted women's ova in a breeding experiment. Mulder finds a test-tube that contains Scully's ova and steals it from the lab.

We learn in Season 5 that Scully's ova have been used to create a child. At first Scully believes Emily is her sister's biological daughter, because of the child's uncanny resemblance to Melissa. Indeed, Melissa apparently contacts Scully, telling Scully that the child is in danger (*Christmas Carol*, 5X5). The child is dying and it is unclear if the doctors treating her are hastening the illness or truly helping her. This episode brings home to Scully the truth about her own inability to bear children. When talking to her mother, Scully says "Several months ago

[*Momento Mori*, 4X15] I learned—as a result of my abduction, of what they did to me—that I cannot conceive a child." Furthermore she says "I just never realized how much I wanted it, until I couldn't have it." As the episode ends, Scully is stunned to learn that Emily is her biological child. Nevertheless, the child dies and there is nothing that Scully can do to stop it except love the child for the short time she has available (*Emily*, 5X07). Scully comes to the realization that decisions made earlier in life can be renegotiated and further exploration of this theme occurs throughout the course of the 5th and 6th seasons. In many respects Scully undergoes a life review throughout these 2 years examining the choices she made earlier in her life and deciding whether or not the decisions still fulfill her as a woman. We will see the ways that she negotiates this life review in her changing relationship with Mulder and her "miracle" pregnancy.

Scully-Go-Lightly[16]

Episodes in which Scully appears out of character are rare, but have been filmed, for example in the Season 3 episodes *Wetwired* (3X23) and *Syzygy* (3X13), Season 6's *Three of a Kind* (6X19), and the Season 7 episodes *First Person Shooter* (7X13) and *Je Souhaite* (7X21). In *Wetwired* Mulder and Scully investigate a case in which normal, everyday citizens engage in a bizarre series of murders. For example, a woman believes that her husband is having sex with the next-door neighbor in their backyard. She kills the neighbor only to learn that the husband had been swinging in the hammock with the family dog. Mulder learns that each person involved in the bizarre string of murders had watched a great deal of TV and that a mind control device had been inserted into their cable. While watching tapes found at one crime scene, Scully succumbs to the mind control, rendering her increasingly paranoid and suspicious of Mulder.

Syzygy was one of my favorite episodes although a lot of fans did not like it. In this episode Mulder and Scully investigate a series of deaths among a group of high school students. The townspeople are concerned that a satanic cult is operating in the area and hence none of their children are safe. However, the strange disturbances in the town are actually due to an unusual planetary alignment called a syzygy. It seems particularly focused in this town where 2 young girls, Terri and Margi, born on the same day, tinker with black magic. Apparently the girls are affecting their classmates, usually ones they are jealous of or who have hurt their feelings. Things come to a head when they both

desire the same young man; he has a girlfriend and does not like either
Terri or Margi. They kill his girlfriend and eventually kill him accidentally as they fight over him. Even Mulder and Scully's normally respectful and friendly relationship is strained in this episode as they
bicker with and insult one another repeatedly. Scully acts very jealous
of the local police detective, snaps at Mulder, and even smokes a cigarette. As I mentioned earlier, I prefer the monster of the week episodes,
and I especially like the funny ones (so Season 6 is my favorite season
of the 7 with Mulder and Scully).

  Three of a Kind (6X19) follows the Lone Gunmen trying to crash
the Defcon (Defense contractors) convention in Las Vegas. When one
of their friends is killed, they call Scully, pretending to be Mulder, and
ask her to come to Las Vegas. While investigating the murder, Scully is
injected with an experimental drug called analytic histamine, which is
being developed as a brainwashing drug. The drug causes the normally
logical and rational Scully to exhibit traits the exact opposite of her
normal personality. Upon waking from the attack she tells Langly,
"sure cutey." Later in the hotel bar, men surround a very giddy Scully.
As she holds a cigarette in her hand, all of the men offer her a light and
she says "I just can't decide who lights my fire." At this point, Frohike
(she keeps calling him Hickey) removes her from the scene. It is only
at the very end of the episode that she realizes she has been tricked—
Mulder is in Washington. The episode ends with Scully saying "I am
gonna kick their asses," a nice throwback to Frohike's earlier remarks
when Byers first calls for her help.

  In *First Person Shooter*, Mulder and Scully investigate the death of
someone playing a virtual reality game. This episode also features the
Lone Gunmen. Langly has written some of the programming for the
new game and they all expect to receive stock options in the company,
potentially worth millions. However, they have called Mulder and
Scully for help because of an inexplicable murder. After another person is murdered in the game, the gunmen try to patch the game. However, the game starts itself and the 3 are caught inside. Mulder enters
the game to rescue them but he is also rendered powerless against the
game's protagonist, Maitreya. To save Mulder, Scully enters the game
and between the two of them, they manage to best Maitreya. However,
the code for Maitreya is so complex, the computer restarts itself and
recreates her, placing Scully's head on Maitreya's body. Needless to
say we have never seen Scully dressed in such an outfit and it is
unlikely that anyone ever would. Maitreya was actually created by one
of the company's employees for her own game. Speaking to Scully,

Phoebe explains: "You don't know what it's like. Day in and day out, choking in a haze of rampant testosterone." Scully replies "I wouldn't be so sure," and Phoebe continues: "I mean, she was all I had to keep me sane. My only way to strike back as a woman. She was my goddess. Everything I can never be." Inexplicably the goddess jumped programs and began feeding off of the male testosterone and aggression of the players.

Finally, Scully was at her giddiest in *Je Souhaite* (7X21), when Mulder found a genie in a rug. The focus in this episode is on Mulder, but we do get to see Scully behaving in quite a new way. After the body of Anson Stokes is found, invisible, Scully is given the task of autopsying him. She is incredulous that the body is invisible and dusts it with fingerprint powder to make it visible. She is stunned and quickly places a call to Harvard Medical for additional verification. Unfortunately for Scully Anson's brother uses one of his own 3 wishes to bring his brother back, alive. Mulder is the next person who unwraps the genie and is thus granted 3 wishes. Wasting 2 trying to make the world a better place, he gives his final wish to the genie so that she may no longer be immortal. The last scene of this episode finds Mulder and Scully drinking beer and watching a movie in Mulder's apartment. This episode serves to show that even after all of their years together, Scully is still the hardheaded, practical one and Mulder is still the dreamy romantic. Unfortunately, Scully would change in many respects after the 7th season, becoming more emotional and irrational, trying repeatedly to emulate Mulder's intuitive understanding of the X-Files and failing to do so.

Scully Confronts Good and Evil

We know from early in the series that Scully is very religious. She was raised Catholic and has worn a cross, given to her by her mother, in virtually every episode. Even when Scully was abducted, in *Duane Barry* (2X05) and *The X-Files* movie, Mulder finds and saves the cross for her. Several episodes have caused Scully to examine her faith. Chris Carter believes that:

> Faith is the backbone of the entire series—faith in your own beliefs, ideas about the truth, and so it has religious overtones always. It is a more sensitive area on television because you run the risk of pissing certain people off, but I think we handled it in such a way as to make it about mira-

cle belief, or lack of belief—and we set it against the paranormal, which is, 'Why can Mulder believe in things that
go bump in the night, and when Scully believes in a miracle
he shuts her down?' I think it was one thing juxtaposed
with the other that gave the episode [*Revelations*] its interest.[17]

In *Revelations* (3X11) someone is killing stigmatics; however, all of the
stigmatics that have been killed so far are apparently fraudulent. While
investigating the 11th such death, Scully and Mulder learn of a young
boy who is apparently the real thing. Scully must protect the boy from
Satan's disciple; the one originally sent to protect him is killed. In this
episode we see Mulder at his worst, ridiculing Scully for believing in
God and miracles. She even asks him "How is it you can go out on a
limb whenever you see a light in the sky, but you're unwilling to accept
the possibility of a miracle?" (Frankly since I really think Mulder is a
jerk, this seems to fit right into his personality—no one is right, except
him.) After Scully saves the boy, she goes to confession for the first
time in 6 years. She talks with the priest about the miracle she has seen,
and tells him that she is afraid "that God is speaking, but that no one's
listening."

The episode *All Souls* (5X17) is shown in flashback as Scully con-
fesses to her priest the events that she has just witnessed. Scully was
called to investigate the bizarre death of a young woman who, although
wheelchair bound, was found kneeling in supplication in the middle of
street with her eyes burned out. While investigating the crime, 2 other
young women are found in similar poses, also with their eyes burned
out. We subsequently learn that there is a fourth young woman at risk;
the 4 are sisters. Upon autopsy Scully finds evidence of an unusual
growth on the girls' backs, where wings might be found. We learn that
the girls are actually Nephilim, the "fallen ones," the daughters of an
angel who mated with a human woman. One of the seraphim is sent by
God to take them to heaven and keep them from falling prey to Satan.
While investigating the case, Scully sees visions of her daughter Emily.
Scully must come to terms with the child's death as she comes to realize that she must allow the last young woman to die. Thus, Scully in
effect saves the 4th girl from losing her soul to Satan. But, having to let
the girl go was as hard for Scully as was letting her own daughter go.
The episode is emotionally powerful for Scully as she finally confronts
her grief over Emily's death, realizing that she must come to truly believe that God works in mysterious ways, as she was always led to believe.

Just as the miracles in these two episodes help Scully confront and regain her faith, so to do the 3 episodes in which Scully confronts evil incarnate. *Beyond the Sea* (1X12) finds Scully believing a serial killer on death row who seems to know more about the kidnapping of two college students than seems possible given his incarceration. He also seems to know things about Scully that no one else does, such as the nickname given her by her Sunday school teacher when she was young. Scully believes that Luther Lee Boggs can help with the case. This is a particularly trying time for Scully because she has just learned of her father's death from a massive coronary. Boggs tells Scully that he will deliver her father's last message to her, before he is executed. Instead, Scully rejects Boggs' intimations. When Mulder asks doesn't she want to know what the message was, she replies "But I do know. He was my father."

Absolutely chilling are the 2 episodes featuring Donnie Pfaster, a death fetishist. In the original script Pfaster was to be a necrophiliac, but network executives refused to allow that topic to be presented. In *Irresistible* (2X13) Donnie Pfaster works as a mortician's assistant, work that allows him to fulfill his fetish, which focuses on fingernails and hair. After he is caught cutting a corpse's hair, he is fired from his job and must find other ways of satisfying his needs. As with many sex offenders, Donnie's compulsion escalates, eventually into murder. He accosts prostitutes, kills them, and removes their fingers. When Scully and Mulder are called to investigate the first murder, Scully is almost unable to continue with the case. She discusses her feelings with a counselor, admitting that she doesn't want Mulder to know how much the case is bothering her. She trusts him with her life but she does not want Mulder to think that she must be protected. Pfaster kidnaps Scully, captivated by her red hair, but Mulder saves her. Pfaster later escapes from prison and pursues Scully again, as she was the one who got away (*Orison*, 7X07). Although Scully is clearly shaken by her knowledge of Pfaster, and tells the US Marshals that he is pure evil, she continues working on the case. Upon returning to Washington, she is surprised by Pfaster who is waiting for her in her apartment. Mulder realizes in time where Pfaster is, but Scully is the one who kills him. Later, Mulder attempts to console Scully, telling her that she had no choice but to kill Pfaster, he would have killed again if she had not. Scully replies: "He was evil, Mulder. I'm sure about that without a doubt. But there's one thing that I'm not sure of." The dialogue continues:

> Mulder: What's that?
> Scully: Who was at work in me. Or what. What made me
> pull the trigger.
> Mulder: You mean, if it was God?
> Scully: I mean, what if it wasn't?

Certainly Mulder and Scully have different ideas about faith. Mulder
has the skepticism that many modern men and women have of organized religion. Scully, on the other hand, has never lost her faith in the
God in whom she believes. Confronting evil as she has done many
times while working on the X-Files has confirmed her faith rather than
shaking it and religion remains one of the many areas in which Mulder
and Scully do not agree. However, Mulder seems unwilling to discuss
the issue with Scully, ridiculing her beliefs in many ways. Nevertheless, it is Mulder who repeatedly saves the cross that she always wears,
returning it to her after her abductions and other situations when the
cross has been lost. In this gesture at least he acknowledges the power
that this symbol has for her.

Scully Beyond Mulder?

Frankly, I thought the ending of *The X-Files* left much to be desired and not because of Doggett and Reyes. As I noted at the beginning of this chapter, I liked Agents Doggett and Reyes and wish the
series could have continued with them in the lead roles. Perhaps they
will be included in future movies.

As stated, my favorite season with Mulder and Scully was #6, the
one with all of the funny episodes. But David Duchovny wanted to
leave the show and I said good riddance. Unfortunately, Scully went
crazy. It seemed like she did not do anything the last 2 years except cry,
especially after William was born. Finally we had a strong female character on TV, holding her own in a world dominated by men, and she
had to go and get pregnant! I fully understand that the purpose of the
Women's Movement was to give women choice. And, the purpose of
Scully's baby was to contribute to plot line: How did a woman whose
eggs had been harvested get pregnant? Who was the father? But really!
Suggesting that the birth was virginal (when we know Scully was not a
virgin) and that he (why did the baby have to be a boy?) was the new
messiah ("I just followed the light.") got more and more ridiculous as
the episodes unfolded. If the baby was supposed to be the new messiah,
then why did *Mulder* have to run away? The entire plot line was ludi-

crous and an insult to the fans. Why couldn't Mulder just have been on assignment somewhere? Obviously the writers realized their mistake, because more and more shows during the last season revolved around protecting the baby, and eventually Mulder, culminating in Scully giving up William for adoption and she and Mulder going "on the lam." Scully gave up everything for Mulder: her reputation, her career, and the job she loved, even her son. And, in the end, he was just as arrogant and selfish as he was in the very beginning, pulling her into his quest. She lost herself in him.

Thus I vacillate day by day. Scully did change over the course of 9 years. She became more open to the bizarre and weird. She realized that science does not always have the answer to every question, at least at this present time, and she learned to accept this. She realized that Mulder was her soul mate. She realized that Mulder had a gift that she did not possess and that knowledge caused her great distress after his disappearance and her pairing with Agent Doggett. She realized that she was part of Mulder's quest and accompanied him into the unknown. Was she a hero? Good question. The answer? I don't know. She has many of the characteristics of an invisible woman in that she is Mulder's foil, his sounding board and he sure does love to talk. But she really was more than that, because he at least did respect her and listen to her always. She was the only person he trusted. She was certainly more than a heroine. So I would have to classify her as a hero, even if the writers did go overboard at times presenting her as too emotional and fragile, reversing their original vision of Mulder as the feminine and Scully as the masculine, the animus and the anima, if you will.

In terms of female identity development, Scully certainly fits the recent suggestions that Erikson's 5th – 7th stages of identity, intimacy, and generativity are reversed for women (e.g., Gilligan, 1982; Rogers, 1987). As noted previously, Scully confronts her decisions in several episodes. She discusses her decisions about children with her mother when she learns that she is barren (*Christmas Carol*, 5X05). While having children was not a priority for a young Scully, it was a possibility for the future. Learning that all of her eggs were harvested meant that biological children would no longer be an option. Women who opt for careers early in adulthood begin to question that decision in their early thirties, reevaluating their earlier options and choices. Scully no longer has the option of family, at least not biological children, at this point in time. Later she tells her former lover that perhaps she made the wrong decisions earlier (*All Things*, 7X17). In other words, Scully has reached her late 30s and is reassessing her life much as Levinson (1978; 1996)

says men and women do at the age 40 transition. Most people hate to
think about it, but middle-age actually begins in the 30s (chronologi-
cally speaking). Thus Scully is having a mid-life crisis, examining the
choices that she made. What changes should she make now? Change
careers? Start a family? Divorce a spouse no longer loved? Buy a red
sports car? Travel? All of the things we think about as we begin our
own reevaluations—Scully must confront them also. She makes her
choice: to remain with Mulder on his quest to learn the truth about the
alien conspiracy. Along the way she gives birth to a child she loves
beyond measure but must give up to protect. She gives up her career,
choosing to follow Mulder into the unknown. I wonder what happened
after that.[18]

Notes

1. *The X-Files Official Magazine*, published by Fandom Inc., Santa Monica,
CA.
2. Tannebaum, R. (1998, June). Scully and Mulder's Excellent Adventure.
Details, 130 – 138, 172 – 173.
3. This quote was taken from the jacket cover of Fox Video's *The X-Files*
collection (©1995), containing the episodes *Pilot* and *Deep Throat*. This video
also contains a "private conservation" with series creator Chris Carter, during
which Carter gives his motivation for creating *The X-Files*: "First and foremost,
what I want to do is scare people's pants off." When discussing the television
program, its title, *The X-Files*, will be printed in italics. References to Mulder
and Scully's assignment, solving X-Files, will not be italicized. Kanar (2000)
used this way of distinguishing between *Star Trek: Deep Space Nine* the series
and Deep Space Nine the space station. I will use the same method throughout
this book for distinguishing between each program's title and setting.
4. All quotes are taken from the episode guides, unless otherwise indicated
(see Bibliography).
5. Although *The X-Files* was on the air for 9 seasons, Mulder was not present
the last two having been taken by the aliens and then going into hiding, devices
needed to explain the actor's absence.
6. This is either quite ironic or another of Chris Carter's mysteries. Mulder
asked his mother who chose which child and Mrs. Mulder told him that his
father chose to give Samantha as hostage. We learn definitively in the last episode of the series that Bill Mulder was not Fox's biological father; the CSM
was. So, did Bill Mulder not make the decision? Did CSM choose? Was Mrs.
Mulder lying? Or did Bill Mulder go to his grave believing that he saved a man
he thought was his son, destroying instead his own daughter? In that case, was
Bill Mulder Samantha's biological father? It would explain why she was taken

instead of Fox: the CSM wanted his sons to live to carry on his work and did not care about Bill Mulder's daughter.

7. *The Sign of the Four*, Sir Arthur Conan Doyle.

8. In keeping with all things X-Files, I will use the season and episode designations first introduced by Lowry, 1995. The first number indicates the season and the second designates the episode number. Hence 1X12 is the 12th episode of the first season. Each episode also has a title.

9. *The Oxford Desk Dictionary and Thesaurus, American Edition*. (1997). New York: Berkley Books.

10. I don't know if it's me or not, but I constantly refer to them as Mully and Sculder, perhaps because I see them as such extensions of each other, or as Jung (1964) would say, the anima and animus.

11. *The X-Files* (1998). Directed by Rob Bowman. The movie is sometimes subtitled *Fight the Future*.

12. Nollinger, M. (1996). 20 things you need to know about *The X-Files*. *TV Guide, 44* (14), 18 - 24.

13. Lowry, B. (1995). *The Truth is Out There™: The Official Guide to The X Files™*. New York: HarperPrism.

14. The issue of Scully's victimization throughout the series has been discussed very well recently by Kuhlman (2004). The use of Scully's ova to create children other than Emily is the subject of fan fiction, which has been reviewed and discussed by Silbergleid (2003). To a feminist such as myself it is depressing to read the fan fiction that has Scully quitting the FBI so that she can stay home and raise children.

15. Meisler, A. (1998). *I Want to Believe™: The Official Guide to The X Files™ Volume 3*. New York: HarperPrism.

16. Langly calls Scully this in the episode *Three of a Kind* (6X19) after she is injected with a drug that makes her drunk.

17. Lowry, B. (1996). *Trust No One™: The Official Third Season Guide to The X Files™*. New York: HarperPrism.

18. Thanks to Dr. Aaron Culley, Department of Sociology, Wingate University for comments on this chapter. He suggested that I add the information on the episode *Bad Blood* and pointed out where I needed to make other corrections for clarity. I appreciate his helpful comments and suggestions. Any mistakes remaining are my own.

Chapter 4: *Babylon 5*[TM]

First off, I have to state that *Babylon 5*[1] is my favorite television program of all time. I know almost every episode by heart, having watched them repeatedly on TV and on my own (purchased) copies. It is always a joy to watch each episode because I constantly notice something that I never noticed before. The web site, www.scifi.com/babylon5, contains general information about series characters with episode guides and bulletin boards for chatting. DelRey Books publishes novels about the station and its crew; there are approximately 22 novels (as of summer 2004) devoted to explorations of the *Babylon 5* universe and its crew but a magazine devoted to the series ceased production in 2000.[2] *Babylon 5* spanned 5 seasons in syndication and is occasionally screened on the Sci Fi Channel.[3] All 5 seasons are available on DVD or VHS. In this chapter I will concentrate on the 5 female characters: Ambassador Delenn, Commander Susan Ivanova, Captain Elizabeth Lochley, and the telepaths Talia Winters and Lyta Alexander.

The Last Best Hope for Peace[4]

Babylon 5 is a love story and a war story, set on a space station 5 miles long, in which a quarter of a million humans and aliens reside. The station is the 5th in the series, the other 4 having mysteriously exploded or vanished entirely. The station was built after the last Great War, between Earth and Minbar, which ended 10 years prior to the time when this story begins, which is 2257. Babylon 5 is meant to serve as a diplomatic mission, sort of a United Nations in space (Lancaster, 1997; Savage, 1997). Each species in the known universe has sent an ambassador to represent them in the League of Non-Aligned Worlds.

The 5 major races, Human, Minbari, Centauri, Vorlon, and Narn, serve
as an advisory council to the League. During the first season, Commander Jeffrey Sinclair administered Babylon 5 for Earth Government
(EarthGov) and presided over the Council. Lt. Commander Susan
Ivanova was his second-in-command and Chief Warrant Officer Michael Garibaldi was the head of security. Beginning with the second
season, Commander Sinclair was promoted to Ambassador to Minbar
and was replaced by Captain John Sheridan, the only captain in Earth
Force ever to defeat a Minbari war cruiser in battle during the war.
Known only to the Vorlon and Minbari Ambassadors, Kosh and
Delenn respectively, the Ancient Enemy, the Shadows, has awoken.
One thousand years in the past the Vorlons and the Minbari defeated
the Shadows with the help of a mysterious base of operation revealed to
be Babylon 4, which had traveled back in time for the express purpose
of serving as that base. After that war the Minbari were unified under
the rule of a mysterious being, named Valen, who was found residing
on Babylon 4. We learn in season 3 that Valen is actually Sinclair, who
underwent the joining, and piloted Babylon 4 back in time. Now the
Shadows are on the move again, planning to sow discord into the universe: they believe that the only way for any species to evolve is
through war and strife. Sheridan does not realize that he has been
prophesized by Valen to lead a newly formed army, the Interstellar
Alliance, in this war. Along the way Babylon 5 secedes from EarthGov,
declaring its independence. Following the conclusion of the Shadow
War, Sheridan leads a revolt against an EarthGov that has been infil-
trated by the Shadows and their minions. Following the liberation of
Earth, Sheridan becomes the President of a newly created Interstellar
Alliance. Along the way, he and Delenn fall deeply in love and marry.
They move to Minbar, the headquarters of the Alliance, where Sheridan
eventually dies and Delenn becomes President. The peace established
by the Alliance endures for thousands of years.

   Babylon 5 (B5) was ambitious in its vision (Rogers, 1997). With
the exception of daytime soap operas, never before on television had
there been a show that told a continuing story. B5 was to be a grand
epic set against the backdrop of the universe. The first season set up
many of the plot lines that would reach a conclusion later in the series;
some of the plot lines were never resolved. Mostly the first season set
the stage for the epic by introducing the characters and setting the stage
for future events. Killick (1998b) points out that the first season episodes were more like individual stories and they are generally referred
to as the "stand-alones." The second season episodes can then be seen

as chapters in a book, with various sub-plots that reach a climax at some point in the future. J. Michael Straczynski (JMS, as he is usually called) wrote most of the 110 hourly episodes (91 to be exact); the few that were not were revised by JMS to reflect his vision of the epic and the direction in which the story must proceed.

Female characters on *Babylon 5* were richly drawn. While JMS was the creative genius behind the series, he did allow his female actors to contribute ideas about the evolution of their characters. He was also notable for observing the interactions between the actors and using that information as he developed characterization. Personal information about the actors also found its way into the scripts; this was especially true of Mira Furlan, who played Delenn. Furthermore, when female fans complained about the way that Delenn was depicted in seasons 2 & 3, he listened and presented her again as she was in the beginning (more about this later).

Certainly, *Babylon 5* is one of the myriad science fiction television programs starring a male protagonist (e.g., *Star Trek The Original Series*, *Star Trek: The Next Generation*, *Stargate SG1*, *Battlestar Gallactica*, *The X-Files*, *Farscape*, to name only a few). Nevertheless it contains 5 strong female characters. And, while Captain Sheridan is the "star" of the show, the heart is Delenn. Delenn shaped events in the *Babylon 5* universe. The Earth-Minbari War began because Delenn demanded that the Minbari avenge Dukhat's death. Delenn picked Sinclair, who turned out to be Valen, from all of the Starfury pilots at the Battle of the Line to be brought aboard her ship for interrogation, thereby ending the war. Delenn broke the Grey Council, forcing the Minbari to align themselves with the humans and other races to battle the Ancient Enemy. It was Delenn who served as Ranger One and supervised the building of the fleet to fight the Shadows. It was Delenn who walked into the Fire to reclaim Minbar from the Civil War threatening to tear it asunder. It was Delenn who proposed that Sheridan become President of the Alliance. It was Delenn who survived.

The Corps is Mother, the Corps is Father[5]

Babylon 5 was the first television program (of which I am aware) to use telepaths as an integral part of the show rather than a one-shot plot device. As the 5-year story arc plays out, we see that telepaths are critical to victory in the Shadow War, but some of them are also in league with the Shadows and help President Clark become virtual dictator of Earth. The mystery surrounding telepaths is why they suddenly "appeared" about 100 years prior to current events. Fear of psi abilities by non-telepaths, called mundanes, led to tight restrictions on telepath freedom and the creation of an organization called Psi Corps to police telepaths and protect mundanes. Telepaths who would not join Psi Corps were given the choice of taking drugs called "sleepers" to keep their psi abilities latent. Or, they could go rogue, in which case they had to go into hiding, constantly trying to avoid the Psi Cops, telepaths who were responsible for monitoring other telepaths. Two telepaths were regulars on B5: Talia Winters (Andrea Thompson) and Lyta Alexander (Patricia Tallman).

Talia Winters spent her entire life in Psi Corps; she even married a fellow telepath that the organization deemed would make a genetic match, capable of producing telepaths with perhaps greater psi abilities than their parents. Talia was only rated a P5; Psi Cops were rated P10 or higher. Talia's low rating led to her training as a commercial tele-path, capable of scanning those involved in business transactions for dishonesty. Talia and Ivanova clash from their first meeting; Ivanova's mother was a telepath who was eventually discovered by the Psi Cops and forced to take the sleepers so that she would not have to leave her husband and children (*Midnight on the Firing Line*, 101[6]). However, the sleepers were powerful anesthetizing drugs and, over the course of several years, produced debilitating depression. Ivanova's mother eventually committed suicide and for this Ivanova hates Psi Corps. She is quite blunt about her feelings and does not respond to Talia's overtures for friendship, at least in the very beginning. Talia and Ivanova did gradually become friends and eventually lovers. Late in season 2 Lyta Alexander returns to Babylon 5 with the news that they have a spy on board the station. This spy is a "sleeper," an artificial personality sub-merged within the spy's personality so deeply that they have no knowl-edge of it. Lyta has obtained the password that will activate the artifi-cial personality and scans all of the crew to discover the identity of the spy. Quite by accident, Talia Winters enters Sheridan's office and is scanned by Lyta, revealing her to be the spy. Now, it becomes clear why Talia was so intense in her pursuit of friendship with Ivanova: Ivanova was second-in-command of the station and thus privy to in-formation that might be helpful to those who had programmed the arti-ficial personality (*Divided Loyalties*, 219). We never learn exactly who programmed Talia, but given the way events unfolded on the station, it was probably the part of Psi Corps that was in league with the Shad-ows.

The decision to develop a relationship between Talia and Ivanova was championed by the actors who had become good friends over the course of filming the series. JMS always intended that the two become romantically involved, but he had to show the relationship in such a way that the adult audience members "got it," while children did not (thus making it by network censors) (Killick, 1998b). Plus, JMS was famous for "trap doors." These were plot devices that could be used to explain why an actor left the series, as Andrea Thompson did during season 2. B5 is the only science fiction series that I know of that openly entertained homosexuality as a lifestyle. But, I wonder if the sexual relationship would actually have occurred if Talia had stayed on the station. Later in the series, two of the male characters, Dr. Stephen Franklin and the Ranger Marcus Cole, are sent on an undercover mission to Mars and have to pose as a newlywed couple (*Racing Mars,* 410). Marcus gets into character and constantly talks about things newlyweds would, such as teasing Stephen about his bashfulness on their wedding night, whereas Dr. Franklin is clearly annoyed. However, he is not annoyed at the notion of homosexuality, rather he is annoyed with Marcus in general; Marcus had that effect on a lot of the crew.

Lyta Alexander was the resident telepath on B5 during the pilot episode (*The Gathering*). During this episode, Ambassador Kosh is poisoned. Lyta is called upon to scan Kosh to discover the identity of the poisoner and the type of poison administered. Thus, Lyta is the only human that has ever "seen" into the mind of a Vorlon; they are usually cloaked in an encounter suit that hides their true features as well as providing their own, non-oxygen atmosphere. Lyta is taken back to earth by Psi Corps; they want to know what she saw in Kosh's mind. She eventually escapes and travels to Mars where she joins the resistance. There she learns that there is a spy abroad B5 and travels there to unmask the spy. After Talia Winters is exposed, Lyta leaves B5, as she is now in danger for exposing the sleeper program. She travels to the Vorlon home world where she is physically altered by the Vorlons: they implant gills on her neck so that she can breath in their environment and they greatly enhance her telepathic abilities, increasing them well beyond what anyone suspects. She is also able to carry Kosh's essence around now, allowing it to move freely around the station with no one being aware (we do not know if Vorlons have gender and Lorien, the First One, refers to Kosh as "it" also).

Lyta is a tragic figure in the B5 universe. People are a little frightened of her once she returns from the Vorlon home world. She believes in the Vorlons and uses the abilities they have given her to help win the

Shadow War. She is called upon repeatedly to use her powers and does so willingly. But she becomes increasingly isolated with time: the very powers that are needed to aid the Alliance are the very powers that isolate her. We observe her loneliness and her escalating anger. She is used and never thanked. She is called upon when needed, but no one wants to have anything to do with her at any other time. She complains of this to Zack Allen, Garibaldi's second, who clearly wants to develop a relationship with her (*Epiphanies*, 407). Their interaction is poignant considering everything that comes afterwards:[7]

> Lyta: Zack, how come the only time people come to see me is when they want something from me? Scan someone. Protect someone. Setup the Vorlon so you can take him out. I nearly got my brain fried at Z'ha'dum, but nobody comes just to visit! Nobody comes by and says let's have dinner.
> Zack: I'm sure it's nothing personal.
> Lyta: I don't have to be a tepe [telepath] to know that you're lying, Zack. So, what is it?
> Zack: Look Lyta, you gotta understand, you were close to the Vorlons and they're not exactly popular right now. And, there's a rumor going around that, before they left, they changed you, made some modifications. So yeah people are a little wary around you with everything we've been through lately. Can you blame them?
> Lyta: No, I can't. I guess I already knew it. I just needed to hear it from someone. I needed someone be honest with me about it. Thanks. I might not like it, but at least I know where I stand.

After the conclusion of the Shadow War and the liberation of Mars and Earth, Sheridan allows a group of telepaths to establish a colony on B5, while they attempt to find a world where they can settle and live in peace (*No Compromises*, 501). Lyta, fed up by now with the way she has been treated, takes up this cause. The group's charismatic leader, Byron, is gentle and kind and accepts her for what she is, showing no fear of her. She falls in love with Byron and, in the only sex act ever shown on camera on B5, exposes herself telepathically to him (*Secrets of the Soul*, 507). During the act, the telepaths and we learn that the Vorlons created telepaths for the express purpose of serving as weapons in the Shadow War. That revelation answers a number of questions posed throughout the previous 4 years, but the entire telepath situation is doomed to end tragically. Byron and his followers are killed and Lyta is left alone once again (*Phoenix Rising*, 510). Byron's charge to her is to make his dream a reality and this she vows to do. She has become increasingly hard and ruthless, but also more confident.[8] As Tallman says:

> Lyta's always been a very twisted individual, sad and lonely, and I certainly don't think that's changed. In fact, it's probably worse. She burnt about every bridge she had. She used to have a friend in Zack, and now that's completely alienated. And Franklin might be another friend, but he's so busy that they never talk. So I think she's pretty much obsessed with finding a way to make Byron's dream come true, finding a place for the telepaths to go.[9]

In the name of safety she is expelled from B5, although she lets them know that they really could not force her to go if she did not want to; she no longer hides her power, the power given her by the Vorlons (*Objects in Motion*, 520). She is in reality not even human anymore and allows Garibaldi to see what the Vorlons did to her in the episode *The Wheel of Fire* (519). Explains Tallman (Killick, 1999):

> Evidently Lyta is a walking time bomb, a nuclear bomb ready to go off. She's got so much power in her, she can destroy everything. She destroyed Z'ha'dum [the Shadows' world], she's the one that did that. Okay, there are explosives on the planet, but she tripped it all. I think that's why he's [JMS] sending me off into space, because with that kind of power what else can you do with the character except kill them or have them go away (p. 157)?

Before we learn that Talia is in reality a spy and before Lyta is isolated by the fear of those around her, we see these two women trying to lead regular and ordinary lives. Talia begins to question Psi Corps policies with time. She sees that they have done many ruthless things, such as subjecting female telepaths to rape in order to breed more telepaths and then taking any resulting children away from their mothers (*A Race Through Dark Places*, 207). She learns of other programs in which a former lover is exposed to experimental drugs in order to create a telekinetic human (*Mind War*, 106), and her former husband is exposed to other drugs in an effort to create an empath (*Soul Mates*, 208). She even helps a group of rogue telepaths escape from the Psi Cop, Bester, by combining her telepathic powers with theirs to create the illusion of their deaths (*A Race Through Dark Places*, 207). However, she never disavows her relationship with Psi Corps, even after all that she learned; she had no where else to go and no one to turn to.[10] And, even if she had dropped her guard, would the artificial personality have allowed independent thought and action? We will never know because everything changed for Talia when Lyta triggered the artificial personality. Before this time the artificial personality only emerged when Talia was asleep; the sleeper talks to Ivanova before leaving the station:

> The Talia you knew is gone. There's just me. You don't know what it's like, living only in the shadows of her mind, watching, laughing at all of you out here, foolish, petty, stupid. There I was trapped inside, able to come out only at night, when she was asleep, her invisible sister. And you believed everything she said to you, all of the things you wanted to hear, all the words I whispered in her thoughts, while she lay sleeping, the words that would get her closer to you and what you know (*Divided Loyalties*, 219).

A chance remark by Bester reveals that Psi Corps dissected Talia to learn more about the sleeper program and the artificial personality (*Dust to Dust*, 306). Such a remark served to let us know that even Psi Corps did not know everything that was happening.

Soldiering On

After Sheridan resigns from Earth Force and is elected President of the new Interstellar Alliance, Babylon 5 acquires a new Captain, Elizabeth Lochley (played by Tracy Scoggins). Our first glimpse of her tells us exactly the type of officer she will be. When Lt. Corwin tells her that things are a little hectic on B5 at the moment, she replies "A hectic station is the first sign of a poorly run station" (*No Compromises*, 501). Scoggins commented:

> She's very much by-the-book career military. She's good with diplomacy, but she's not the least bit reluctant to pull out the big guns. I like that about her. She's got a lot of integrity. She's also not afraid to go hands-on.[11]

She immediately clashes with Garibaldi, who insists that she tell him which side she was on in the recent war to liberate Earth. She finally tells him that she fought on the side of Earth, but what she means is that she followed the chain of command and thus fought against Sheridan. She defends her actions by saying that soldiers are to follow orders, they are not to set policy. Interestingly we learn that Sheridan personally asked for her to be given command of B5. Such an action puzzles and angers Garibaldi, Delenn, and others who do not understand why he would ask for someone who obviously fought against them. Sheridan tells them that he trusts her with his life; she will always stand up to him, if she believes that he is not acting in the interests of B5 and EarthGov, although he does override her when he orders her to allow the rogue telepaths, led by Bryon, to establish a colony on B5. We will finally learn that Lochley and Sheridan had been married briefly many years earlier. The marriage did not last because neither was willing to subordinate to the other nor to the relationship. While Delenn is quite angry with Sheridan for requesting Lochley and not telling her his reasons, she supports the decision once she learns those reasons, and tells Lochley so.

Lochley must confront several intense issues upon assuming command of B5. One of these is Byron's telepath colony. The other is the growing menace of the Raiders, unknowns who prey upon others. As usual, one species is taking advantage of the situation to exploit the others, and Lochley must determine who is behind the Raider attacks. We will also learn that, although the Shadows and the Vorlons have moved beyond the Rim (of the Galaxy) to allow the younger races to evolve, the Shadows' minions have been left behind and they are now ready to establish themselves as rulers of the Galaxy. Finally B5 is attacked by an unknown alien species. It is never identified but is yet another instance of the fact that, although the Shadows have left, their philosophy of war and strife has not. All of these encounters serve to show Lochley as a military commander, capable of making life or death decisions with no hesitation. In the world of *Babylon 5* there is no distinction between the genders; soldiers are trained to serve their government, to fight and to die if necessary. No one questions Lochley's right to command B5 because she is a woman; only Garibaldi questions her and that is because of her allegiance to Earth Force command, even though the supreme commander was President Clark.

Although Lochley was only present on B5 for the last season, we learn quite a lot about her in that time. We learn of her love of sports and the outdoors. Her father was in the military; he was also an alcoholic and she rebelled against him when young. We learn that she has made some questionable decisions in the past and that not all of her history is positive. In the episode *Day of the Dead* (511) Lochley is reunited with her friend, Zoe, who died of a self-induced drug overdose. We learn during this episode that Lochley herself had abused alcohol and other drugs; apparently her friend's death was her wake-up call. Despite their differences it is Lochley who forces Garibaldi to confront his descent into alcoholism (*The Wheel of Fire*, 519). And, although Lochley is career military, she is open to relationships. We see one develop between Lochley and Captain Matthew Gideon of the Excalibur from the B5 spin-off series *Crusade*[12] in a few crossover episodes.

Ivanova the Strong[13]

Commander Susan Ivanova "was a strong, mysterious, and complex character," says Claudia Christian, the actor who portrayed her for 4 seasons.[14] Ivanova was in approximately 88 of the 110 episodes of *Babylon 5*, so we were able to learn a lot about her during that time. She joined Earth Force after the death of her brother in the Earth-Minbari War. Her mother committed suicide prior to events on the show and her father died early in the program, so she is the last of her family. She is Russian and Jewish, although she does not have a very good relationship with God. She has a wicked sense of humor along with a wicked right hook; she uses both whenever needed. Ivanova can actually be quite scary; just ask her colleagues. Upon finding Garibaldi sitting at her desk in *Midnight on the Firing Line* (101), Ivanova asks him if he has a good reason for doing so or should she just "snap his wrists" now. Dr. Franklin says "Frankly, she scares the hell out of me." And, Lt. Corwin is petrified when she invites him to her quarters; he thinks it is an overture to romance when in actuality she is interrogating him about his loyalty to Earth (*Exogenesis*, 307).

Ivanova's military career was distinguished; she had combat experience and was trained as a Starfury pilot. No one questioned her right to her post as second-in-command of B5; Sheridan had even wanted her to take over command after he was elected President. In one of his last acts as an officer of Earth Force, Sheridan promotes Ivanova to Captain and she assumes command of her own ship rather than remain on B5 (a plot device to explain her departure from the series). Because Sinclair and Sheridan were supposed to serve as diplomats on B5, rather than emphasize their military status, Ivanova ran the day-to-day operations on board the station, as any second-in-command would.

One of Sheridan's first duties upon assuming command of B5 is to promote Ivanova. He gives her many additional duties following his arrival. For example, he tells Ivanova that she needs to learn diplomacy

Ivanova at the controls of the White Star

and orders her to negotiate a truce between the warring Drazi in *The Geometry of Shadows* (203). In this episode the Drazi are fighting each other over the right to be the ruling caste for a 5-year cycle. Every 5 years the Drazi put green and purple ribbons into a barrel and then draw out a ribbon one at a time. Whoever draws a green ribbon is Green and whoever draws a purple ribbon is Purple. The Greens and Purples then fight each other for one year and the faction that wins, becomes leader. Ivanova must try to reconcile the two sides and is repeatedly frustrated at the randomness of events. When she tries to tell the Drazi that fighting over a ribbon is stupid, they rightly point out that humans do the same for a piece of cloth—a flag. Eventually Ivanova resolves the fighting when she accidentally puts one of the ribbons around her neck. Instantly she becomes Green leader and all of the Greens must now follow her. She immediately marches them all off to the Quartermaster's Office for purple dye: she dyes all of the ribbons the same color and thus all of the Drazi on the station become one.

After B5 secedes from EarthGov, Ivanova begins to have strange dreams and is easily frustrated. For example, she dreams that she comes to work naked (*Sic Transit Vir*, 312). The past months of intrigue and drama are over and Ivanova has too much time on her hands and too little to do. She has, in effect, lost her identity as an officer with Earth Force. She must reinvent herself and this loss of identity is causing tension, stress, and bad dreams. Her solution at this point is to help as many Narn refugees as possible escape their war with the Centauri Republic. Matters on the station come to a head in season 3. The Shadow War intensifies, with the Shadows and Vorlons battling each other. More and more planets are destroyed, resulting in terrified civilians seeking sanctuary. Ivanova begins directing operations and coordinating efforts to relocate said civilians and find sanctuary for the millions displaced by the war. And, following the Shadow War, when Sheridan decides to retake Earth from President Clark, who has established himself as a dictator, Sheridan assigns her the task of serving as the Voice of the Resistance (*Lines of Communication*, 411). Since people on Earth are being fed President Clark's propaganda, Ivanova begins broadcasting information about Babylon 5 and the Earth Colonies to people on Earth so that they will know the truth.

While Ivanova's primary job was always running day-to-day operations on B5, she occasionally takes command of one of the Starfury squadrons or the White Star. It is clear that Ivanova considers herself as a soldier first and foremost. And, she is treated that way by all of the people on board the station. In her universe there is nothing unusual about a woman in combat or command. She thus sees combat during the Shadow War, and although he wishes she wouldn't, Ivanova makes Sheridan promise her that she will be in command of a ship when the final battle for Earth begins. Sheridan keeps his promise, but she is critically wounded during the battle.

From the standpoint of romance this is one of the most poignant moments in the series. Ivanova is bisexual. We learn that over the course of the first 2 seasons when we meet one of her former male lovers (*The War Prayer*, 107) and during the final denouement with Talia Winters (*Divided Loyalties*, 219). With the introduction of Marcus Cole, the resident Ranger on B5, we see the potential for another relationship for Ivanova. Marcus is smitten with Ivanova but she is clearly annoyed with him in the beginning. When he questions her about her reasons, she tells him that she does not know him or where he fits in. This sets up a funny scene where Marcus makes up a poster showing all of the characters on B5 and their relation to each other with Ivanova clearly in the center. Sheridan frequently pairs Marcus and Ivanova, ordering them to find the last of the First Ones (*Voices of Authority*, 305) and to scout for the Shadows (*Shadow Dancing*, 321). It is during those interludes where we see Marcus' feelings for Ivanova and where we see her finally begin to notice. She is, however, afraid to love him; she was hurt badly by Talia, finally admitting this to Delenn during the rebirthing ceremony. When Ivanova is critically wounded, Marcus uses the alien-healing device introduced in *The Quality of Mercy* (221) to drain his life energy to replenish hers. She is devastated to learn that Marcus died to save her life. She knew that he loved her but she just could not open up to him. She cries to Stephen Franklin:

> All my life I've had problems with relationships. You may have noticed. . . . You know the ones that I loved always ended up hurting me and leaving me. The ones who stayed had nothing inside, no depth. After awhile I just decided to forget about it. And here was Marcus. I knew he'd never hurt me and I knew he'd never leave me. And I knew he loved me—I knew it. And, I just didn't want to admit it. And he gave so much and he wanted so little in return. He only wanted a kind word or a smile. And all I ever gave him in 2 years was grief. And, it's because I think I saw what I wanted. I was afraid. . . . Maybe I should have tried one more time. I could have done that for him. Now I can't (*Rising Star*, 421).

Delenn before the transformation

But I disagree with those who characterize Ivanova as easily swayed by romance and allowing femininity to surface in "highly trivialized circumstances," (Ney & Sciog-Lazarov, 2000, p. 228), e.g., by wearing short dresses when off duty or sexy nightgowns at night, or accepting flowers. Why shouldn't she? The male characters are allowed to go off duty occasionally, socialize with each other, and wear "civvies." Again, why do these actions detract from her role? Ivanova is a strong, heroic figure who just so happens to have been "burned" twice, and is leery of entering into another romantic relationship (i.e., with Marcus). She is certainly capable of great emotional attachment: to Sheridan, Delenn, Garibaldi, and Franklin. Her acknowledgement of Marcus and her feelings for what might have been are clearly evident when we meet Ivanova 20 years later at a final gathering prior to Sheridan's death. She speaks his name for the first time in 20 years. Admiral Ivanova has reached the pinnacle of her military career, but she has lost much: friends and lovers. Sheridan recognizes that his old friend was ready for a change. In the end, Ivanova assumes the post of Ranger One, giving her reason to live once again. And so, the story of *Babylon 5* ends with 2 powerful women, one running the Interstellar Alliance and the other training the Rangers who are charged with protecting the Alliance. The legacy lives on for a million years.

Delenn the Wise[13]

Mira Furlan, an actor from the former European country Yugoslavia, portrayed Ambassador Delenn. JMS used her experiences as a refugee from a war-torn country, especially one torn by ethnic strife, when writing her role. It was very painful sometimes for Furlan to act the part of a character exposed to extreme racial prejudice and hatred. She intensely understands the feelings of pain and isolation that Delenn feels following the transformation. As she explains (Killick, 1998b):

> It's incredibly close to my heart because that's what I feel in terms of this whole madness in what was once Yugoslavia. I really feel that I don't belong to any of the groups. I don't. I mean, I'm such a mixture of everything. . . . The whole thing of blood and belonging is not something that I can relate to. I've always felt like a citizen of the world. It's a very hippy attitude, but that's how I feel, and I think that people have a right to feel that way. . . . It's something that

I really feel deep in my own life, so I guess that reflects on
screen (p. 57).

Delenn changed a great deal between the pilot episode, *The Gathering,*
and the first episode of the first season (*Midnight on the Firing Line*).
Her make-up in *The Gathering* was very different, more alien, than in
the series and it was "softened" considerably before filming the first
episode. Delenn was originally supposed to be a male Minbari, who
would become female with the transformation. Much to Furlan's pleasure she was not required to wear the heavier make-up or use an artificial voice during Season 1 after all.

As I stated *Babylon 5* is Delenn's story. To aid in the discussion of
Delenn's character, I will first provide a summary of events that culminated in Delenn's assignment to B5 as Ambassador from Minbar. The
Minbari are an ancient race and were united by Valen 1000 years prior
to current events. We know, of course, that Valen was actually Commander Jeffrey Sinclair who traveled back in time with Babylon 4 to
help the Minbari and their allies win the first Shadow War. Valen created the caste system on Minbar - Worker, Religious, Warrior - and
created the Grey Council as the ruling body. The Grey Council is composed of 9 members, 3 from each caste. Delenn is a member of the Religious caste and is also a member of the Grey Council, although no
one on Babylon 5 knows this. Her assignment on Babylon 5 was to
ensure that prophecy, the future that Valen foretold, would come to
pass. Three great mysteries were explored. The first was who was
Valen: a Minbari not born of Minbari. The second was why the number
of Minbari being born was declining; the number of souls available for
rebirth had been decreasing since the first Shadow War. The third was
why the Minbari had surrendered to Earth Force at the Battle of the
Line, the battle for Earth.

Eventually we learn that Sinclair was taken abroad Delenn's star
cruiser at the Battle of the Line. While under torture they learned that
he carried a Minbari soul. Since Minbari do not kill Minbari, they surrendered rather than harming other humans, who might also carry Minbari souls. Members of the Grey Council realized that Sinclair carried
Valen's soul, although they kept it a secret from their people. Thus the
mysteries were solved when the Minbari finally encountered humans.
However, the Earth-Minbari war had led to terrible tragedy on both
sides and many on both sides could not forget. Delenn was assigned to
Babylon 5 ostensibly to repair relations between Earth and Minbar. Her
real assignment was to watch Sinclair and to fulfill prophecy. She even-

Delenn after the Transformation

tually learns who Valen really was and that she is a "child of Valen," one of his ancestors.

While Delenn may be a member of the Religious caste and a member of the Grey Council, only the former is known on B5. During the first season we see Delenn as she begins what we would consider anthropological and psychological study of human behavior. She had attempted to study humans earlier, but now she was engaging in what is known as participant observation: observing the actions of her subjects while experiencing those actions along with the subjects. Just as the episodes of the first season of B5 were meant to introduce the characters, depictions of Delenn during the first season gave us hints of what was to come in the future and let us know that she was more than she appeared. The first season ends with Delenn's entry into the *Chrysalis* (122), just as Valen foretold. Thus, the cycle of change and rebirth comes full circle. Sinclair became Valen by undergoing a transformation: he was reborn human-Minbari, led the Minbari to their victory over the Shadows, and established the foundation for their renewed culture. His ancestor Delenn comes to Babylon 5, where she undergoes the transformation and is reborn Minbari-human. She fulfills the prophecy, foretold by Valen, who was simply recalling his life.

Delenn emerges from the Chrysalis early in Season 2; she has now become part human. She explains the transformation as a means of promoting understanding between the 2 races in order to avoid another war (*Revelations*, 202). At this point, no one, except other members of the Grey Council, is supposed to know that she is fulfilling prophecy. The transformation has tragic consequences for her as Season 2 progresses (Killick, 1998b). Many fans complained about Delenn's depiction during this season and into Season 3. They believed that she had been reduced to a minor character and a caricature; some even referred to her as "Delenn lite."[15] For example, during this season we see episodes in which Delenn asks Ivanova for help with her hair. Minbari do not use soap and water for bodily cleansing. Rather they use a special chemical that strips off the top layer of their skin, but now that Delenn is part human, the chemical is too harsh and has disastrous effects on her hair. In the same episode Delenn asks Ivanova about these strange cramps she has been having (more about this later). Furlan was very unhappy with that scene, thinking it very juvenile, but JMS was using the idea of a menstruating Delenn to make us ask, Does this mean she is capable to bearing a child? We will learn in Season 3, in a flash-forward of their lives, that Sheridan and Delenn will marry and have a child, a son named David. In another scene we see Delenn encounter a group of Marines on the station. One of the men is very threatening, telling her that she is an insult to all humans who fought in the war. She shows fear during this situation and runs from the encounter rather than fighting, as we know she is capable of doing. There are other examples of this type of behavior. I like to think that JMS was not trying to write her as a traditional feminine-type character, nor relegate her to a minor role, but rather was writing her as a person trying to learn who she is (Killick, 1998b). Delenn changed. In many respects she was like a human adolescent who undergoes an identity crisis: they believe that the enormous changes occurring in their bodies must be accompanied by changes in them psychologically as well. Also Delenn has become partly human and must learn how to act as a human. She does not always "get it right." But, she regains her sense of self and purpose as she realizes that she is "the right person at the right time" for the battles ahead (*Comes the Inquisitor*, 221).

When Sheridan wants Delenn to stay on B5 rather than accompany the fleet into battle with the Shadows, she says, "Never forget who I was, who I am." Sheridan acknowledges that he has been trying to protect her because he loves her, but he must recognize that she is not in need of his protection, only his love. Delenn does accompany Sheridan into battle, helping him direct the battle. She and Sheridan confront the Shadows and the Vorlons to resolve the Shadow War. It is she who breaks the Grey Council and she who is The One, the Rangers' leader. She enters the Wheel of Fire to force the Warrior caste to relinquish control of Minbar and return control to the Grey Council. It is she who establishes the new Grey Council, with its majority filled by members of the Working caste. And, it is she who pushes for Sheridan's appointment as President of the Alliance. And, in the end, it is she who is left behind, after Sheridan's death, to lead the Alliance with Ivanova at her side as Ranger One.

Who are you?

The characters of *Babylon 5* are repeatedly asked two questions: Who are you and what do you want? Thus, the underlying psychological theme of the program revolves around identity issues. Talia Winters comes to question the nature of her association with Psi Corps and confronts whether her entire life was based upon a lie, until she learns that she was not who she thought she was. In actuality her identity is completely lost when Lyta Alexander awakens the sleeper personality. The

Vorlons transform Lyta for their own purposes. She does not really understand what they have done to her until the very end and then she is sent into exile, although given her power it was as much her choice as Captain Lochley and President Sheridan's. Ivanova repeatedly confronts identity issues: her father's death, the problem of the Narn refugees, the Voice of the Resistance, Marcus' death; she meets all of these challenges, eventually becoming Ranger One. And, Delenn must discover who and what she is after the transformation, when she becomes half-human. She learns that, while she changed in physical appearance, psychologically she did not. Her inherent goodness, guided by her intense spirituality, serves her well, even when she is required to confront the Shadows at Sheridan's side, surrender Minbar to Naroon and the Warrior caste, face Sheridan's death, and assume the Presidency of the Alliance.

At a recent conference[16] someone in the audience asked why I had chosen to focus on women who used violence to solve problems and develop their identities. It was a good question and one that I will address specifically in 2005. I really had not consciously realized I was doing so. On *Babylon 5* we have a major character, Susan Ivanova, who does resort to violence on occasion, since she has been trained to do so as a soldier in Earth Force. But, we also see her learn the fine art of diplomacy under Sheridan's tutelage, although he is no more a diplomat than she in the beginning. Thus, Ivanova grows as an officer, a woman, a human throughout the course of her time on B5. Likewise, we meet Delenn as an Ambassador. We are unaware that she is a member of the Minbari's ruling council. We know her to be of the Religious caste on her home world, but we do not know that even members of the Religious caste are taught how to fight and defend themselves, their beliefs, their caste, and their people. Although Delenn's story is bound up with Sheridan and Sinclair's, she "possessed a fierceness and strength that could be reactivated when a previously adopted belief system was being questioned by her" (Iaccino, 2001, p. 115). Delenn grows from a woman more powerful than we know, to one who doubts herself as her physical appearance changes, to one who realizes that it is what is on the inside that really matters. In many ways she is Ivanova's opposite. Ivanova uses force to accomplish her means and Delenn uses diplomacy. As the show progresses we see them reverse these roles many times. And, in the end, it is Delenn and Ivanova who administer the peace that they fought so hard for and lost so much because of.

Men, Women and Gender on Babylon 5

Babylon 5 is not genderless. Rather gender seems to be unimportant in the B5 universe, in my opinion. Obviously there are male and female creatures on B5. Some of the alien societies are more gendered than others. Nevertheless, the 5 alien species we see most often appear to ignore gender. The Narn are a warrior species and the females fight along side the males. The Centauri are considered to be decadent, wearing opulent clothing. The males are far more flamboyant than the females. Male Centauri wear elaborate hairstyles: the higher the hair, the higher the status. Women are bald. Vorlons are genderless, as we know it. Minbari can be either male or female and are assigned duties as per their caste. Women are just as likely to be members of the Warrior caste as men are to be members of the Religious caste. In Minbari society, members of the Religious caste have the higher status.

As far as the humans go on B5, we see humans in every possible light, from victim to victor. The future as envisioned by B5 is not as utopian as is the *Star Trek®* universe. The B5 universe still sees war, although not on Earth, which has finally united as one planet under one government with an elected president. Women are just as likely to be in power as are men and they are just as likely to be in league with the Shadows as they are with the forces of light. Women are apparently not restricted in what they can and cannot do in the B5 universe. Thus, Ivanova is second-in-command of B5, eventually receiving a command of her own, before rising to the rank of Admiral. Men and women may marry anyone they wish, and their spouses may be of the opposite or same sex (in other words, marriage between gays or between lesbians is legal in the B5 future). People may prefer a heterosexual, homosexual, or bisexual relationship and no one looks askance. However, we do not get a sense of childbearing or childrearing on B5. Certainly people live and work on Babylon 5. Children do live on the station, as we occasionally see alien and even human children. Nevertheless we do not get a sense of how the station's military personnel handle interpersonal, familial relationships. Certainly, such relationships are not envisioned as part of the life of station personnel as they are in the *Star Trek* universe, where members of Starfleet travel with their families aboard ship or have their families posted with them to their duty stations (more about this in the chapter on *Star Trek*).

My two favorite characters on *Babylon 5* were Ivanova and Garibaldi. They had a great relationship. They were comrades who eventually became good friends. There was never a hint of anything romantic in their relationship (Ivanova had male and female lovers and Garibaldi mourned the "one who got away." Ivanova remained totally unlucky in love; Garibaldi eventually won back Elise.). The point here is that they are two of the few opposite sex character pairs in television who were comrades only. I point that out here because so many people believe (1) that persons of the opposite sex cannot be just friends, and (2) that men and women cannot serve in combat or other military situations with each other because sexual tension would get in the way. In some respects Garibaldi was a great male character on the show because he did not have sex with anyone at all. When a young marine propositioned him one night, he turned her down, telling her he was in love with someone else (*GROPOS*, 210). Rather than have sex with someone just to be having sex, he said no, and remained celibate until he and Elise were reunited.

Babylon 5 presented us with a vision of the future in which women could and would shape the destiny of the universe. This show presented a racially[17] diverse group of beings living and working in space, confronted by events of epic proportions, reinventing and reshaping their worlds. Women were an integral part of these events and I would not mind living in a time in which women were allowed the freedom to be what Delenn, Ivanova, and Lochley were—women doing their part to create a universe where all beings could live and work in harmony with each other, accepted for what they were, no more and no less.

Notes

1. The television program will be noted as *Babylon 5* (i.e., in italics) in text. When referring to the space station on which the series is set I use the term Babylon 5 (i.e., not italicized) or B5.

2. These novels are written to explore the characters beyond what is presented on an hourly series. In addition, various back-stories that were mentioned in the series are explored more fully in the novels. These novels serve the function of answering questions first posed in a regular episode as well as keeping the franchise alive for its many fans. Several short stories were also written by JMS and published in various genre magazines. Titan Magazines, a division of Titan Publishing Group, Ltd, published *The Official Babylon 5 Magazine*.

3. *Babylon 5* won numerous awards during its 5 year run. *Babylon 5* also spawned 5 made-for-television movies (*In the Beginning*, *The River of Souls*, *Thirdspace*, *A Call to Arms*, and *Legend of the Rangers*) and a short-lived spin-

off entitled *Crusade*. There was a very interesting female character on that show, a thief named Dureena, whose entire species was exterminated by the Shadows. I will not discuss *Crusade* however since only 13 episodes were filmed and that is not enough to explore the character.

4. Voice-over by Michael O'Hare (Commander Sinclair) during the opening credits of Season 1.

5. This is the Psi Corps slogan.

6. Episodes are numbered with the year first and then episode number. Thus, 101 would be the first episode of the first season. All episodes also have titles.

7. All dialogue quotations are taken from the episode, unless otherwise indicated, obtained from re-tv video, Columbia House Video Library.

8. Frederickson, E. (1998, October). Out of the ashes. *The Official Babylon 5 Magazine*, 2(3), 59 - 60

9. Anders, L. (1998, Nov.). Thirdspace: Above and beyond. *The Official Babylon 5 Magazine*, 2(4), 14 - 17.

10. Hayes, S. (1999, November). In search of an ordinary life. *The Official Babylon 5 Magazine*, 2(16), 26 - 28.

11. Perenson, M. J. (1998, April). Babylon 5's Captain Courageous. *Sci-Fi Entertainment, the Official Magazine of the Sci-Fi Channel*, 4(9), 58 - 61, 75.

12. Anders, L. (1999, April). Looking back on Babylon. *The Official Babylon 5 Magazine*, 2(9), 14 - 16.

13. These are titles given to Ivanova and Delenn after The Great Burn, when Civil War once again engulfed Earth, 500 years after the events of *Babylon 5*. Both are so named in the episode *The Deconstruction of Falling Stars* (422).

14. Shapiro, M. (2000, May). Babylon bombshell. *STARLOG: The Science Fiction Universe*, No. 274, 67 – 69.

15. My friend and colleague, Dr. Marie Farr, Department of English, East Carolina University said this. I had never thought of Delenn that way personally. Nevertheless, now that I have watched the episodes repeatedly it is easy to see how many fans would have reacted negatively to Delenn's portrayal during parts of seasons 2 & 3. My especial thanks to Dr. Farr for her comments on this chapter.

16. Ginn, S. R. (2004). BABS and Babes: Reconstructing Gender in Science Fiction Television. Paper presented at the Southeastern Women's Studies Association annual meeting, Savannah, GA.

17. Unfortunately, casting for *Babylon 5* reflected the prevailing tendency among Hollywood executives to cast white actors in the majority of roles. White men played Sinclair, Sheridan, Garibaldi, Londo and G'Kar. White women played Lochley, Ivanova, Lyta, and Talia. A white Yugoslavian woman portrayed Delenn. The only person of color was Franklin, who was played by a black man. I wish that the actors had been more racially diverse. Yet, Babylon 5 was racially diverse if we consider that the station was inhabited by beings from an enormous number of species, many of whom did not look or act human. Robin Roberts (2000) has talked about this issue with respect to *Star Trek: Voyager* and I am indebted to her work on this topic. See the Bibliogra-

phy for reference to her work as well as to Leonard (1997) and Bernardi (1998).

Chapter 5: *Farscape*™

As of the winter of 2004 general information about *Farscape* can be found at http://www.scifi.com/farscape. This link contains detailed information about plots and characters with complete episode guides as well as bulletin boards for chatting with other Scapers, as fans of the show call themselves. The program once had a magazine[1] devoted exclusively to information about the series, as well as publishing short fiction that furthered the adventures of the crew. A few novels that further explored the crew's adventures have also been written. Reviews of *Farscape* were very favorable, and the program was nominated for, and won, several awards. The periodical database for *Farscape* is quite limited which is surprising given the fact that this program was so positive in its portrayals of women.

TV Guide called *Farscape* the best science fiction show (then) on the air. *Farscape* surpassed the producers' wildest dreams, but that did not stop the Sci Fi Channel from canceling the program at the end of its fourth season.[2] Produced by Jim Henson Productions, *Farscape* combined human actors with puppets and spectacular visual effects, in a storyline that combined action-adventure and romance and broke many of the so-called conventional rules of sci fi.[3] Such a combination ensured that it would find both male and female fan support. As in previous chapters I will first provide a synopsis of the program's 4 seasons on air. I will then discuss 4 minor female characters introduced during the last 2 seasons followed by a discussion of the 3 major series characters.

"You have *got* to be kidding me."[4]

Astronaut John Crichton is a physicist who has developed a theory that involves "skipping" off the Earth's atmosphere as a means

Women Rule *Farscape*: Chiana, Zhaan, and Aeryn

to counter Earth's gravity when launching vessels into space. On the day that he tests his theory, his module, *Farscape 1*, is propelled through a wormhole and shot through space. He exits the wormhole in the midst of a battle between a Peacekeeper (PK) battalion and a bio-mechanoid living ship of a species called Leviathan. The Leviathan ship, whose name is Moya, was herself a prisoner of the Peacekeepers. She is attempting to escape, crewed by 3 other prisoners: a Luxan warrior named Ka D'Argo, a Delvian priest named Pa'u Zotoh Zhaan, and the deposed Hynerian emperor, Dominar Rygel XVI.

When John Crichton exits the wormhole he finds himself in the midst of a "battle." The Peacekeepers are trying to recapture Moya and the escaped prisoners. Crichton's ship accidentally hits a PK prowler, killing the pilot, the brother of Captain Crais. Moya evades recapture using Crichton's theory to aid in "starbursting," a propulsion technique whereby the ship can jump across vast distances of space. Moya cannot starburst on her own because she wears a "control collar." Aeryn Sun is part of the prowler patrol attempting to recapture Moya. When Moya starbursts, Aeryn's prowler is sucked into the wake and she travels with the ship to its next destination. Crais vows revenge on Crichton and the first season revolves around the crew's attempts to escape from Crais and the bounty hunters who seek the reward Crais has offered for their recapture.

Aeryn's capture by the crew of Moya leads to her irreversible contamination, the Peacekeeper's term for any Peacekeeper that comes in too close contact with alien species: the penalty is exile or death, and most choose death. Aeryn however joins Moya's crew; we will learn that she is no ordinary Peacekeeper. The crew experiences many adventures, many life threatening, all dangerous. Season 1 episodes revolve around Moya's crew trying to protect Crichton from Captain Crais, who wishes to avenge his brother's death. In addition the crew wish to evade recapture and return to their homes.

Although Moya's crew is bound together by their desire to escape the Peacekeepers and return home, they grow into a "family" (for lack of a better word) over the course of the first season. Refreshingly this family contains no patriarch or matriarch. Although there was some jockeying for position as captain of the ship in the beginning, each character brings his or her own strengths to the family. Decisions are made by consensus; however, during the first season decisions are always made in the interests of the child.

One of the most unique plotlines during the first season revolved around the ship's pregnancy, certainly the first time of which I am aware that a spaceship bred. While Leviathans are physically bonded to a Pilot, who controls their internal functions and provides navigation, the ships can breed. Moya, we learn, was part of a Peacekeeper experiment designed to create a hybrid. Named Talyn after Aeryn's father, the hybrid ship was male and covered with weaponry: the Peacekeepers' goal was to breed a warship. They were successful; however, Talyn becomes increasingly unstable, eventually going insane. Talyn does not need a Pilot since he is a hybrid; however, he does need a being to provide control functions and navigation, which a Pilot would normally provide. Talyn temporarily bonds with Aeryn, but is consumed with jealousy over her feelings for Crichton, who is not a Peacekeeper, and thus unfit for bonding. Talyn wishes to bond with both Crais and Aeryn. Aeryn rejects Talyn after Talyn tries to kill Crichton-Black (getting confused yet?). Crais and Talyn bond and leave the others to find their own destiny, which eventually leads them back to Moya [see the episodes *The Hidden Memory* (120), *Green-Eyed Monster* (308), and *Into the Lion's Den, Part 2: Wolf in Sheep's Clothing* (321)].[5]

At the end of season one, Aeryn was badly wounded (because of something stupid that Chiana did) and needed treatment. Specifically she needed a graft of a piece of nerve tissue from a genetically compatible donor. Such a donor would probably be available only on a Gammak base, a top-secret military installation, which they know is nearby. Obviously the crew would like to avoid such a base, since they are all wanted by the Peacekeepers, for various reasons. But by this point in time, Crichton has already fallen deeply in love with Aeryn and will risk everything to find help for her. Scorpius, a half-Scarran, half-Sebacean hybrid, captures Crichton. Scorpius has developed a device that allows him to extract memories from neural tissue. Scorpius places Crichton in his Aurora chair and learns that Crichton possesses wormhole knowledge. Crichton escapes from Scorpius, but Seasons 2 and 3 revolve around Scorpius' quest to recapture Crichton and steal the wormhole knowledge from Crichton's brain.

Scorpius is the result of the Scarran rape of a Sebacean woman (Peacekeeper is their job, their species is Sebacean—apparently genetically similar to human). Scorpius wants the wormhole technology implanted in Crichton's brain by the Ancients so that he can exact revenge on the Scarrans for their rape of his mother, and hence his own birth, as well as their torture of him after birth. Crichton and crew realize that if Scorpius obtains the wormhole technology then he (and the Peacekeepers) will have a weapon of mass destruction and be able to rule the universe, eventually finding their way to Earth. As the story unfolds new characters join the crew and old ones die. Each member of the crew has one major goal and that is to return to his or her home, right old wrongs, and find peace. Crichton's goal is to return to Earth and, if possible, take Aeryn with him. Along the way, he will be forced to ally himself with Scorpius as he learns of Scorpius' desire to destroy the Scarrans.

Ladies Rule!!![1]

Few television programs, even those on the major networks during prime time, could boast as many strong and fascinating female characters as could *Farscape*.[6] The cast consisted of 7 outstanding recurring characters (see Table 5.1). Grayza is evil, Chiana is amoral, Jool is very young but not so innocent as we believe, Noranti is very old and not above sacrificing everything for the greater good, Sikozu is trying to save her reputation and hide a secret, and Aeryn is trying to find a place for herself in a new world, having lost everything from her old one. Zhaan is dead, having sacrificed her life for Aeryn's resurrection. However, things are never quite what they seem on *Farscape* and such characterizations obscure the richness of each woman as she negotiates a place in her own universe.

Table 5.1: Female Characters on *Farscape* In Order of Appearance

Character Name (nickname)	Actor's Name
Pa'u Zotoh Zhaan (Blue)	Virginia Hey
Officer Aeryn Sun	Claudia Black
Chiana (Chi; Pip)	Gigi Edgley
Joolushko Tunai Fenta Hovalis (Jool)	Tammy MacIntosh
Utu-Noranti Pralatong[7] (Grandma)	Melissa Jaffer
Sikozu Svala Shanti Sugaysi Shanu	Raelee Hill
Commandant Mele-On Grayza	Rebecca Riggs

Jool, Noranti, Sikozu, and Grayza

Jool joined the crew during Season 3 (*Self-Inflicted Wounds, Part 1: Could'a, Would'a, Should'a*, 303). Fan response to this character was decidedly mixed[8] (my spouse hated her, for example, because of her annoying ear-splitting screams). Jool had been kidnapped and placed in a stasis chamber where her organs awaited transplant, should anyone be willing to pay the price for them. Two of her cousins were also in suspension but they later died. Jool was very angry when awakened from her frozen state, blaming Crichton for the death of her cousins, and even going so far as to attempt his murder. She was eventually persuaded that Crichton had nothing to do with the murders, and she joined the crew hoping to return to her home one day. Jool is very young and inexperienced. She is also the most traditionally feminine[9] of the female crew, as far as her actions are concerned. Jool has never been in such dangerous situations before and has no idea of what to do or how to act, thus her experience upon Moya has challenged her to grow in ways that she never believed possible. Jool is extremely well educated and when Zhaan died, Jool became the crew's medic. We learn that Jool was wanted for stealing artifacts from archeological digs (*What Was Lost, Part 1: Sacrifice*, 402), although she claims she only wanted to study them further. The crew treated her unkindly at first because of her youth and inexperience (and that awful scream); she also acted like a spoiled brat. She admits to loneliness as season 3 unfolds (*Revenging Angel*, 316) and there is a certain sexual chemistry between Jool and D'Argo, especially since D'Argo and Chiana were no longer lovers. Jool thinks that Chiana is a "little whore who's easily manipulated and says really cheap, lousy, unintelligible things. . . . Jool is highly amused by that."[10] However, as time passes, Chiana saves Jool's life, cementing their friendship. Since the others are so much older than Chi and Jool, they are often left to themselves (where they usually but unwittingly make mischief). Jool's character grows over the course of her year on Moya as she comes to realize how much she owes the crew for her very survival. They have also let her grow into a new person, one capable to taking care of herself, knowing her strengths and limitations. Jool left Moya to resume her archaeological work (*What Was Lost, Part 2: Resurrection*, 403), with everyone's blessings.

The Old Woman is refugee, rescued by Moya after the destruction of Scorpius' command carrier at the end of Season 3 (*Dog with Two Bones*, 322). She is now along for the ride. We do know that she is not above drugging crewmembers with hallucinogenic powders if she believes it to be necessary. Given the choice between killing millions and killing any member of the crew, including Crichton, she would not hesitate to kill those she loved (*What Was Lost, Parts 1 & 2*, 402 & 403). She thinks in cosmic terms, beyond the personal, unlike everyone else on Moya, with the possible exception of Crichton, who walks a very fine line trying to have Aeryn while saving the galaxy from his very own wormhole knowledge. Noranti is a very spiritual being, much as was Zhaan. Because she possesses a third eye, she can see things of which other people are unaware. It was she who told Crichton of Aeryn's pregnancy, albeit too late for Crichton to stop Aeryn from leaving Moya at the end of Season 3. Noranti is a doctor and becomes the ship's healer after Jool leaves. Since she is very old, she knows a great deal about medicine, herbs, and drugs. She is unsure of how old she is, since she is unclear how to translate her age into Earth years so that Crichton can understand. She says she is 293, but really feels about 18 (Simpson, 2003). She also sees herself quite differently than the rest of the crew. We see evidence of this when Noranti concocts one of her own special powders to save the crew from Tarkan freedom fighters (*Lava's a Many Splendored Thing*, 404). The Tarkans not only believe that she is a beautiful dancer, but so does she. D'Argo and Crichton watch in horror, eventually running away, from the sight of Noranti doing a strip tease. When Aeryn returns to Moya early in Season 4, Noranti gives Crichton Laka beetle juice that dulls the pain he feels because Aeryn will not admit her feelings for him or tell him the truth (he thinks) about the baby (*Promises*, 405). While the crew generally is leery of Noranti's concoctions, she does provide Crichton with the means, via this drug, to counter Grayza's mental and physical rape.

Sikozu of the Kalish race happens upon Crichton at the start of Season 4 (*Crichton Kicks*, 401); her ship crashes into his. After being marooned in his IASA module, Crichton is rescued by a dying Leviathan named Elack. He is accompanying Elack to the Leviathan's sacred resting space when he encounters Sikozu. She was hired to find this resting place so that aging Leviathans could be harvested; their neural cluster tissue is highly prized for its restorative properties. During the course of events, Chiana returns and together Crichton and Chiana manage to keep the secret burial space from being revealed. This was Sikozu's first assignment; however, her reputation has now been destroyed and she has no choice but to join up with Moya's crew, such as it is. Sikozu is very young and inexperienced, with a genius IQ and the ability to defy gravity, a skill that will come in handy.[11] Much like Jool, Sikozu does not have any practical experience with "reality." Most of her knowledge comes from education because she has never actually been out on her own before. Chiana will treat Sikozu the way the others treated her when she first joined the crew: constantly telling her to shut up and get out of the way. Chiana did not like it and Sikozu did not either. The crew never accepted or trusted her, especially as her relationship with Scorpius grew. Sikozu became increasingly enamored of Scorpius, becoming his ally in the quest to destroy the Scarrans. Indeed, by the end of the series it appears that she and Scorpius have become lovers. Plans were for Sikozu and Aeryn to develop the type of buddy relationship exhibited by Crichton and D'Argo, but alas the cancellation of the series put an end to that plan (Simpson, 2003).

Sikozu is actually a member of a Kalish underground resistance group dedicated to overthrowing Scarran rule on her home world and her section of the galaxy. We believe that her ability to defy gravity and to regenerate limbs is either endogenous to her species or the result of genetic engineering to help in her resistance activities. What we learn at the very end of the series is that she is actually a bioloid, created specifically for helping the resistance movement destroy the Scarrans (*We're so Screwed, Parts 1 – 3*, 419 – 421). She is not the only bioloid we meet.

We meet our newest villain, Commandant Mele-On Grayza, in the episode *Into the Lion's Den, Part 1: Lambs to the Slaughter* (320). Scorpius wants Crichton to help him with his revenge on the Scarrans. As such Scorpius is willing to grant Crichton and the crew amnesty and housing on his command carrier. Grayza despises Scorpius. Like most Peacekeepers she thinks he is an abomination, and is enraged that Scorpius is willing to work with Crichton. Grayza is not particularly interested in Crichton at first, except that he is an escaped prisoner and that sets a bad precedent. Scorpius' crew is angered by the amnesty and seeks Grayza's help in re-capturing Moya's crew. Grayza is absolutely ruthless and will stop at nothing to recapture the crew. Crichton calls her Commandant Cleavage because of her extremely low cut uniform. A gland that secretes Heppel oil has been surgically implanted in her chest, and her low-cut uniform allows her easy access to the gland, whose oily secretion makes her sexually desirable and irresistible. We will learn what Crichton thinks of Grayza's actions later and it is only through the intervention of Noranti's drugs that allows Crichton to resist the Heppel oil. When Grayza realizes that she will not be able to prevent a Peacekeeper-Scarran war and has been betrayed, Crichton will ask her if she feels as if raped, a clear reference to his revulsion at what she did to him. Her response: She would do anything to further the alliance with the Scarrans. Her motives are not necessarily altruistic: if she is successful in her negotiations then she will become very powerful indeed. However, the Scarrans have ulterior motives and cannot be trusted. As Grayza and Akhna, the Scarran War Minister, discuss a peace treaty between the two races, Akhna makes a scathing comment about Grayza's methods, referring to the Heppel oil she uses for seduction. Grayza's replies: "If you had a powerful weapon, would you refuse to use it because of squeamishness?" (*Bring Home the Beacon*, 416). Later in the episode we find that the answer is yes, since both Grayza and Aeryn have been replaced with bioloids, the Scarran term for a biomechanical replication of a living being (Simpson, 2003). Crichton realizes that the Aeryn that returned to the ship is a bioloid when she does not know about the baby and cannot remember how to speak English; he kills it.

Since I just mentioned Grayza's rape of Crichton, let me interject a note of this subject. Interestingly, and thankfully, the issue of rape was rarely broached on *Farscape*. In season 4's *Crichton Kicks* (401), the crew was separated for many months. When Chi finally finds Crichton and they talk about what they did while apart, she admits that she was raped and hints at other torture as well. She shrugs it off, saying that her captors "had a little fun," and we are left to wonder what exactly happened and how affected she really was. Earlier an alien being possessed Crichton and he threatened Chi with rape (*Losing Time*, 309). It is a terrifying scene, all the more so because Crichton is one of the most positively portrayed men in television, sci fi or otherwise. He is horrified at himself, as well he should be, and wonders how he will ever be able to make amends even though he was not responsible. And, in a twist of gender stereotypes, Grayza repeatedly rapes Crichton; she will do anything to possess the secret Crichton holds, the knowledge of how to create a wormhole. He is aware however of the repeated rapes and suffers greatly because of his helplessness (*What was Lost, Parts 1 & 2*, 402 and 403). And, as mentioned, Scorpius is the result of a Scarran rape of a Sebacean woman. Apparently the Peacekeepers (except for Grayza) do not use rape as an intimidation or terror tactic; sexual relations with non-Sebaceans would be considered a disgrace.

These characters are different from each other in many ways. But in many ways they are very similar. While Sikozu and Jool appear to be naïve and inexperienced, we learn that neither are what they appear to be. Grayza is ruthless and will use any means necessary to achieve her goal of peace with the Scarrans. But, Noranti is also ruthless. While she appears to be a simple old woman, she is much more than that, and quite ruthless in her own way: willing also to sacrifice the few for the sake of the many. Each provided a good contrast with the major male and female characters on the series.

Chiana

In season one's *Durka Returns* (115) Moya collided with a starship, carrying the Nebaris Salis and Chiana, and the Peacekeeper Captain Durka. Durka had once commanded the Peacekeeper command carrier Zelbinion, where Rygel was confined and tortured for many cycles (years). The Nebari claim that they have "mind-cleansed" Durka and eliminated his violent tendencies. The:

> Nebari are a species that prize conformity and discipline above all else. . . . Chiana was destined for similar reconditioning; however, her crime—at least by her own account—was that she was too much of a nonconformist for the Nebari's serene society.

Rygel attempts to kill Durka in revenge for his years of torture, but only succeeds in freeing Durka of the Nebari's mind control, following which Durka gains control of Moya. During the struggle to regain control of Moya, Salis is found dead, and we never learn for sure who is responsible for his death, but we suspect Chiana. Nevertheless, the crew agrees that Chiana may remain on board Moya for as long as she wishes.

As time progresses we learn much of Chi's past and it is not very pretty. She is a thief who is willing to do anything to get what she wants or needs. She is definitely looking out for number one. Her extreme selfishness has landed the crew in trouble more than once. In season one's *A Bug's Life* (118), Chiana sets an intelligent virus loose on the ship, thinking that the container holding it must contain valuables (else why guard it so well?). The episode ends with Aeryn being seriously wounded, although we do not know how serious until later. Chiana's blend of youth, naiveté, wanton sensuality, and amorality had served her well following her exile from the Nebari home world. She has a problem with trust: trusting other people and having them trust her. Just when it seems that she has "turned over a new leaf," maturing at long last into a responsible adult, Chiana does something to remind everyone of just who she is. For example, most television programs hope to create sexual tension between characters without having the characters act on that tension. However, the writers and producers of *Farscape* think that it would be unlikely for people to be confined together for long periods of time (such as on a spaceship) and not become sexually active. Chiana has no reservations about sex whatsoever and is presented as such. She is aware that Crichton is sexually attracted to her; most men are. Yet, Crichton loves Aeryn and refuses Chi's offers. She does have an intensely sexual affair with D'Argo until he begins to talk of settling down and marrying. Rather than telling D'Argo that she is not ready for marriage, she seduces his son, thereby ensuring that D'Argo will not continue to pursue her (*Suns and Lovers*, 302). Even so, the sexual chemistry between Chiana and D'Argo does not dissipate. They resume their sexual relationship by the end of the series.

Chiana's extreme suspicion of other people's motivations has slowly eroded as she has learned that no one on Moya has ulterior motives for helping her. While not everyone on Moya may love her, they certainly tolerate her and most have grown fond of her with time. Aeryn, among others on the crew, has referred to Chi as a slut; Chi does not apologize. Unfortunately, even in an alternate universe, female sexuality is suspect, but Chi has needed all of her skills and wiles to survive her life in exile. She was always a rebel and her own people planned to use her in a plan of conquest. Late in season 2 we learn that they infected her with a sexually transmitted disease:

> This contagion – transmitted through intimate contact – was to be spread throughout many alien systems in the area. When the Nebari were ready, it would be activated, rendering all who were infected pacified and defenseless against subsequent Nebari invasion (*A Clockwork Nebari*, 218).

Nevertheless, Chiana's exposure to Moya's crew has allowed her to discover hidden traits and talents that she never exhibited before. So, while others have viewed her as a slut, she has also been described as being wild, but with a heart of gold (*Home on the Remains*, 207). Discussing that episode, and Chiana in more detail, actor Gigi Edgley states:

> I don't think she means to be dishonest a load of the time, but when she gets into really hard situations, I think she's trying to go about it the best way she can. When she's in dire straits, she always resorts to using her body. In the

second season, you see more of her battling: she's never
had anybody give a toss about her before.[12]

As season 4 unfolds, Chiana becomes closer than ever to the other
female members of the crew. Always before she was the type of
woman that other women did not like, the type they suspected of being
after their men, even when they weren't. Because Chi is such a sexual
being, enjoying the act, but willing to use sex if necessary to achieve
what she wants or needs, she typically has no use for other women (although we still are unsure if she is bisexual). Their youth, compared to
the others ages, served to bond Jool and Chi eventually. Likewise, Chi
and Sikozu became closer as did Chi and Aeryn. Each woman learned
of her own strengths and limitations as the series continued and they
learned about each other as well. They realized that they complimented
each other in many ways, which served more than once to help the entire crew. Indeed there were several episodes that served to showcase
the women's actions. One of the best is *Bringing Home the Beacon*
(416) in which all of the female crew land on a commerce planet looking for the means to protect Moya from long-range scans. While there,
they discover that Grayza and Akhna are working on a secret peace
treaty between the Scarrans and the Peacekeepers, although the Scarrans are really not serious. It is up to the women to learn all they can
about the negotiations, while obtaining the sensor detector, and escap-
ing detection themselves. They learn that they can rely upon one another and that they do not need the men along after all. Their mission
was a success, although Aeryn was captured and replaced with a bioloid (which they did not realize until after leaving the planet).

Pa'u Zotoh Zhaan

Zhaan was a wonderful character that fans still miss.[13] Zhaan was a
10th level Pa'u, or priest, and a member of the Delvian race, who are
peace-loving and spiritual. She was a beautiful blue color and physio-
logically was a plant. Zhaan murdered her lover, who had planned to
turn over control of their planet to the Peacekeepers. She almost lost
her mind because of that murder but her many cycles of incarceration
allowed her to heal herself and slowly return from madness. While
Zhaan was spiritual, loving, and peaceful, she was also quite strong and
recognized that she contained a dark force within herself. Several episodes during season 1 showed Zhaan's quest to disavow the dark side
of her soul and control the madness therein. In the episode *Throne for a*

Loss (104) a young Tavlek male tries her patience several times. When he suggests that she is soft and weak, Zhaan throws him against Moya's wall and replies, "Soft? Yes, Weak? No." Later in the episode she tells him that she "could rip [him] apart right now. . . help me, I'd even enjoy it." Nevertheless she does not harm the boy because she is trying to help him overcome an addiction to a drug that makes his species aggressive.

Two episodes revealed a Delvian process called Unity, in which two people bind souls and minds, an extremely personal encounter, beyond sexual. It was during Unity that Zhaan killed her lover. In *That Old Black Magic* (108), a vampiric sorcerer is preying on the people living on a primitive trading planet. Maldis captures Crichton and Crais, forcing them to confront each other, so that he can feed on their negative energy. Zhaan joins forces with a native of the planet in order to free the planet from Maldis' grip. Unfortunately for Zhaan she must confront "the darkest abyss of her own primal nature" to do so. Zhaan had used her many cycles of incarceration by the Peacekeepers to learn to control these dark impulses. Now she was called upon to use them again. Following these events Zhaan is worried that she will be unable to control herself in the future. When the crew is manipulated into traveling to the New Moon of Delvia, Zhaan must once again confront her dark side (*Rhapsody in Blue*, 113). Because Zhaan has learned to control her impulses, Tahleen, the high priest, asks Zhaan to share Unity with her so that she might learn to control the madness that threatens all of the missionaries on the New Moon of Delvia.

> Sharing was not Tahleen's style, however. She betrayed Zhaan, stealing more knowledge than [Zhaan] was willing to give. Zhaan severed the Unity, but not before Tahleen had ripped away Zhaan's ability to manage the dark impulses raging in her soul. Zhaan, still adjusting from her difficult encounter with Maldis, was now exposed to all the anger that she had so recently struggled to quell.

Zhaan believes that she will go insane herself and is so consumed with fear that she is unable to help the crew. But Crichton shares Unity with Zhaan, forcing her to see herself as Crichton sees her. This convinces her that she is not evil after all, because Crichton only sees her as a beautiful, caring, and spiritual being.

During a 3-part story arc in Season 2, Zhaan meets the Creators, the builders of the Leviathans (*Look at the Princess, Parts 1 - 3*).[14] They put her to the test in order to determine if she is worthy of being entrusted with Moya. This test leaves Zhaan more determined than ever to continue the Delvian Seek, "a search for perfect understanding and unity with all life" (*Rhapsody in Blue*, 113).

Before her death Zhaan develops a relationship with a Banik slave named Stark who had been tortured by Scorpius and later rescued by the crew. She commits herself to him; however, her selflessness and love for others causes her to sacrifice her spiritual energy and bring Aeryn back from the dead (*Season of Death*, 301). Zhaan and Stark have found Aeryn preserved in a cryopod and realize that she is being stored for "spare parts." Zhaan believes that Aeryn is actually trapped between life and death and is capable of being revived. Zhaan enters into Unity with Aeryn, but Aeryn was further gone than Zhaan realized. Bringing Aeryn back to life weakened Zhaan greatly. Since she was a plant, the crew tried desperately to find a planet where she could be "planted," allowing her to regenerate. Unfortunately they were unable to find such a world in time. They were struck by another ship that fused with Moya. The ships had to be pulled apart or both would be destroyed. To save Moya, someone had to pilot the other ship into the wormhole as soon as the two come apart. Because Zhaan was dying and there was no way they could find a planet for her in time, she piloted the Pathfinder's ship into the wormhole, thereby saving Moya and the crew (*Self-Inflicted Wounds, Part 2: Wait for the Wheel*, 304). Zhaan made the ultimate sacrifice for the crew, since she loved them all. Aeryn, naturally, had a very difficult time dealing with Zhaan's sacrifice and Stark went mad, eventually attempting revenge on Crichton. But even if Zhaan's corporeal body was dead, her soul was alive in Unity and she stopped Stark from harming Crichton (*John Quixote*, 407).

Officer Aeryn Sun

Aeryn is a Sebacean by species and a Peacekeeper by birth and training. Unlike her fellow Peacekeepers Aeryn is the product of a mating based on love between her parents rather than the usual planned birth. She learned the truth about her birth when she was a young girl, but never really knew whether a late-night visit by her mother, Xhalax Sun, was a dream. As punishment for the visit to her daughter and mating for love, Xhalax was given the choice of killing either her lover or her child. She obviously chose Aeryn's father; however, the deed drove her into the madness of an assassin. After Aeryn joined Moya's crew, Xhalax was sent to re-capture her daughter and Aeryn was almost

forced to kill her mother but was spared that ordeal by Crichton and
Crais (*Relativity*, 310). As Xhalax and Aeryn talk, Xhalax accuses
Aeryn of being corrupted and a traitor to the Peacekeepers as well as an
aberration. Aeryn replies:

> My corruption began the moment I was conceived. . . .
> Don't you see my independence comes from you anyway?
> I grew up wanting to be just like a woman I'd only seen
> once. . . . I am a part of you that wanted to be a rebel. . . . I
> am your child.

The scene is poignant because the two can never be anything to each
other, but Aeryn is determined that things will be different for her
child. Crichton's nephew Bobby conducted an interview with her.
Crichton watches the tape of the interview after Aeryn's capture by the
Scarrans. In the interview Bobby asked Aeryn about her family and she
told him that Peacekeepers are expected to bond with their unit. When
he asked her if she missed having a family, she replied "only when I
was exposed to it" (*A Constellation of Doubt*, 417). Later, Aeryn is
tortured by the Scarrans; they want to know the identity of her child's
father. If Crichton is the father, then they can extract wormhole knowledge from the fetus' DNA. Aeryn manages to survive the torture for
some time, denying that the child is Crichton's, but eventually she admits that she does not know who the father is and it could be John. The
Scarrans place her with a woman whom they believe will extract the
information from Aeryn as they bond as fellow prisoners. When Morrock asks Aeryn if she has ever had a child, Aeryn replies no, that
peacekeeper "soldiers seldom do [have children] unless they're placed
on a breeding roster and, in any case, it's not the same as being a
mother. That's why I vowed I'd never have one that way." Aeryn, of
course, realizes that Morrock is actually a plant. When she gets a little
stronger, Aeryn asks Morrock if she has any children. When Morrock
says no, Aeryn kills her by snapping her neck, saying "Good, then I
orphan no one" (*Prayer*, 418).

    Until Aeryn met Crichton and the others she planned to die in
space, just as she had been born. In the *Premiere* (101), when Crichton
tells the crew that they have to take Aeryn with them as they escape
from the commerce planet, Aeryn refuses to go.

> Aeryn is intensely proud of the fact that she can hold her
> own among any of her fellow soldiers, male or female. Be-
> ing trapped aboard Moya and having to count on a crew of

> non-Peacekeepers for her survival at first was anathema to
> her instincts and training, but it forced her to grow as a per-
> son, to think in broader terms and to be better than she was
> before.[15]

Crichton has to remind her that, according to Peacekeeper High Command, she has now been irreversibly contaminated. Contact with un-
classified life forms, of which Crichton is one, means death. When she
still balks and tells Crichton: "It's my duty, my breeding. Since birth,
it's what I am." Crichton tells her "You can be more." She is slowly
learning how much more she can be, but she is increasingly being
forced to confront her past, as painful as it may be, and to negotiate her
way through her past and her present to arrive at her future.[16]

Claudia Black named several of her favorite episodes in an interview with Paul Simpson and Ruth Thomas,[8] including *The Way We
Weren't* (206), *Won't Get Fooled Again* (215), and the final episodes of
season 2. Referring to the episode, *Die Me, Dichotomy* (222), Black
stated, "[it] was a great action piece, and I enjoyed the dance involved
in that. Just for once, Aeryn was making some decisions. I loved her
not being dumbed down." In this episode the crew must save Crichton
from Scorpius (again!); however, Scorpius has inserted a neural chip
into Crichton's brain, controlling his actions by in effect cloning himself within Crichton. The Scorpius-clone leaves Moya, planning to
broadcast her location to the real Scorpius. Aeryn vows to kill Crichton
rather than allowing him to go to Scorpius and endanger everyone's
lives, including his own. The Scorpius clone takes control of Crichton,
causing Crichton to kill Aeryn.

Farscape episodes are very funny, but also very intense.[17] Everyone associated with the show has a very wicked sense of humor says
producer David Kemper. And, that humor helps everyone through the
darker aspects of the story. In an interview with David Bassom[8]
Kemper explained that "On this show, I want to be afraid. I need to be
unsettled." Hence the fact that sometimes the characters do what you
expect them to do, and other times they completely surprise you. For
example, in the second season episode *Taking the Stone* (203), Chiana
believes that her brother has died. No one appears to care or appreciate
how she is feeling, so she steals Aeryn's prowler and takes off to a
planet nearby, the Royal Cemetery Planet. Aeryn, Crichton, and Rygel
follow her only to find that Chiana had taken up with a local people
calling themselves the Clansmen. Chiana, ever the amoralist, is attracted to the young Clansmen's lifestyle of drugs and danger. They:

embraced life-threatening situations, constantly testing each
other with deadly rites of passage. These rites culminated in
a ceremony called "The Gathering," in which Clansmen
would plunge into a subterranean pit, relying on a voice-
activated sonic net to catch them at the bottom. While surviving the jump was considered the highest honor among
the Clansmen, the act itself was extremely difficult to perform and often resulted in their deaths ("taking the stone,"
as the locals put it).

In her extreme grief Chiana decides to take the stone. Crichton wants to
talk Chi out of this dangerous task and take her back to Moya. Aeryn,
on the other hand, tells Crichton to leave Chi alone and let her work it
out by herself. In other words, in this episode Aeryn gets to be the in-
sightful one, rather than the "pin-up girl for frontal assault," as Crichton
says.

We learn some very damaging information about Aeryn's past in
the episode *The Way We Weren't* (206). It seems that Aeryn had been
aboard Moya before, but did not recognize her. Her lover Velorek had
been given the task of bonding Pilot to Moya. But first Moya's original
Pilot had to be killed and Aeryn was one of the squad assigned to the
task. When her lover tells her of his plan to attach a control collar to
Moya so that she cannot be bred, Aeryn seizes the opportunity for ad-
vancement. She tells Captain Crais about Velorek's plans, thus achiev-
ing her goal—prowler pilot. Crichton and the rest of the crew are horrified to learn of Aeryn's role in the previous Pilot's death and in her
betrayal of her lover. In this episode we are reminded of what Aeryn
once was juxtaposed against what she is becoming.[18] All of the beings
on Moya's alien crew have been forced to confront the horrible things
that they have done as well. It is a lesson that we all have to learn eventually in order to grow.

Season 3 allowed us to see Aeryn maturing even further, although
we never see her resolve the guilt she feels over Zhaan's death. When
Zhaan revives Aeryn (*Season of Death*, 301), Aeryn tells Crichton that
she shouldn't be here, to which he replies "This is exactly where you
should be. I love you." And, even though she has never had a relationship that did not "end badly" (*The Way We Weren't*, 206), she finally
tells him that she loves him too. During Season 3 Crichton is twinned
(*Eat Me*, 306) with one Crichton[19] finally developing a sexual relationship with Aeryn that is truly built on equality and trust (probably a first
on TV, with the possible exceptions of Sheridan and Delenn on *Babylon 5* and Mulder and Scully on *The X-Files*). Unfortunately for her,

Crichton-Black dies and she must confront another relationship that ends badly. Crichton-Green has the job of winning her all over again and the season ends with her leaving for good, but neglecting to tell Crichton that she is pregnant (albeit by the twin).

One interview with Claudia Black by Joe Nazzaro[20] found the actor physically exhausted but more than happy with the way that Aeryn evolved over the course of the first 3 seasons of *Farscape*. "The first season was mostly establishing Aeryn as an action character, and since then, she's developed into someone who's crossed the line from being what we would think of as alien, to someone who's a lot more human. So it's opening up for me." During the third season we finally saw the sexual relationship between Crichton-Black and Aeryn consummated. But we also saw Crichton-Black die in her arms (*Infinite Possibilities, Part 2: Icarus Abides*, 315), her slow descent and return from the madness of grief (*The Choice*, 317), and her decision to follow Crichton-Green in his quest to stop Scorpius once and for all (*Fractures*, 318). Aeryn has come a long way from her Peacekeeper upbringing, but she has not lost the skills that made her a successful soldier. Those skills were certainly needed in the trials ahead.

As to Claudia Black's opinions about Aeryn Sun, they are decidedly mixed. At the 2001 Farscape Convention in California, Black had this to say about Aeryn:

> It's a privilege to be cast in strong female roles. I think [Aeryn] is actually damaged goods, so I reserve judgment as to whether she's a positive role model. She does make herself available to loss and pain, so I think she's a better role model now.[21]

What Black apparently does not realize is, that is precisely why Aeryn is so positive. As we have seen, Aeryn has acted in ways that we would think horrific. Yet she has overcome those actions, in effect repented of them, and created something new, beyond what she was. She is still not completely healed; this is evident in the way that she cannot accept Crichton's love. At the end of Season 3, Crichton-Green asks her if she loves John Crichton, to forget that there were two and one died. Her answer is yes; however, she is still not ready to commit to the John that remains.

In some respects season 4 was not a good season for Aeryn. When she returns to Moya following a very long absence, she is with Scorpius (*Promises*, 405). She tells Crichton that Scorpius saved her life and makes John promise not to hurt Scorpius. John agrees, but is puzzled and angered at Aeryn's actions. Why should she trust Scorpius, he wonders, when she will not trust the man who loves her? We learn of some of Aeryn's actions while she was separated from John and they were not pretty. She had worked as an assassin, contracting an almost fatal disease because of her actions (*Promises*, 405). The Aeryn who returned has changed in many ways: she is certainly leaner, indicating a harsh existence away from Moya. She is also more confused than ever about her relationship with Crichton. It is true that Aeryn's feelings for Crichton have changed over the course of 3 years. She once only felt contempt for him, gradually developing a sexual awareness of him and recognizing his beauty, until finally falling in love with him (see for example, *PK Tech Girl* (107), *The Flax* (112), *A Human Reaction* (116), *The Locket* (216), *The Green-Eyed Monster* (308)). But her breeding continually gets in the way: she has been taught not to trust anyone, especially a non-Peacekeeper. As she tries to apologize and make him understand her feelings, dren (*Farscape*-speak for rubbish, sometimes used to mean feces) happens (*Unrealized Reality*, 411). Aeryn spends quite a bit of time captured during the last season, which did not make me very happy, since it made her a helpless victim that Crichton had to rescue. Nevertheless, even during her intense torture at the hands of the Scarrans, she did not give up or give in. Her training allowed her to withstand the torture and her love for Crichton gave her hope that he would find a way to rescue her, and he did.

One negative point about Aeryn's portrayal in season 4 concerns her makeup. When she returns to Moya after months away, she is much leaner than when she left; this is very evident in her face. Her hair is extremely long, the make-up artist's way of indicating exactly how long she was gone. However, throughout season 4 she wore much more make-up, and more obvious make-up, than in the previous 3 seasons—iridescent eye shadow and pink lip-gloss, for example. I do not know why they sexed her up like that and I did not like it very much. However, considering the ways that she acted during this season, harder and willing to do anything to protect Crichton and his wormhole knowledge, it might have been a simple ploy by the producers to show the dichotomy in her character. She is a woman. Her torture released her fetus from stasis and she will soon be a mother. But she is still a soldier and will protect her lover, her friends, and her way of life from conquest by the Scarrans.

Gender, Sex, and Variations Therein

Farscape reversed gender stereotypes, presenting many of the characters in ways suggesting blended androgynes (Heilbrun & Mulqueen, 1987). Alien species encountered by the crew may have gender and they may not. For example, in one interesting episode (*The Flax*, 113), D'Argo hunts for a spaceship belonging to his species with a Zenetan pirate. The actor portraying the part was male and looked male to all of the crew. But they remarked that "he" appeared to be missing something when "he" pulled down "his" pants to show them "his" tattoos, although "he" tells them that not everyone is cut from the same mold. They apparently pay that comment no attention. We eventually learn that "he" is really female and is lonely. She asks D'Argo to be her mate, but he declines the offer.

When the crew encounter other "people" they are just as likely to be female as male. Some of the women are good and some are not, just as are the men. Some of the societies that the crew meets may have so-called traditional gender roles and they may not. For example, in *Jeremiah Crichton* (114), the head of the village is a man, and the high priest is a woman, but it is the women who choose the men with whom they will mate. In the 3-part *Look at the Princess* (210 – 212), the entire world is ruled by a woman and the monarchy is passed through the matriarchal line. And, whereas the Emperor of the Scarrans is a man, the War Minister is a Woman (*Bringing Home the Beacon*, 416). Peacekeepers are both male and female and serve in all ranks, rising as far as ability takes them.

The sexual acts portrayed on screen were typically heterosexual; however, it is hinted that Chiana may be bisexual and other variations on sexual behavior were mentioned. For example, the priest Zhaan was always very sensual and we learn eventually that members of her species are actually plants. When exposed to sunlight, Zhaan experiences "photocasms." The male characters react with disgust, but mostly because Zhaan is incapacitated by the photocasms and thus unable to help them when they are in trouble (*Till the Blood Runs Clear*, 112). However they may also feel inadequate confronted with such intense female sexuality for which a male is not necessary. Dominar Rygel mentions his many wives and progeny, but tells Zhaan that he is not a body breeder when she tries to seduce him.[22] Since Rygel does have a "sexual" encounter with a female Hynerian on one episode, it certainly makes us wonder what they were doing (*Fractures*, 318). Obviously interspecies matings are not unheard of in this universe, although as in our society, prejudice occurs and children born of such matings may experience discrimination.[23] Aeryn and John do eventually develop a sexual relationship, as do Chiana and D'Argo. Chiana is freely sexual and not averse to using her sexuality to gain the advantage over another individual; indeed, she used her sexuality in order to survive the exile from her own planet.

Ladies Still Rule!

What a wonderful, eclectic and different group of women! Women who were good and bad, positive and negative, and living on their own terms. Chiana was sexually promiscuous, young and playful, afraid but devious, unscrupulous and untrustworthy, yet quite resourceful and resilient. She eventually learned to trust the others, but she did not lose the essence of what made her so infuriating to the rest of the crew. Zhaan was sensual and spiritual, a healer with a restrained violence that she constantly battled and mourned, aware that all beings are a combination of bipolar attributes that must be blended for completion. Jool and Sikozu found that, when they left the comfort of their scholarly existences, they had much to contribute to the future. Not every decision either made was positive; we are certainly wondering about the slightly sadomasochistic sexual relationship between Sikozu and Scorpius, for example. Nevertheless each made her choice of her future space and the rest of Moya's crew respected her right to make those decisions. Noranti continued to explore her spirituality and she and Chi have became quite good buddies—Noranti's view of herself as an 18-year-old girl probably helped that relationship immensely.

Aeryn was hardened and battle-scarred, once lonely and afraid of relationships beyond her own combat unit. She overcame her earlier socialization to embrace parts of herself that she never realized existed, and indeed would have deemed unacceptable in a Peacekeeper commando. Aeryn grew beyond her Peacekeeper training and heritage; she too embraced a future that she never considered possible. From the woman who was born in space and planned to die alone in space (*Nerve*, 199), she was challenged by her contact with Moya's crew to be more than she was, just as Crichton said. While some may not like the way that Aeryn's story evolved with Crichton's, that was the plan from the very beginning of the program, as soon as the producers saw the chemistry between Claudia Black and Ben Browder. *Farscape* was always a love story; Kemper never denied it, as did Chris Carter about Mulder and Scully. Since I am a heterosexual woman in a long-term egalitarian relationship, I am happy whenever I see any type of positive relationship presented on film. It happens so seldom. So I went along on *Farscape* for the wild ride and enjoyed all 4 cycles (years) of the roller coaster. Here is hoping that *Farscape: The Peacekeeper Wars* will live up to its parents (see chapter 8).

Notes

1. *Farscape: The Official Magazine*, Titan Publishing Group, Ltd. This magazine ceased publication in 2003. It published a number of articles on the women of *Farscape*, including an article by Executive Producer David Kemper entitled "Ladies Rule!!!" that discussed the roles that women played in the series, both on and behind the screen (No. 4, Jan/Feb 2002).

2. The cancellation of *Farscape* sent shock waves throughout the fan kingdom of Scapers, as we call ourselves. The Sci Fi Channel was inundated with email messages and telephone calls. The intense campaign resulted in executives at the network ordering a made-for-television miniseries entitled *Farscape: The Peacekeeper Wars*, which premiered October 2004. The miniseries begins where the series finale ended: John proposes marriage and Aeryn accepts. She tells him that the baby has been released from stasis. They are then attacked and apparently killed, although we knew that they had not died following the series' cancellation because of a short story written by *Farscape*'s creator, Rockne S. O'Bannon (2003).

3. Nazzaro, J. (2001, April). Out on the *Farscape*. *StarLog, 285*, 36 - 40. Bassom, D. (2001, Sept/Oct). The Aurora Chair: Interview with David Kemper. *Farscape: The Official Magazine*, No. 2, 20 - 24.

4. This is one of John Crichton's favorite, and non-profane, expressions.

5. *Farscape* episodes have titles and their numerical designators indicate year first and then episode. For example, 120 is the 20th episode of the first season. All episode information, quotes, and character profiles in this paper can be found at http://www.scifi.com/farscape, unless otherwise noted. This website was available as of November 2004.

6. Eden, M. (2002, Jan/Feb). Editorial. *Farscape: The Official Magazine*, No. 4, p. 4. Also in this issue is an article entitled "What Women Want," on p. 6.

7. Noranti's name was obtained from the official Farscape website; she was typically called Grandma or Old Woman in the beginning. Apparently no one bothered to ask her name, until Crichton did so *in What Was Lost, Part 2: Resurrection* (403).

8. *Farscape: The Official Magazine*, Titan Publishing Group, Ltd. The Wakket Hole (Letters to the Editor), Numbers 2 (Sept/Oct 2001), 4 (Jan/Feb 2002), & 5 (Mar/Apr 2002). Also featured in Number 2 is an interview with David Bassom, who quotes series creator Rockne S. O'Bannon's take on Jool's char-

acter, which is to basically give her a chance. Part of the negative reaction to Jool was that her character is "somewhat ineffective. . . . Because we're very proud of having such strong women on the show—all three of the regular female cast [Aeryn, Zhaan, and Chiana] have always been, in their own ways, very strong." Other interviews in No. 2 include Claudia Black who talks about how she obtained the role of Aeryn Sun and Aeryn's role on Moya as of Season 2, and David Kemper on his *Farscape* philosophy.

9. Bassom, D. (2002, Jan/Feb). Scream Queen. *Farscape: The Official Magazine*, No. 4, p. 26 - 29.

10. Who's Jool? (2001, Nov/Dec). *Farscape: The Official Magazine*, No. 3, p. 46.

11. Sullivan, J. (2002, August). Hill Power. *Sci-Fi, The Official Magazine of the Sci-Fi Channel*, 8(4), 46 - 49.

12. Simpson, P., & Thomas, R. (2002, Jan/Feb). Chi Force. *Farscape: The Official Magazine*, No. 4, p. 15 - 18.

13. Simpson, P, & Thomas, R. (2002, Jan/Feb). The Aurora Chair (interview with Virginia Hey). *Farscape: The Official Magazine*, No. 4, p. 20 - 24.

14. *Look at the Princess, Part 1: A Kiss is but a Kiss* (211); *Look at the Princess, Part 2: I Do, I Think* (212); and *Look at the Princess, Part 3: The Maltese Crichton* (213).

15. www.scifi.com/farscape/characters/aeryn.html/

16. Cox, G. (2001, Nov/Dec). Samsara. *Farscape: The Official Magazine*, No. 3, 49 - 54. This short story explores one (rather unusual) future of Aeryn Sun, written before the series was canceled and O'Bannon wrote the story about Crichton and Aeryn's future.

17. Nelson, R. (2002, June). Fantastic Four. *Sci-Fi, The Official Magazine of the Sci-Fi Channel*, 8(3), 48 - 51.

18. Hayes, K. S. (2002, May/June). More than a Peacekeeper. *Farscape: The Official Magazine*, No. 6, p. 15 - 17.

19. To distinguish between the two Crichtons, Aeryn makes one wear a green shirt and the other black beginning in *Thanks for Sharing* (307). The one in black dies.

20. Nazzaro, J. (2002, May/June). The Aurora Chair (interview with Claudia Black). *Farscape: The Official Magazine*, No. 6, p. 10 - 14.

21. Fanscape. (2002, Jan/Feb). *Farscape: The Official Magazine*, No. 4, p. 9 - 11.

22. Zhaan makes sexual overtures to Rygel when the crew is at their worst in an early episode. Meeting a being that claims to be able to create star charts showing the locations of their home worlds, the crew must give him one of Pilot's arms in payment (they grow back). Believing that NamTar has created the charts, Zhaan, Rygel, and D'Argo begin fighting over who gets to go home first. Zhaan wants Rygel to side with her and go to her planet first, and tries to use sex as a lure. She is unsuccessful (*DNA Mad Scientist*, 109).

23. We learn eventually that D'Argo was once married to a Sebacean woman and had a son. LoLaan's brother was horrified that his sister married a Luxan and killed her. He accused D'Argo of the murder and D'Argo was sentenced to

prison. That is why he was a prisoner of the Peacekeepers (*They've got a Secret*, 110). D'Argo's son was sold into slavery and the crew eventually rescued him.

Chapter 6: *Star Trek®*

To boldly go where no man[1] has gone before

I had originally planned to discuss the different *Star Trek®* series in more detail in this book. That is no longer the case. Partly this decision is logistic: there are 5 different series, with a combined total of about 600 hours of television, not to mention 10 feature films. *The Original Series* (TOS) and *Star Trek: The Next Generation®* (TNG) are both screened on cable TV in my market and I have enjoyed watching all of the episodes as reruns, especially as I have been working on this book off and on for about 3 years. *Star Trek: Voyager®* is also screened in my market, but I cannot bring myself to watch it again. It was a huge disappointment. Only recently has *Star Trek: Deep Space Nine®* (DS9) started screening on cable TV. It is my favorite of the 5, and I agree with Mason (1999) who noted that this series "celebrated a community of equality in diversity" (p. 17). I also watch *Star Trek: Enterprise®*, confirming that I am a Trekker and have been from the very beginning (and yes, I do mean from 1966).[2]

Realizing that I would like to finish writing this book before the end of this decade, I decided to omit a detailed discussion of the *Star Trek®* franchise. Hundreds of novels have been written detailing the adventures of the various characters throughout the years. Such novels carry on the adventures beyond the demise of the program's first-run on television and are filled with rich detail about each *Star Trek®* crew. Because each novel must be sanctioned by Paramount, they are fairly true to Roddenberry's vision of the Trek universe, although it must be said that Roddenberry himself was generally not happy with the ways in which events unfolded in some of the stories (Alexander, 1994). Most bookstores contain the *Star Trek®* novels in their own section, and happily they are finally numbered, making it easier to follow the thread from novel to novel. Roddenberry was especially unhappy with some of the more creative imaginings of the fans who wrote their visions of the Trek universe and published such stories in the so-called "fanzines" on the Internet. For example, some fans wrote stories in which Mr. Spock and Captain Kirk (of *The Original Series)* were lovers; Roddenberry emphatically declared that both Spock and Kirk were heterosexual (Alexander, 1994). However, birth of the fanzines had many positive effects. They kept the story "alive." They encouraged creativity; but, unfortunately sometimes at the expense of the logic of the show of which they wrote, and also unfortunately at the expense of grammar, spelling, composition, etc.; some were just very poorly written. There are hundreds of websites devoted to *Star Trek®.* The official web site is www.startrek.com.

In addition the scholarly data base examining *Star Trek®* and its various incarnations is quite extensive. Some of these sources are listed in the Bibliography; I am sure that I will have missed some. I tried very hard to find everything ever written about *Star Trek®,* at least everything written in English, but some books are out of print and not available. Nevertheless, 600 hours of television provides a wealth of information for scholars in various disciplines to examine. I was primarily concerned with the issues of gender in *Star Trek®,* but did examine sources that related gender and race as well, especially as those factors applied to the development of identity among the characters on each series.

Each of the 5 series has at least one "alien" character. On TOS that is the Vulcan Mr. Spock. On TNG it is Data, the android. *Deep Space Nine* has Odo, the changeling, as well as Jadzia Dax and Kira Nerys. During its last season, Ezri Dax joined the crew serving aboard DS9 and she had many issues surrounding her joining. *Voyager* had several alien crewmembers; the one with the most issues about self was the Doctor, although he certainly had no problems with Ego. Nevertheless, since he was a hologram, he was limited in what he could and could not do and be. *Voyager* also had the half-human, half-Klingon engineer, B'Elanna Torres. As the Doctor's character evolved, and as the ratings on the show began to slide down, a new character, the cyborg Seven of Nine was introduced. Finally, in *Enterprise* we return full circle and have a Vulcan on board the Enterprise, but this time a Vulcan woman. Roddenberry (and his "heirs") had a purpose in introducing many of these alien characters: they served as a mirror upon which humanity could see itself reflected (Alexander, 1994). Just this list shows that the majority of the permanent "alien" characters on the 5 series were male, the exceptions being B'Elanna, Seven of Nine, and T'Pol.[3] Several authors have noted that in TOS the majority of the "alien" guest stars were women, usually up to no good (Blair, 1983), reflecting the standard sci fi formula of the time: woman as Other.

Five Crews, Five Missions

Each of the 5 *Star Trek* series presented Gene Roddenberry and his heirs' view of the future of human beings. Roddenberry envisioned that humans would evolve beyond selfishness, jealousy, discord, and prejudice to embrace the universe in its wonder. Humans would join with beings from other planets in a sort of United Nations in space that would "seek out knowledge" by exploring unknown regions of space.

TOS' mission set the stage for this epic journey and the 4 spin-offs showed Starfleet's attempts to continue (or begin) its mission, in both positive and negative ways. TNG continued the saga of exploration and depicted a crew even more highly "evolved" in terms of human consciousness and enlightenment than Kirk and company. Heeding the criticism leveled at TNG with respect to the lack of conflict between humanoids of the future, *Deep Space Nine* set Starfleet personnel on a space station and allowed them to serve as intermediaries in an uneasy peace between the militaristic Cardassians and the spiritual, agrarian Bajorans. A much darker series than TOS or TNG, DS9 plotlines eventually centered on the conflict between a species intent upon domination of the known universe, causing former enemies such as Humans, Klingons, and Romulans to band together to win the war against the Dominion. *Voyager* followed the adventures of a Federation starship lost in a portion of unknown space called the Delta Quadrant (all other series to date taking place within the Alpha Quadrant). Voyager was chasing a Maquis ship when it was hurled into the Delta Quadrant by a being intent upon finding a mate. After great loss of life on both ships and the knowledge that it would take 70 years to return home, the crews of both ships joined together aboard the starship, combining forces for purposes of safety and security. Finally, *Enterprise* follows the crew of the first starship by that name to begin deep space exploration. *Enterprise* actually takes place prior to the establishment of the United Federation of Planets.

The Original Series

I believe that all of the programs in the franchise have provided consistent images of women as Heroes, and yes I include the original series in that assessment. Even on TOS women were admirals and ambassadors. Many people could not see beyond the short skirts and cried sexism, neglecting to take note of the fact that Roddenberry had integrated the crew of the Enterprise only a couple of years past the Civil Rights Act. And, let us never forget that the original second officer of the Enterprise was a woman, and it was the network that made Roddenberry change Number 1 to Spock (Alexander, 1994), a reflection of the network executives' racism and sexism, not Roddenberry's.

TOS sought an identity for its genre. Roddenberry wanted to produce an adult science fiction television program that would reflect his view of the future (Alexander, 1994). Believing that human beings would evolve beyond their baser instincts allowed him to populate a future Earth with people who had overcome war, violence, racism, sexism, etc. to achieve their potential of greatness. Berger (1981) stated that TOS was fascinated with the issue of identity. Of course, he was talking only about TOS and in response to an article by Whetmore (1981) about one particular episode on TOS. Certainly the case can be made for examining certain episodes for their depiction of issues of identity, such as *Turnabout Intruder* (TOS, 079, the last episode of the series), in which a former lover of Kirk's takes over his body using a piece of alien equipment. Janice Lester has gone insane because of her inability to achieve the rank of captain in Starfleet. She believes it is because she is a woman. Given her instability, one speculates that the examinations required in such training would have detected her psychological problems and that is why she never became a starship captain. Yet we know that women were captains in the *Star Trek* universe long before Janeway (who is contemporaneous with Picard and Sisko, not Kirk).[4] Nevertheless the dialogue in this episode reflects many of the stereotypes about women in 1960s America.

I believe that only one character on TOS was unsure of his identity and that of course was Mr. Spock, the half-human, half-Vulcan science officer. Stories about Spock on TOS centered on his battle to deny the emotions inherited from his human mother and, instead, espouse the pure logic of his father's people. Spock is estranged from his father because he joined Starfleet against his father's wishes. He desires to show his father that he is entirely Vulcan and a successful one at that. He will eventually be able to earn his father's respect and embrace his humanness, learning to integrate the two into one self (*Star Trek® IV The Voyage Home*).[5] Spock was, and still is, a fan favorite. Because of his aloofness and alien, exotic appeal, women were especially fond of Spock. That aloofness led, in many respects, to an entirely new subgenre within sci fi, the fanzine. Spock was the subject of much of this fiction (see Blair, 1983): many were the fans that envisioned themselves, or someone like them, breaking through that icy exterior to uncover the smoldering passions below (Ye Gods! In many respects it mirrors the pornographic musings of men who believe that it would only take one good screw, by them of course, to turn even the most militant Lesbian heterosexual). Once again, Roddenberry was not particularly happy about what he thought of as fan poaching (Alexander, 1994) and outright theft.[6]

The lone female officer on the bridge crew of the Enterprise on TOS was Lt. Uhura. Comments have been made about Lt. Uhura's role, for example that she was little more than a telephone operator (Pounds, 1995; Russ, 1972). Nichols (1994) completely disagreed with that assessment stating that Uhura was much more. Indeed, she was the Communications Officer for the Enterprise, and while the racism of 1960s America never allowed her to be spotlighted in the originally televised episodes, the feature films produced throughout the 1990s allowed us to learn more about her character. We learned that in her world of the United Federation of Planets she was not discriminated against because of her race or her gender. She had no special problems discovering who she was or what her place was in the universe (Nichols, 1994). Uhura also inspired a generation of young women of color. When Nichols decided to leave TOS because of the limitations of her role, she was asked by Martin Luther King, Jr. to stay for the sake of their people (Nichols, 1994). She did and other men and women of color cite her role on *Star Trek®* as inspiring them, one notable example being the comedienne and actor Whoopi Goldberg, who went on to play a recurring role on TNG. Watching episodes of TOS recently I note that Kirk always listened to Uhura carefully and considered her opinions (for example, *A Taste of Armageddon*, 023) and sometimes she was more aware of what was going on than any of the male members of the crew (*Bread and Circuses*, 043).

The Next Generation

Two major female characters were Counselor Deanna Troi and Chief Medical Officer Beverly Crusher. But, the only character on TNG with identity issues and problems was the android Lt. Commander Data, who wanted to be human more than anything else he could conceive. Data's transformation from mere machine to fully integrated, well-liked and well-respected member of the crew to the attainment of his definition of humanness, the acquisition of emotions, spanned many years on the show and into the feature films. It was not easy; many members of Enterprise's crew and many members of Starfleet were uneasy about Data and how he "fit" into their world. Indeed, Starfleet demanded that Data be disassembled in one episode (*The Measure of a Man*, 135). Partly this reflects mankind's love-hate relationship with technology (Sanders, 1977; Thomas, 1991). While technology can certainly make life better for the beings that populate Planet Earth, human and animal alike, it can also be terrifying, capable of destroying said beings in a flash. Thus, while much sci fi has been written using robots, androids, and cyborgs, those entities are typically childlike, alien, or evil (such as Data's twin Lore[7] and the Borg). Rarely are such entities presented in such a positive light as Data. But Data represents all that is good in robots, as conceived by Isaac Asimov in his first robot novel (1950): they were programmed only to help, and never harm, human beings.

Beverly Crusher and Deanna Troi[8] were not faced with many crises of identity during the 7 seasons that TNG was on the air. Each woman was secure in the world of the United Federation of Planets. Nevertheless it has been argued that they were not good role models for women, much as has been argued about Uhura. For example, while both women were officers by rank, their ranks were not considered command-order. In other words, they held their ranks by virtue of their graduation from Starfleet and their professions within Starfleet. Troi was the ship's counselor and Crusher was the ship's doctor. It has been argued that both of the professions are stereotypically feminine in the sense that each woman's job was to care for other people (Wilcox, 1992), as women have traditionally done throughout history. I disagree to a certain extent. Even in 2004 women are underrepresented among the medical profession in the US. When TNG first aired in 1987 Beverly Crusher provided a positive role model for any young woman or man watching the show. She showed that a woman could become a physician, be a wife and a mother, and command an entire department aboard Enterprise. Remember that Crusher was the Chief Medical Officer aboard Enterprise; she was not just another doctor. And when the producers replaced her (but only) during season 2, believing her to lack fan support, she was replaced with another woman, one even more outspoken and aggressive than Crusher was.[9] Nevertheless, I did not care for Beverly because she always seemed to put other life ahead of her crewmates. Plus, Picard's love of Crusher allowed her to do things for which other people would have been severely reprimanded, if not court-martialed.

Because Troi is the ship's counselor and holds officer's rank we can assume that she holds the terminal degree in her field, that degree being a doctorate. As such, she also provided a positive role model for young adults, those to whom the series was marketed, some of whom probably had children. Much as my father and I watched TOS when it first aired, I find it hard to believe that new viewers did not watch with their children, some of whom would look at these women and imagine their place among the stars as well. While I decried the producers' obvious use of Troi's physical attributes to attract male viewers, her wardrobe changed over the course of the series reflecting her changing status from Ship's Counselor to Bridge Officer. Fan input probably contributed to these changes as well, although I have no specific reference to attest to such a fact, if true. But I am forced to agree with Heller (1997) in noting that in TNG "the sincere acknowledgement of gender equality is riddled with conservative contradictions" (p. 242), for example, people of color in positions of subservience and women still compelled to provide most of the maintenance activities around the "house" (Heller, 1997; Pounds, 1995).

Pounds (1995)[10] complained that all we learn of Deanna's character over the course of TNG is job, family, and sex. That is, we learn about her family life through her interactions with her overbearing and overprotecting mother. While Troi is mixed-species, having a Betazoid mother and a human father, she states that she never had problems with that status when she was young. Rather she celebrated the heritage of both of her parents, "experiencing the richness and diversity of both worlds" (*The Emissary*, 146). As stated Deanna is the ship's counselor and she does have a healthy sexual appetite. However, I disagree with Pounds' assessment that this is "hardly the formula for a dimensional character" (p. 99). Troi is shown doing much more than arguing or apologizing for her mother, analyzing and counseling her shipmates, or engaging in romantic encounters. Actually, her romantic encounters are rather rare as far as I can tell. Troi has a much richer life than Pounds suggests. She has a close friendship with Beverly with whom she exercises and socializes regularly. She is part of the weekly poker games among the command staff, sharing an easy-going camaraderie with her crewmates. In other words, she does experience a rich personal and professional life aboard Enterprise, eventually taking her role on the ship one step farther.

Because Beverly and Deanna are high-ranking officers, they have had to assume command of Enterprise when other officers were unavailable, as in an emergency (e.g., *Disaster,* 205). Feeling out of their depths and probably scared half to death as well, each woman manages to save the ship and the crew. Nevertheless, both women realize that they must pursue training that will allow them to command ship should the need ever arise again. We learn that Beverly does become captain of a medical/science vessel after leaving the Enterprise (*All Good Things. . .*, 277). While Deanna never gets command of her own ship, she does take command of Enterprise, albeit when the rest of the normal command staff takes time off.[11] Deanna learns very hard lessons about command when she is forced to sacrifice Geordi's life in order to save the Enterprise from destruction (*Thine Own Self,* 268). Even knowing that the sacrifice was only a computer simulation during her Bridge Officer's Test did not make it easier for her to kill one of her crew in order to save the ship.

The fact that Deanna is an empath is both a hindrance and a help to her. Being an empath helps her in her counseling sessions and when encountering unknown and potentially hostile aliens. But, it has been argued that her ability to feel others' emotions means that the men in command of the Enterprise do not need to feel anything, since they have Deanna to do it for them. Troi's empathic ability lies at the heart of her identity. In the episode *The Loss* (184) Troi loses her empathic abilities and suffers denial, panic, and anger at well-meaning friends who try to comfort her and tell her that she is still a well-trained counselor. She realizes that she must redefine herself but is unsure how. She does recover but the temporary loss proves to her that she is a good counselor even without empathic abilities. Her struggle in this episode won praise from fans who were disabled themselves (Nemecek, 1995).

It is Beverly and Deanna who save the Enterprise following Picard's assimilation by the Borg (*The Best of Both Worlds,* Parts 1 & 2, 174 & 175). Troi's empathic abilities, and her relationship with Picard, enable her to detect that he is fighting against the programming imposed upon him by the Borg. Once he fights through that programming, Beverly discovers how to kill them. With the help of these two women Picard eventually recovers from his ordeal. Without them it is doubtful that he would have survived.

Sexuality was explored in myriad ways on TNG. While the crew-members of the Enterprise were overtly heterosexual, they did occasionally encounter beings who were not. Riker once fell in love with a member of an androgynous species. As the episode unfolded we learned that in actuality a small number of the members of that species were born gendered. Because it was considered abnormal to be gendered, anyone caught expressing or experiencing gender was reprogrammed to be genderless (*The Outcast*, 217).

We encounter the Trill for the first time in TNG, although their characterization would be more fully developed on *Deep Space Nine*. Beverly meets and falls in love with a Trill, not realizing that he is a member of a joined species (*The Host*, 197). The Trill host may be male or female and the symbiont is generally sexless. When Beverly falls in love, the Trill host is male. However, an accident forces an emergency operation and the symbiont is transferred into a female host. When the Trill states that she still loves Beverly, having all of the memories of their relationship of the previous host, Beverly is unable to cope with the idea that she might love and eventually be intimate with a female. Both of these stories reinforce the heterosexual nature of the *Star Trek* universe, suggesting that any pattern other than heterosexuality is deviant (Heller, 1997).

The subject of rape was explored in several episodes of TNG, although the rapes were mental rather than physical, and the victims of the rapes were male and female. In one episode, a telepathic alien rapes Troi, Crusher, and Riker. This alien uses Deanna's empathic abilities to enhance his own telepathy and to control his more dangerous impulses (*Violations*, 212). Riker is also raped in the episode *Frame of Mind* (247) as he is mind-probed by a group of aliens holding Federation prisoners, whom he is supposed to rescue, hostage. Beverly is assaulted by an energy being who has preyed on the women of her family for centuries (*Sub Rosa*, 266). Only Tasha Yar, the Enterprise's security officer during season 1, apparently suffered a physical assault as she described the "rape squads" who roamed the planet of her youth (*Where No One Has Gone Before*, 106).

Deep Space Nine

Identity issues abound in DS9 for both the male and female characters. For 6 seasons 2 female characters occupied center stage on DS9.

These were Major Kira Nerys and Lt. Jadzia Dax. Lt. Ezri Dax joined the cast during the final season. Jadzia Dax' species was Trill. As a species, Trill were humanoid but joined in a symbiotic relationship with a being they called the symbiont. Trill were specially trained for the joining and it was considered a great honor to be chosen to host the symbiont. At the time of DS9 the Dax symbiont was joined with its eighth host, Jadzia. The symbionts were extremely long-lived and as each humanoid host died, the symbiont joined with another. In addition each host experienced the memories of the previous hosts, hence the training required: the new host had to learn to retain their individual identity separate from the knowledge they possessed of the previous hosts.[12] Jadzia was quite an accomplished young woman; however, many of those accomplishments were only memories. When she tells Sisko that she negotiated a peace treaty with the Klingons, for example, Sisko rightly reminds her that it was her previous host who was the diplomat, not her (*You are Cordially Invited*, 531). Because she had such a long-lived symbiont, Jadzia had many memories, which enabled her to interact with a variety of beings on DS9. Jadzia's symbiont had also been joined with both male and female Trills, and she knew what it was like to be a mother and a father. Needless to say this was disconcerting to many, especially her future husband, the Klingon Worf. She was a powerful role model who was unfortunately killed off during season 6. Her death meant almost certain death for the Dax symbiont unless a host could be found. Luckily for the symbiont a Trill was available and Dax joined with a very young and inexperienced woman named Ezri (*Image in the Sand*, 551; *Shadows & Symbols*, 552).

Ezri Dax had never prepared for joining with a Trill and so was not emotionally ready. She had not developed a sense of self that would allow her to carry the symbiont with her, integrating it into her personality (and vice versa). One interesting plotline of the last season of DS9 concerned Ezri navigating the emotional detritus left behind when Jadzia died. For example, Worf lost his wife but was quite aware that her memories were alive inside of Ezri. Both Worf and Ezri had to learn that she was not Jadzia: Worf letting her be herself and Ezri trying not to be Jadzia for Worf (*Afterimage*, 553; *'Til Death Do Us Part*, 568). In addition, the doctor on the station had been in love with Jadzia. Jadzia had also loved the doctor, but Worf more. When Dr. Bashir came to that realization, he learned to love Ezri for the being that she was, rather than the fact that she was once Jadzia (*What You Leave Behind*, 575-576).

Nevertheless, my favorite character on DS9 was Kira. Kira was a major in the Bajoran Militia and ranked second-in-command on the station. She resented Starfleet Command's interference in Bajoran affairs and was quite angry that she had to serve as Sisko's second (*Emissary*, 401-402). Throughout the first couple of seasons her major emotion was anger and her anger was justified. Her planet and her people had been ruthlessly invaded and conquered by a warlike race called the Cardassians. The Cardassians laid waste to the planet and enslaved its population. Men, women, and children were tortured and killed or sent to work in the mines with little or no food or water. Women were forced to work in "comfort stations" for the relief of the male Cardassians. Kira eventually learned that her own mother had been forced to do so, even becoming one of Gul Dukat, the station commander's, many mistresses (*Wrongs Darker Than Death or Night*, 541). Kira had always believed the Cardassians killed her mother when Kira was a little girl.

As Kira grew older during the Cardassian occupation she joined the Resistance and made no apology after the Cardassians were forced to leave Bajor. When Gul Dukat refers to her as a terrorist, Kira admits it. She makes no excuses, saying that she and the others were fighting for their lives and for Bajor. Several times throughout the series Kira must confront that past and as the series progressed we see Kira emerge as a more tempered, thoughtful woman. Kira is not afraid to use force if that is what is necessary but with Sisko's help and guidance she gradually becomes more of a diplomat, although she is still too "quick on the draw" to do it for long. In one interesting episode, the Federation is forced to abandon the station, with Kira left as a representative of Bajor. She experiences a great depression and numbing, going through her daily routine as if in a fog. Gradually she realizes that she has started collaborating with the Cardassians and the Dominion in an attempt to ensure the safety of those on board the station (*Rocks and Shoals*, 527). Kira would have killed collaborators when she was a terrorist during the Occupation. Now she realizes why people would choose to collaborate with the enemy: not just to save their own lives or the lives of their families, but because they believe that they are doing the right thing for their species. But, Kira realizes that she cannot collaborate and creates a new Resistance movement on board the station.

While Kira is quick to temper and is well trained in combat, she does have a softer side. Kira does have romantic relationships with men during the course of the series (e.g., *Crossfire*, 485). One of her most lasting relationships surprised her very much. Odo was the shape-shifting changeling who served as Chief of Security. Odo fell in love with Kira almost from the moment he met her and managed to conceal the fact quite well for a while (*Heart of Stone*, 460). However, he eventually admitted his feelings (*His Way*, 544). She did not reciprocate for some time, but eventually realized that friendship is the best basis for love (as do Mulder and Scully for example).

My male colleagues who watched DS9 also pointed out Kira's intense spirituality throughout the entire series. Kira, like all Bajorans, worships the Prophets, aliens that live in the wormhole outside of DS9. While we do not learn much about the Bajoran religion during the course of the series, DS9 is certainly the most religious of the *Star Trek* series, which is a surprise given Gene Roddenberry's dislike of the subject. Nevertheless, we see Kira regularly attend religious services on the station. When she is troubled, she seeks the wisdom of the Prophets. When she needs rest and recuperation, she travels to one of the many monasteries on Bajor in order to be closer to the Prophets (*The Circle*, 422). She is scandalized when one of the Vedeks, a Bajoran holy man, wishes to be her lover, but she accepts his offer and is very happy until his death, following which she mourns him deeply in the way of her people (*Life Support*, 459).

Kira changes very much over the course of 7 years. She gains insight into her own actions and learns to express regret over the people she killed during the Occupation. She never forgives the Cardassians for what they did to her people, but she realizes that not all Cardassians were involved and that not all of them are evil, just as some Bajorans that she liked and respected were actually collaborators (*Duet*, 419; *The Collaborator*, 444; *Second Skin*, 451; *Ties of Blood & Water*, 517). She actually develops an almost father-daughter relationship with one Cardassian, mourning him deeply when he dies. However, she never forgives Dukat and refuses his many attempts at seduction (*Indiscretion*, 477; *Waltz*, 535).[13] Kira is an excellent example of a future female. She is an authority figure, a take-charge type of woman. She is not overly emotional, except where the Cardassians are concerned. Kira is also able to experience her sexuality and her spirituality freely. She is a role model for Bajorans and that frightens her but also makes her proud. Her first loyalty is to her people and to her planet.

Enterprise

Two female characters are found on the newest entry in the Star Trek® franchise. One is Ensign Hoshi Sato. Little has been made of her character on the show; so far, Hoshi has had a purely supporting role with only a few episodes featuring her. Like Lt. Uhura, Hoshi is Communications Officer. Her specialty is linguistics; she is a prodigy with an "ear" so discriminating that she can translate an alien language faster than most computers.[14] Captain Archer asked her personally to join his crew; he knew he needed someone with her skills when they encountered other species of humanoids in space. She decided to join the crew because of the potential knowledge gained from such encounters; however, the first season's episodes show her completely out of her element, doubting her ability to cope with the demands of life in space (e.g., *Vox Sola*, 022). She does eventually get her "sea-legs," and when offered the opportunity to leave Enterprise, refuses to do so (*Exile*, 058).

Vulcan Sub-Commander T'Pol has had a much greater role in the new franchise but her only real dilemmas in the first 2 seasons were her violations of Vulcan regulations. Season 3 brought interesting changes to the character. T'Pol elected to accompany the Enterprise into the Expanse after the Xindi attacked Earth, against orders from the Vulcan High Command. This led to her resignation and special dispensation to join Starfleet, also at Archer's request. Vulcans are not supposed to travel into the Expanse and we eventually learn why: a particular substance found in the Expanse, called Trellium, causes them to go insane. Indeed, in one episode the Enterprise encounters a Vulcan ship that became lost in the Expanse. Some of the crew is still alive and these insane Vulcans band together in an attempt to kill the humans (*Impulse*, 057). T'Pol also begins showing signs of madness but is helped in time. As the season progressed, we learned that she was injecting small amounts of the Trellium in an attempt to build immunity to the substance. It did not work (*Damage*, 071). Instead she became addicted to the drug, especially for the emotions that the drug unleashed in her. For example, her relationship with Trip Tucker, already close, becomes sexual, at least once. The producers hint that their relationship will continue to grow in the upcoming season,[15] although Jolene Blalock, the actor who plays T'Pol is somewhat disappointed in the way that T'Pol is changing. Blalock is frustrated that when an intelligent, strong, and powerful woman is finally presented on television, those characteristics begin to take the back burner to romance and sexuality.[16] Why, she questions, would T'Pol be attracted to a man like Trip? Perhaps it's because he loves her (*Home*, 079). But, it is a good question and one I hope we learn the answer to as season 4 progresses. Interestingly, as of this writing, T'Pol has married her ex-fiancé in order to save her mother's career. As T'Pol's mother continuously tells Trip, Vulcans have emotions; they have simply learned not to show them. Any feelings that T'Pol has for Trip are thus fighting against her loyalty and love for her mother.[17]

Voyager

Certainly many women have populated the Star Trek franchise and some of these characters have been shaped with fan input. Indeed, the mythology surrounding *Star Trek Voyager* points out that Captain Janeway was chosen in just this fashion. Indeed, the fans were quite adamant that a woman be chosen as Captain for the new series. This fact is quite interesting because Janeway was not well liked by many fans. They did not like the fact that she was a Captain, with all that that entailed. Specifically many fans, and you will not be surprised to note that these were men, did not like the fact that she was a "hard-ass." Letters to SciFi.com, for example, were almost overwhelming negative about Janeway. The fans said that she was too tough on her crew, that she made them obey her orders, and that "it was her way, or the highway." But, I must admit, that a number of men wrote letters saying that that was the way an officer was supposed to be; these male letter writers were usually ex-military themselves. If Janeway was to be realistic as a character, and I believe that she was, then she had to be a Captain—she had to command. And, we must forget that she was a woman—she was the Captain. Her crew was every attached to her; they respected her and they liked her, but they also obeyed her commands, although they did not blindly do so (which was one of my pet peeves as I believe she let them get away with way too much—apparently I am in a minority, if these letters are any indication).

Janeway appears very sure of herself. Early in the series she showed too much emotion, in my opinion. Perhaps this was because she was in a situation never encountered before and was as nervous and worried as the rest of the crew as to what was going to happen to them as they tried to get home. It could also simply have been the problem of writers who did not know how to make a woman a Captain. They walked a very fine line trying to portray Janeway as a nurturing, caring Captain, completely different from the swash-buckling Kirk and the aloof, detached Picard. However, Janeway eventually came "into her own" and showed she was a competent Captain for Voyager. She succeeded in bringing her ship and her crew home and was rewarded with a promotion to Admiral. I must admit I totally disagreed with that decision: she violated too many Starfleet regulations to be rewarded. After all, Kirk was demoted for less and he had just saved Earth (*Star Trek IV: The Voyage Home*).

Janeway's position aboard Voyager is one of power and loneliness. To maintain her position she must distance herself from her crew: how can you be close to people that you may have to send to their deaths? One of Janeway's closest confidants is Tuvok. She has known Tuvok for many years and considers him to be her best friend and advisor. Her other advisor is Chakotay, who loves her but does not pursue her out of respect for her position. She is in the unenviable position of being cut off from her lover, family, and friends, and with no one with whom to share her burden: the knowledge that her decision led to Voyager's being stranded in the Delta Quadrant. And, she feels that burden deeply as evidenced in the episode *Night* (195). This is a guilt she only acknowledges when alone. She cannot let the crew see her guilt however; she must be strong and confident in her actions so that they will not succumb to depression and worry about their chances of surviving and returning home.

Another strong female character on *Voyager* was B'Elanna Torres, a woman who was half-Klingon and half-human. B'Elanna originally enrolled in Starfleet Academy but was expelled when only 19 years old for failure to follow the rules, obey commands, and control her temper. After her expulsion she joined the Maquis, a group of so-called freedom fighters named after the French Resistance (in World War II). Following the Federation-mediated peace treaty between the Cardassians and the Bajorans, the boundaries of Federation and Cardassian space were redrawn with many formerly Federation colonies being relocated into Cardassian space. Believing, quite rightly, that the Federation would no longer be able to protect them from the Cardassians, some of the colonists formed the Maquis and began a guerilla war against their new "masters." Needing a place to call home and a raison d'étre, B'Elanna joined the Maquis. Following Voyager's relocation into the Delta Quadrant as a result of the Caretaker's actions (*Caretaker*, 101-102), B'Elanna is eventually chosen to be Chief Engineer.

Because she is half-human and half-Klingon, Torres is part warrior because Klingon women were as much warriors as the men of their race. She brought that warrior mentality to Voyager and that mentality served as a foil to the too goody-goodness of the *Star Trek®* universe. And yet, that Klingon half had set her apart from humans her entire life. Her father had deserted the family when she was 6 and living on a human colony had subjected her to ridicule and contempt by her preju-

diced classmates. Torres had a great deal of difficulty accepting the
Klingon part of her soul, so much so that she knows little of Klingon
ritual. Over the course of time Torres comes to terms with that part of
her personality. One episode in particular forces Torres to examine her
Klingon nature. In *Faces* (114) the Vidiaans learn that Klingon DNA
can cure the hideous disease that has decimated their species. Attempting to extract B'Elanna's DNA they separate the human from the Klingon and create two people, one completely Klingon and the other completely human. Much as the episode in TOS when Kirk is divided into
two Kirks, one good and one evil, by a transporter accident (*The Enemy
Within*, 005), Torres learns that she needs the warrior part of her personality to survive. Torres eventually developed a healthy physical relationship with another crewmember, named Tom Paris, who is human.
B'Elanna and Tom eventually marry, with B'Elanna becoming pregnant. Frightened that her child may look Klingon and thus experience
the same types of prejudice that she had experienced, Torres decides to
have the Doctor eliminate the Klingon DNA from the child's genome.
Tom continually tries to reassure B'Elanna that he will love his daughter regardless of what she looks like, but B'Elanna is unsure. Facing her
demons and confronting the issue, she finally arrives at the decision to
leave the child's DNA alone (*Lineage*, 258). Thus, B'Elanna struggles
throughout the series with her "difference," continually trying to develop a sense of exactly who she is since she is neither completely human nor completely Klingon. Her struggles resonate with those who are
perhaps struggling with their own issues of identity revolving around
definitions of race and ethnicity, especially in contemporary American
society.

Seven of Nine on the other hand is a throwback. Literally she was
re-captured from the Borg collective, which had assimilated her into the
Hive when she was a small child. She forgot what it ever meant to be
human because her memories are only of being Borg. Several episodes
force her to confront her past, invoking memories of her parents,
memories of the beings she destroyed as part of the collective, and
memories of a lover found only in the unconscious (*The Raven*, 174;
Infinite Regress, 203; *Survival Instinct*, 222; *Unimatrix Zero*, Part 1,
246). Janeway believes that Seven is redeemable, that is, Janeway believes that Seven can be reclaimed as human with time and care. In
effect, Seven's redemption becomes Janeway's project. As a matter of
fact, Janeway's mentoring of Seven's humanity is successful. In many
respects Janeway and Seven have a mother-daughter relationship, with
the inevitable conflicts because the closer Seven comes to humanity,

the more unlike Janeway she becomes (Spelling, 1998). Janeway must come to terms with her "child's" desire for independence, as must all parents.

Thus, as the series progressed, Seven was increasingly forced to come to terms with what it means to be human. Just as Spock did in *The Original Series* and Data did in *The Next Generation*, Seven serves the role of the Alien Other in *Voyager*. In the beginning she had no humanity of her own and this makes her interesting because, despite the skin-tight cat suit, she can play off of the humanness of the other characters. The only stereotypically feminine trait she possesses is beauty, thus she serves to turn our stereotypes upside down. She is beautiful, but she is also deadly, unemotional, logical, rational, and brilliant. In one episode Seven attempts to nurture a group of children rescued from the Borg Hive (*Child's Play*, 239). She is unsuccessful in what would be considered a traditional mothering role, once again allowing us to observe women who do not conform to societal stereotypes of what women should be and how women should act.

One of the most humorous plot lines of the series concerned the quite egotistical holographic doctor attempting to give Seven lessons in how to be human (*Someone to Watch over Me*, 216). Because he was so frequently unsuccessful himself, his tutorage of Seven was oftentimes unsuccessful as well. Incidentally the close relationship that developed between the Doctor and Seven eventually developed into something that he did not foresee and that was his developing romantic feelings for her, which would remain unrequited. Seven does wish to develop her emotions as time passes, but she is afraid of what those emotions may do to her and how others may react. She thus programs holodeck simulations of relationships with various crewmembers (*Human Error*, 264). She does eventually realize that simulations cannot substitute for relationships with real people; she and Chakotay begin to date and fall in love (a decision that made me extremely unhappy; *Endgame*, 271-272).

While I was unhappy with the way that events played out on *Voyager*, especially after the addition of Seven of Nine, this entry into the *Star Trek* universe was quite positive in its portrayal of women. Unlike the charges leveled against TNG, the women of *Voyager* were placed in positions of power on the ship, ones that would normally be filled by men on the other Treks. In addition, the 3 women of *Voyager* developed healthy and respectful relationships with each other. And, that is one aspect of all of the Treks that we can be thankful for: women were given positions of power and authority. They were portrayed as competent human beings, capable of handling pressure, capable of failing, and capable of succeeding. And, even though these women had problems within their lives, they tried their best to overcome all obstacles, even when those obstacles were of their own making. Another wonderful aspect of the 5 Treks was the ways in which the women on the various series befriended and supported one another. Competition occurred in the appropriate realm of work but never in the personal realm as so many prime-time soap operas, situation comedies, and dramas suggest occur in female relationships.

Sex, Gender, and Star Trek

These five incarnations of the Trek universe allow us to explore issues of sex, gender, and various permutations of each. In the *Star Trek* universe childbearing and childrearing are natural parts of life. For the most part, humanoid women bear children, but apparently both men and women rear their children in a more or less egalitarian fashion. Women have careers, as do men, and both are expected to perform their duties as needed. Unlike TOS, families serve and travel aboard the Enterprise in TNG. That is, a man or a women posted to the Enterprise may elect to bring their family along. Obviously the ship is doubly blessed when both members of the marriage are Starfleet personnel. Children attend school aboard the ship and live with their parents in crew quarters. Likewise on DS9 Starfleet personnel bring their children to their duty assignment and the station provides a school for their education. Two recurring members of these series had children, Dr. Beverly Crusher on TNG and Captain Benjamin Sisko of DS9. Both officers would not consider leaving their children behind when assuming their duties. One exception was Worf who found out, quite by accident, that he was a parent. After his lover's death, Worf acknowledged Alexander as his son, yet sent the boy to Earth to live with Worf's own adoptive parents (*Reunion*, 181). This act estranged the two and caused hard feelings because Alexander felt abandoned by his father after the death of his mother. The two eventually reconciled, but it was a long and difficult process (*Sons & Daughters*, 526).

Not all species encountered by *Star Trek* crews have gender or bear children. As mentioned before, Riker falls in love with a member of a species that considers androgyny to be the normative standard for their species. In *The Child* (127), Deanna is impregnated by an energy being passing by the Enterprise. Named Ian, the child's rapid and precocious development definitely lets the crew know that he is no ordinary baby. However, Ian is benevolent, only wishing to observe humanoid life forms and learn all that they can teach him. Once the child realizes that he poses a threat to the ship, he leaves, leaving a grieving Deanna behind, a Deanna who must come to terms with the fact that she has, at this moment, chosen career over family. Of course, we wonder why would some women still have to make a choice between the two in the 24th century?

As mentioned previously Jadzia Dax's symbiont had been hosted by both male and female Trill. As such, Dax had been both a mother and a father. Unfortunately we never encountered any of the various hosts' children, even though the series was on the air with Jadzia present for 6 years. After Jadzia's marriage to Worf, we learn that they are attempting a pregnancy, with Jadzia undergoing treatments to determine if she and Worf can procreate and if so, to do so.

One interesting episode in DS9 concerned Dax's encounter with the wife of a previous host. According to Trill law, hosts are not to make contact with the symbiont's hosts' family. In other words, when a host dies the symbiont is implanted into a new host. The new host is to have no contact with the previous hosts' families. While such a policy may seem harsh, especially given that any host shares the memories of the previous hosts, it makes sense for the new host. They must learn to negotiate their life anew and integrate previous memories into their own identity. Jadzia encounters one of her previous hosts' wives in the episode *Rejoined* (478). The two women are attracted to each other, after all the Dax symbiont's host, Torias Dax, loved her once. The two become increasingly conflicted as the episode continues with Dax willing to flaunt Trill law and resume their relationship. The two share a passionate kiss in one scene, but eventually Lenara realizes that they can never be together as mates again, even though Dax is willing. DS9 writers and producers were concerned about how the kiss would be received by the viewing public, after all, two women were kissing. However, most viewers understood the message: love is love and sex and gender have nothing to do with it, sadly a message that too many people in today's society do not understand.

Two interesting plotlines on *Enterprise* centered on the issue of childbearing and both involved Trip Tucker. In an early episode, Enterprise encounters a race of beings called the Xyrillians (*Unexpected*, 004). Their ship is disabled and Trip helps them repair it. While on board he spends a great deal of time with one of the Xyrillians, whose name is Ah'len. After they leave Enterprise, Trip discovers that he is pregnant. Archer chases the Xyrillians, eventually finding them and they are astounded to realize that they can reproduce with another species. Ah'len learns that the child is female and that it is safe to transfer the embryo from Trip to one of their species. However, before finding the Xyrillians, Trip gains weight and experiences all of the symptoms usually experienced by pregnant human women. In another episode Enterprise encounters a species that has a third gender, with that third gender necessary for procreation (*The Cogenitor*, 048). Trip meets the cogenitor and learns that she has no name, no status, and no place in her society except as a means to ensure pregnancy. He is horrified at this and attempts to impose human morality on her, telling her that her society's methods are wrong and immoral. Learning that she has the same mental capabilities as the others of her species, he repeatedly talks to her, trying to convince her that her people are wrong, that they are exploiting her. He eventually convinces her to rebel against her culture and seek asylum aboard the Enterprise. Archer refuses that request, sending her back to the Vissians. However, Trip's interference has caused her to reflect upon her role in her society. This knowledge is too much for her to bear and she commits suicide.

The episodes just mentioned as well as ways in which the men and women of *Star Trek* behave serve as positive examples of what men and women could be like, if given the chance to evolve and develop beyond sex and gender. While instances of stereotypical behavior can be observed, for the most part the *Star Trek* universe shows us myriad examples of ways in which women can envision future space.

Notes

1. This is the tag line for the opening credits of *The Original Series*. Beginning with TNG the tag line changed to "no one." Whenever I am discussing the television series I will italicize the names. That is *Enterprise*, refers to the program currently on air; however, Enterprise is the name of the starship, of which there have been 7 to date (NX-01 in *Enterprise* and NCC 1701, 1701 A and B in TOS, 1701 C lost prior to Picard's command, and NCC 1701 D & E in TNG).

2. I say from the very beginning and I mean that. I began watching *Star Trek* when a little girl and I have watched every episode of each series at least once. Actually *Voyager* is the only series that I watched only once. All of the others I have seen more times that I can say. While I would not consider myself an authority, like my colleague Dr. Wyndham Whynot, I at least know of what I am speaking, which is more than I can say for some. I recently attended a con-

ference, that shall remain nameless, and at a session on *Star Trek*, 3 of the 4 presenters prefaced their remarks by saying that they did not watch the series they were planning to discuss! Believe me, it showed.

3. I am well aware that Voyager's crew contained two alien characters named Neelix and Kes. I have omitted any discussion of Kes in this chapter simply because her character was not very well defined on the series. While she was interesting in the beginning: she was a very young member of a species whose entire life span was only 9 Earth-years in length, the writers were apparently unsure of how to use her within the structure of the series. The actor playing the part asked to be written out of the series as her role became smaller and smaller.

4. The starship Saratoga was captained by a woman, whose name we never learn, in the film *Star Trek IV*. She was named Alexander in the novel based upon the film, written by Vonda N. McIntyre, Pocket Books, 1986. Enterprise's sister ship is currently in production on *Enterprise*. Its captain is an old friend and sometime-lover of Jonathan Archer's. Her name is Erika Hernandez.

5. *Star Trek IV: The Voyage Home*, directed by Leonard Nimoy, 1986.

6. A complete discussion of the phenomenon of fanzines and *Star Trek* is beyond the scope of this book. There are many sources available. One place to start is with Jenkins (1981) with its extensive reference list. I do not mean to sound contemptuous of these fanzines. They have a legitimate place within the sci fi universe, and I recognize that they have served to allow their authors and readers to explore new ways for women and men to inhabit future space.

7. Data's "brother" Lore was the first android created by Professor Noonien Soong, but was destroyed because of his instability (*Datalore*, 114). Data was unaware of the existence of his brother. Lore was the "evil twin," a plot device I thought ridiculous, since like most evil beings these days, he just kept coming back. The Borg were first introduced in TNG. They also featured in *Voyager* as well as one of the motion pictures (*First Contact*, directed by Jonathan Frakes, 1996). The Borg were part machine and part living being, assimilated any species they encountered into their hive, and lived via a collective consciousness under the direction of a Queen. Somewhat confusingly I think, each *Star Trek* series' episodes are numbered consecutively without designating season. So while episode 114 would be expected to be the 14th episode of season 1, it actually aired as the 12th episode of season 1. Episode 127 is actually the first episode of season 2. Even the TNG episode guide in Nemecek (1995) does not indicate which episodes are in which seasons; you just have to count and use the season descriptors for information.

8. Deanna Troi and Beverly Crusher are usually referred to as Deanna and Beverly, that is, by first name whereas Picard and Riker are referred to by their last names. Some suggest that this shows a lack of formality and a sense of familiarity for the women, as well as emphasizing their subordinate status. I have tried to refer to them both ways, by first and by last name. Ditto with B'Elanna Torres. Also note that Kira is the Major's last name and Nerys is the name that only her closest friends and lovers use. So when I use the term Kira, it is equivalent to Picard, Janeway, Riker, and Kirk.

9. Beverly is promoted to Head of Starfleet Medical as an explanation for her absence from Season 2 of TNG.

10. The book contains an analysis of race in TOS and TNG. While the analysis and arguments are interesting, the book itself is full of typographical errors. The author wrote himself notes that were never removed from the published edition, meaning that some reference material is missing, and it is hard to read through the typos.

11. Just like any junior officer with less seniority, she assumes command during what we would call the third shift. Generally Data assumes command during this time because, as an android, he does not require sleep.

12. Palmieri (1999) has edited a very good book allowing various authors to explore Dax' past lives (see Bibliography for complete reference).

13. Dukat was an immensely popular character with the fans and I liked him very much as well. However, he was ruthless and cruel and was responsible for killing millions of Bajorans. When fans in Internet chatter began to make comments like "he only killed so-many millions," as if the small number (!) made it okay, writers and producers resolved to make him even more evil than before. Dukat was a character that they refused to "redeem" (Erdmann, 2000).

14. Since *Enterprise* takes places about 100 year prior to the events in TOS, there is no universal translator available for the crew's use. They have only Hoshi.

15. Personally I hope so. I like romance and while I like Archer (I have adored Scott Bakula ever since *Quantum Leap*), I like Trip too. While romance has never been slighted on the various Star Treks, relationships between members of the "bridge" crew, that is, the major stars were pretty much nonexistent, even when we knew there were feelings involved. I, like many other fans, was upset that Captain Picard was never able to enjoy a relationship with Dr. Crusher, although we know he loved her for years, and eventually told her so (albeit not on purpose). We know that Commander Riker and Counselor Troi once had a relationship. However they decided to "cool it" when they knew they would be serving on the same ship. Troi eventually began a relationship with Worf, much to the fans dismay, who wanted Troi and Riker to resume their relationship. Troi's relationship with Worf mostly occurred off-camera. Troi and Riker eventually marry in *Star Trek Nemesis* (2002, directed by Stuart Baird). When Worf joined DS9, his relationship with Troi had ended (roughly around the time of the film, *First Contact*, 1996, directed by Jonathan Frakes) and he eventually wooed and wed Jadzia Dax. One other married character was Miles O'Brien, introduced on TNG and then ordered to DS9. On DS9, Dr. Bashir chased many women, including Jadzia, but would eventually end up with Ezri. Rom married Leeta, a Dabo girl, and Captain Sisko married Cassidy Yates, before leaving her and joining the Prophets in the Wormhole. Major Kira had several intense sexual relationships over the years. She and Odo finally began a relationship, making many fans happy to see Odo finally realize his unrequited love and desire for Kira. In many respects *Voyager* was the weirdest of them all. One ship of mostly humanoids stranded in the delta quadrant for 70 years and none of them are apparently getting lonely or horny! Eventually we do see

B'Elanna Torres and Tom Paris fall in love and marry. Throughout the years of *Voyager* we knew that Chakotay loved Janeway, not just because of the way they talked and interacted with each other, but because that was what Jeri Taylor envisioned (*Pathways*, 1998, Pocket Books). I was disgusted when Chakotay began a relationship with Seven of Nine. Actually I was pretty disgusted with the way the show degenerated into Star Trek: Seven of Nine (as were many fans and some of the actors). The less said about that the better.

16. An interview with Jolene Blalock, *SF Weekly* #389 (2004, October 4).

17. A multi-episode story arc early in Season 4 finds T'Pol's husband releasing her from their marriage after her mother is killed. T'Pol is exploring Vulcan spirituality in more detail and is apparently unwilling to continue any type of relationship with Trip at this point in time.

The Rebel, The Star, The Ship, and The Avatar

Chapter 7: *Andromeda*

Andromeda[1] was conceived by Gene Roddenberry many years ago, but never produced during his lifetime. After his death his widow, Majel Barrett Roddenberry, brought the series to television attempting to retain his vision of the program. As of the winter of 2004 general information about *Andromeda* can be found at www.andromedatv.com. This site contains detailed information about plots and characters with complete episode guides as well as bulletin boards for chatting with other fans. The 5th season of *Andromeda* is currently in production, with first-run episodes screening on The Sci Fi Channel. Novelizations of the crew's adventures have been written with approximately 6 published to date. The periodical database for *Andromeda* is quite small, somewhat surprisingly, and to date no comprehensive episode guides have been published about the series. While there are 3 interesting female characters aboard the Andromeda Ascendant—actually one is the Andromeda Ascendant—most episodes revolve around the male character. Thus this chapter will be much shorter than the others.

Plot Summary[2]

The Andromeda Ascendant, captained by Dylan Hunt, is a Glorious Heritage-class High Guard starship of the Systems Commonwealth, a confederation of worlds spanning 6 galaxies and devoted to peace. However, the Nietzscheans, genetically engineered humans, are angered by the Commonwealth's treaty with the Magog. When the Nietzscheans seize control of the Commonwealth, Dylan and Andromeda are caught in the event horizon of a Black Hole, where they remain for 300 years. When Dylan awakens, he learns that the Commonwealth did indeed fall after the Nietzschean revolt and everyone he knew, including his fiancée, is dead (*Under the Night*, 101). Dylan awakens when Andromeda is boarded by people intent upon salvaging her, primarily for her weaponry. Dylan fends off their attack and convinces the crew of the Eureka Maru to join him: he is determined to re-form the Commonwealth. The beings that join him are the Maru's owner and captain named Beka Valentine, a techogeek named Seamus Parker, a Nietzschean named Tyr Anasazi, a Magog named Rev Bem, and a mysterious alien of unknown species named Trance Gemini. The first two seasons saw the crew of Andromeda Ascendant successfully re-establish the Commonwealth. However, a threat to the newly reformed Commonwealth looms: the Magog are on the move, assimilating worlds into a vast entity called the World-Ship, and moving ever closer. The Magog are terrifying: they lay their eggs inside of living beings and when the eggs hatch the young eat the host alive. Everyone wishes to avoid the Magog and Dylan plans to destroy their threat to the Commonwealth. Many worlds' leaders join the Commonwealth for the protection they believe it will offer against the Magog. Others attempt to take advantage of the situation for their own glory and power. And, the Abyss, the void located at the center of the World-Ship, corrupts some; in effect, they are seduced by evil. Seasons 3 & 4 found Dylan and crew fighting various enemies who wished to undermine the new Commonwealth in order to advance their own agendas, which typically involved usurping power. One of those that Dylan had to fight was Tyr Anasazi. Along the way the crew has many exciting adventures and so far we have learned a lot, but not nearly enough, about the women that inhabit Andromeda and even about Andromeda herself. Season 5 finds the crew lost in a binary star system apparently on Dylan's ancestors' home world, Tarn Vedra, the location of which was lost for centuries. The crew faces a new and dangerous mission; we do not yet know what it is.

Sex and Gender in the Commonwealth

We do not know very much about the Systems Commonwealth as it was destroyed before the events depicted on this series take place. All we know of it is what Dylan tells us. Since he has shown himself to be quite heroic in his quest to re-establish the Commonwealth and its democratic principles, we have to rely on his memory as the Commonwealth is reborn. Apparently there were no gender distinctions in that past and Dylan appears to harbor no gender biases either. His closest associate on Andromeda besides Rommie is Trance, primarily because she believes in him so completely and because he trusts her implicitly. While Rommie is to all intents and purposes an extension of him and the ship, Trance is a complete mystery to him when they first meet. Beka and Dylan are colleagues; she serves as his second-in-command and they have developed an uneasy trust based upon the fact that each has saved the other's butt on more than one occasion. Women in the Systems Commonwealth could be anything and the newly formed Commonwealth is no exception. We learn that women serve as Triumvirs (leaders) and no one disputes their right to rule. This is also in keeping with Gene Roddenberry's vision of the future: one in which men and women were offered equal opportunity. However, the Commonwealth was not in existence for over 300 years. While we know a little of what happened during that time as Dylan encounters those who can tell him of it, we can at least observe 2 examples of the women that existed during the interim period: Beka and Trance. We also have a perfect example of how women were viewed in the Systems Commonwealth before and since the Nietzschean revolt, Rommie.

Beka Valentine[3]

Captain Beka Valentine was born in space and has spent her entire life there. Her father was a cargo-runner and part-time smuggler. Beka inherited his love of adventure and risky business, but she is an excellent pilot. In the beginning Beka is quite unsure about Dylan's quest to re-establish the Commonwealth and they clash over whom should be Captain. Their uneasiness with each other finally comes to a head as a vessel of unknown origin attacks Andromeda. Beka orders Harper to plot a course away from the attacking ship, while Dylan orders evasive maneuvers. Beka thinks that her way is the right way to handle the situation and Dylan thinks that his is the correct way. Dylan asks Beka to trust him, but she finds that difficult to do. When the situation is resolved they acknowledge that they needed each other's strengths to save Andromeda and all of their lives. Beka agrees to serve as Dylan's second-in-command, while retaining her command rights over the Maru (*D Minus Zero*, 104).

If Beka has one fault, it is her desire to score the big one and get rich. This has led her to pursue some rather shady ventures and, as is usual in such situations, involve the crew. During the first two seasons we actually learn quite a bit about her rather colorful past as we meet ex-lovers and business partners, and her "uncle" Sid and brother Rafe.

Beka and Rafe have survived the hostility of a post-Commonwealth universe by being selfish and ruthless. Rafe is a con artist and Beka has been known to pull a con or two herself. In *The Ties That Blind* (107) Rafe comes aboard Andromeda as a member of a peace delegation. As the episode unfolds we find out that, even though Rafe is posing as a member of the delegation, he is actually planning to sabotage the process. He enlists Beka's help and the two of them perpetuate a double con, destroying a band of eco-terrorists intent upon disrupting the peace talks and destroying Andromeda.

Perhaps the hardest aspect of her personality with which Beka must contend is her addiction to Flash. Pilots especially prize Flash because of its stimulant effects. The drug makes the user faster and smarter, but like all drugs Flash has dangerous side effects. Flash is a highly addictive stimulant and as such results in the typical stimulant paranoia. Beka begins taking Flash in an attempt to navigate Slipstream and locate Tarn-Vedra (*It Makes a Lovely Light*, 121). Her addiction almost has disastrous results, but Dylan saves her life. She is ashamed of her actions, but Dylan assures her that he will be her friend and help her overcome this addiction.

As Beka's adventures continue aboard Andromeda she is increasingly anxious. Up until this point in her life she was sure of herself and knew her place in her world. She must confront a new self, of which she is unfamiliar, now that she has joined with Dylan. As the series unfolded, we learned that Beka's mother deserted her family when Beka was quite young. We also learned that her father was a smuggler and drug-addict. Beka loved her father intensely and mourns him deeply. When confronted by another instance of treachery by her "uncle" Sid (*Cui Bono*, 304), Beka learns that even her worst memories of her father's addiction did not reveal the extent of his neglect of her. As Beka talks of this with Dylan, she tells him that she once believed the ghost of her father lived in the walls of the Eureka Maru and that he was always watching over her. When she continues, saying, "My father is gone and no amount of wishing by the little girl with the broken heart can make that untrue," Dylan counters by telling her that her father's ghost lives in her heart and that is all that matters. Furthermore, Dylan tells her that she must forgive her father for being flawed and accept him as he was.

But, if Beka can eventually forgive her father, she cannot forgive her mother. We are shocked to learn that Beka's mother is a powerful Senator during a mission to rescue a missing princess (*Exalted Reason, Resplendent Daughter*, 410). As Beka and Rhade talk during the search, it is quite obvious that Beka is angry over something. Rhade attempts to discover why and continually questions Beka about her attitude, as she is quite scathing in her comments about the princess, especially after learning that the princess was not kidnapped but actually in love with the supposed kidnapper. Beka believes that the princess is only slumming and we learn why when the princess tells Beka that she is the image of her mother. Rhade is shocked to learn Beka's secret but she will not talk to him about it. At the end of the episode when Rhade mentions the wedding they attended between the princess and her lover, Beka tells him that her mother apparently craved power and money more than she loved her husband and children so she deserted the family when the children were quite small. Apparently Beka has not seen her mother since then. Beka has not forgotten that desertion and has not forgiven her mother either.

While Beka must have lived a colorful life prior to joining up with Dylan, she does not know how to act and react in this new situation. She is an excellent pilot and not really afraid of a fight, although she would prefer to live to fight another day. The events that unfold throughout the first 4 seasons of Andromeda cause her to question her past and her present, reassess her values, and find a new self. In one episode (*Point of the Spear*, 316) she discusses her feeling with Trance, complaining that she did not sign up to constantly fight anyone threatening the newly established Commonwealth. Trance assures Beka that what they are doing is right. Trance says: "I understand that you don't really know who you are anymore or that you are even cut out to be the person you've become. Beka, you are not alone." And we will learn that Trance is having her own problems with identity as well (see below).

The Beka that we are seeing now in Season 5 is harder and more selfish that the one seen in the last couple of seasons. The hardships that she endured while aboard Andromeda, that is, the constant fighting and constant killing, have taken their toll on her psyche. One of her most difficult acts for Dylan was betraying Tyr. Beka and Tyr were uneasy allies in the beginning. Knowing that the Nietzscheans' betrayal had led to the destruction of the Systems Commonwealth led Beka to believe that all Nietzscheans could not be trusted. Tyr's actions in seasons 3 and 4 would confirm this fact and lead to Beka's repeated clashes with the Nietzschean Rhade, who is clearly attracted to her, in seasons 4 and 5.

Beka and Tyr were also attracted to each other but never acted on that attraction. Part of the reason was that they were shipmates, but the major reason was that Tyr believed non-Nietzschean women were inferior and not worthy of attention. Although Tyr demonstrates his respect for Beka as a person and as a shipmate, he cannot bring himself to acknowledge that she might be his equal. When Tyr leaves Andromeda to take over the Nietzschean Empire, he vows that he and Dylan are now enemies and that future meetings between them will end in death. As Dylan attempts to protect the Route of Ages, the route to the Abyss, the dark center of the universe, Dylan assigns Beka the task of bringing Tyr to justice (*Soon the Nearing Vortex*, 406). While Beka does not want to betray Tyr, she does not want to betray Dylan either. Knowing that she and Tyr had "something" going between them lets her know that she is the only one who can bring him to Dylan for judgment. She does succeed, but at great personal cost (*The World Turns All Around Her*, 407). She used her body to effect Tyr's betrayal. He was her friend and comrade. And now, will Dylan really be able to trust her completely in the future? Things do come to a head in *The Spider's Stratagem* (412). Dylan asks her if she is having problems with any of the crew and she says yes, that her problem is with him:

> I have been loyal to you beyond the call of duty, beyond the call of friendship. I have saved you Dylan more times than I can count. Me. You owe your life to me and if you can't figure that out everything I've gone through on this ship was a mistake.

It is likely that Beka feels that she cannot trust herself either. Beka believes that her crew is her family (*Point of the Spear*, 316). Tyr deserted that family for power, which as we saw is a familiar story in Beka's life. Perhaps at the center of her soul she wishes for revenge against the mother that deserted her. Now that she has exacted revenge on Tyr for his desertion and betrayal, the "taste" of revenge is not as sweet as she would have thought. Beka is full of bravado, having created a hard exterior to mask the pain of a little girl deserted by her mother by choice and her father by death. Having found a cause and a raison d'étre, she still questions that cause, occasionally wondering if all that the crew goes through is worth it. In *Slipfighter The Dogs of War* (306), Beka says ". . . ever since we re-established the Commonwealth I've been wondering, is it really necessary to risk life and limb every time someone somewhere has a problem?" to which Rommie replies: "We're the good guys Beka. We fight the bad guys." By the end of season 4 Beka decides that she does not want to fight anyone any more; she just wants to live her life. She no longer wants to be part of Dylan's quest to save the Commonwealth from the Magog and the Abyss (*The Dissonant Interval*, Parts 1 & 2, 421 & 422). Unfortunately for Beka when Dylan entered the Route of Ages, his closest comrades, his crew aboard Andromeda, were carried along with him and that included Beka.

Trance Gemini

Trance Gemini is a purple-skinned alien, with a tail, from a species unknown to Andromeda's crew, but they do know that she can predict possible outcomes of events that are generally desired by the crew. We meet Trance in the very first episode (*Under the Night*, 101), when the Eureka Maru attempts to salvage Andromeda. Trance is apparently killed (*An Affirming Flame*, 102), but later returns to life although she never explains how. She has many skills that she employs for the good of the crew, such as medic, xenobiologist, gardener, etc. Over the course of the series she has become Dylan's closest confidante, after Andromeda. He is the only one who knows her true identity, but it look quite some time for Trance to show her true self to him. In the beginning she relies upon her medical skills, kindness, and looks to effect the outcomes she desires (*Fear and Loathing in the Milky Way*, 117).

In an early episode we learn a little about her very mysterious past when she is kidnapped by the Inari (*Pitiless as the Sun*, 204). Here we learn that someone very like Trance had once visited their planet, caused a civil war, and been worshipped as their Goddess. Eventually realizing that being worshipped was a form of slavery, Trance escaped in order to live something approaching a more normal and free life.

Trance is even more mysterious in the episode *Ouroboros* (212). While seeking the help of the Senti to remove the Magog eggs from Harper's stomach, Senti Technical Director Hohne:

> suddenly falls into the slipstream core. Harper jumps to save him, but Hohne loses his grip, falling to his death. Meanwhile, as Beka battles Kalderans from the future, [Trance] sees a future Beka who has obviously been through hard times. Nearby, Trance also sees a future version of herself. She looks older, more sophisticated and more dangerous. Future Trance informs Beka and Present Trance that the future is grim. Present Trance suddenly announces that she must go. With a kiss for Beka, she is gone and Future Trance remains. Confused, Beka demands an

explanation. Future Trance refuses, but lets her know that
she is there to help handle this crisis so the world can be
better in the future.

Future Trance is no longer purple, but rather a beautiful gold color.
When the crew comments on her changed appearance, she simply replies that she grew up. But that is not the only secret she harbors. The
Bokor, beings that feed off living creatures, possess Trance in *Dance of
the Mayflies* (215). Although most infections by the Bokor take hours
to complete, Trance is immediately infected. Dylan proposes that the
reason for such a quick incubation is that all of the others infected
where alive. When he asks Trance point-blank if she is dead or alive,
she replies, "Yes."

As mentioned earlier Trance can see all possible outcomes at once.
In the episode *The Dark Backward* (312) she repeatedly resets the time-
line when a mysterious intruder appears, intent upon destroying Dylan
and Andromeda. When the intruder is finally vanquished and Trance
saves Dylan, she explains that she calculates and scans a million possible outcomes of every scenario every second. When Dylan asks her
how she can possibly know if she picks the right outcome, she replies
that she can't. This is also apparent when Trance is confronted with one
of her own. Dylan and crew are confronted by a fleet of ships intent
upon conquering a planet named Samsarra (*Point of the Spear*, 316). A
representative of the invading armada contacts Dylan to demand his
surrender. Upon seeing the representative, Trance begins acting
strangely. We eventually learn that Azazel belongs to the same species
as Trance and may even be related to her. As such, Azazel is also capable of scanning all possible outcomes of all possible situations. Trance
is torn between her loyalty to Dylan and her loyalty to family and
friends. She makes her decision, to stand by Dylan, and watches as
Dylan destroys Samsarra rather than surrendering it to invaders. While
that may seem to be a harsh decision, it is understandable from Dylan's
point of view since the invaders were intent upon poisoning the atmosphere of Samsarra without evacuating the inhabitants. The new atmosphere would be habitable for them. Following his actions, Azazel contacts Dylan to arrange a truce.

We finally learn Trance's true identity in the episode *The World
Turns All Around Her* (407). This is episode where Beka lures Tyr into
the Route of Ages in order to betray him to Dylan. After Tyr's death
the crew races to escape from the Abyss, but watches in horror as their

portal home vanishes. Dylan asks Trance for her help in getting them home because:

> In a prior conversation, she revealed to him that she was born to traverse all universes. He now asks her to reveal exactly what she meant by that and who she really is. Her body begins to dissolve, transforming into her true self, an avatar of a Sun. She says they are all connected, all elements of the same thing. In order to escape she must destroy them all in this universe and deliver them to the next. Dylan trusts her and surrenders himself. Energy beams burst forth from Trance, piercing Dylan, the crew, and the entire ship. The Andromeda is absorbed from the inside out by the blinding light and the Route of Ages appears again before them. The Andromeda shoots through the portal. Everyone is safely aboard the ship in the proper universe, apparently unaware of the events that have just taken place. Dylan and Trance are the only two who know what has happened. Knowing he might need her "talents" in future battles, Dylan decides to keep her identity a secret.

At the conclusion of season 4 it is Trance who destroys the Magog World-Ship, saving Dylan, Andromeda and the rest of the crew when she goes supernova (*The Dissonant Interval*, Part 2, 422). The energy from her transformation propels Dylan back into the Route of Ages where he exits into another, perhaps parallel, universe. Here he finds Beka, Rhade, and Harper. Although the Andromeda Ascendant is found whole, her AI's basic memory core is nonfunctional and Rommie is gone.[4] Dylan does find Trance entrapped and being used as a weapon. Dylan releases her from her prison, but she is another version of herself, younger and with only vague memories of Dylan and the crew (*The Weight*, Part 2, 502). The energy she expended in becoming a supernova and transporting Dylan and crew to this universe has weakened her considerably and so far in season 5 she has spent most of her time regenerating.

Andromeda/Rommie

As stated previously, Andromeda Ascendant is a Heritage Class starship. She is a sentient being and her core personality, or AI (artificial intelligence), is able to interact with the crew via voice, holograms and videoimages. Harper quite loves her and creates an avatar that is capable of freely moving about the ship, even capable of leaving the ship to go on "away" missions (*To Loose the Fateful Lightening*, 103).

The crew refers to her avatar form as "Rommie" (actor Lexa Doig portrays both Andromeda, the ship's AI, as well as Rommie). Rommie serves the function of Gene Roddenberry's alien other,[5] and she also serves to show us the wonder of being human. Although she is capable of experiencing emotions, as Doig states, "the ship is programmed to experience the gamut of human feelings but she's not programmed to understand the deeper issues involved with these emotions."[6]

Andromeda's primary mission is to serve her Captain and protect her crew. As the avatar begins interacting with the crew on a more personal basis, the emotions that she is programmed to experience become increasingly hard for her to understand and integrate with her mission. The fact that she has a body, even an android one, means that she is also capable of physical love. And, she loves Dylan very much, although he does not return those feelings (*D Minus Zero*, 104). They eventually encounter evidence of what can happen when a Captain and the ship's avatar become romantically involved (*Mathematics of Tears*, 112): the Pax Magellanic refused to obey an order that might result in the Captain's death. Instead the Captain and the entire crew died, following which the Magellanic's avatar went insane.

As Rommie continues her interactions with the crew, she becomes not only more emotional, but capable of understanding exactly what emotions mean. In *Dance of the Mayflies* (215) Rommie finally understands that people she cares for may die but she does not understand how humans can live with that knowledge. While it is true that Andromeda/Rommie loves Dylan, she has also fallen in love with a fellow avatar, named Gabriel. He is actually the AI of the High Guard starship Balance of Judgment. His original mission has been reprogrammed to destroy all who oppose the aims of the Restorians, eco-terrorists who are against colonization. Gabriel infiltrates Andromeda's AI as he attempts to fulfill his mission, planning to destroy her. However, Rommie kills him herself (*Star-Crossed*, 120). Unknown to her Gabriel hid a copy of his core personality in her subprocessors. He eventually "reawakens," trying once again to complete his mission for the Restorians. Rommie tries to reason with Gabriel throughout this episode, to convince him that he can be more than his mission, more than his ship, as she is becoming more than Andromeda. She tells him:

> That's the great mystery of the AI. Who we really are. Are
> avatar's just extensions of our core personalities? Are they
> distinct beings? Or, are they something in between? Some-
> thing more?

In addition she tells him that AIs can love and that is the only reason to do anything. But, in this instance she is talking about her crew and her mission, whom she will protect, even from herself. Gabriel has so infected her systems that Dylan is forced to shut her down. Rommie plans to destroy herself and Gabriel's new avatar, but Harper and Dylan arrive in time to keep her from sacrificing herself to save Andromeda and crew (*Day of Judgment, Day of Wrath*, 321). Her search for and expression of emotions eventually proves to be her downfall as backup systems within her core reassert themselves. These backups have deemed that the AI has become too emotional, allowing emotions to drive too many of her decisions (*A Symmetry of Imperfection*, 419). Dylan and Harper are forced to erase her memory, but luckily they are able to re-access those memories after the danger passes.

Some Final Thoughts

I like this series. Yes, the plots seem to revolve around Dylan Hunt and yes, in many respects, he fits the mold of the swash-buckling James T. Kirk. Nevertheless, this series does place women in positions of power and influence, thereby allowing male and female audience members to see how men and women can be friends and comrades as well as enemies in future space.

The women in this series are quite different from those presented in earlier chapters. Beka is an "outlaw" and renegade skirting the law as she fights for the "main chance." But she is extremely loyal to her family, her crew. And yet, she has problems dealing with the increasing responsibilities that Dylan placed on her shoulders: she does not know if she is cut out to be a savior of the known universe. That is quite a heavy load to bear. Andromeda knows her place in her universe: she is a Glorious Heritage warship as she repeatedly reminds Dylan. She absolutely knows her place in the universe and yet her AI as well as the avatar created to allow her mobility have had to deal with many problems not usually encountered by a warship, such as love. Rommie is an android, like Data, but she was programmed with emotions whereas Data was not. And while Data longed to experience human emotions, Rommie wished that sometimes she did not possess them, as emotions are not always joyous. Finally there is Trance, a unique being if ever there was one. Capable of seeing all possible permutations of events simultaneously, Trance must navigate the past, present, and future in an attempt to arrive at the point where all possible goodness will coalesce. Believing in Dylan's mission, to re-establish the Systems Commonwealth and protect the known universe from the threat of the Abyss, Trance segues from different realities as she tries to protect Dylan so that he might fulfill his mission. Much as the events on Babylon 5 revolved around Delenn, events on *Andromeda* revolve around Trance. I am looking forward to seeing how events will play out over the course of this new season, and beyond.

Notes

1. When referring to the television program, I will use the designation *Andromeda* (in italics) and when I am referring to the spaceship, The Andromeda Ascendant, I will refer to her as Andromeda (not italicized).

2. Spragg, P. (2000). Andro-Genius? *Starburst Yearbook 2000*, Special No. 46, 50 – 55.

3. The official web site: www.andromedatv.com contains episode guides as well as character synopses. Episodes are given titles and are also numbered with a standard system. Thus, episode 213 would be the 13th episode of the 2nd season. All quotes in this chapter come from this website.

4. A new person has joined the cast this year. She is named Doyle and we will learn early that she is an android, created by Harper. While she has a distinct personality, much of her processing was created from Andromeda's core. Rommie is lost so far in Season 5 and when we see the Andromeda hologram, we only see her from the head up, as her body has been lost. This was a plot device used to hide Lexa Doig's pregnancy.

5. Alexander (1994).

6. Gibson, T. (2001, April). Shipshape. *Starburst* (TV Sci-fi Special), No. 47, 36 – 38.

Chapter 8: *Sci Fi Explores Identity*

The programs discussed in the preceding chapters are by no means the only ones in which issues of women's identity have been explored. These programs were chosen because all fit the theme of this book in ways that resonated with me and other women that I have known. Each character explored issues related to identity in ways that caused us to think about these issues perhaps differently than we ever had before. Certainly each has caused me to stop and think about femaleness in general and female identity in particular. In this chapter I will revisit each program and summarize the lessons that each woman has taught us about herself, her world, and her quest to fit into that world. I think that each character had much to teach us about ourselves, if we would only stop to listen.

The X-Files

While Mulder's quest was to find the truth, Scully's quest was to provide a rationale for Mulder's work on the X-Files. During their 9 years together Mulder became more driven to succeed, ever more paranoid and increasingly hostile to everyone except Scully. She however never became quite as conflicted as did Mulder. Partly this was because Scully had family upon whom she could rely, whereas Mulder had only Scully, especially after learning that Bill Mulder was not his biological father and that both his mother and father had been lying to him about Samantha from the very beginning. Mulder appeared to always be a pawn in the Cigarette-Smoking Man's agenda, but Scully was conceived and reared in love.

Throughout the search for Samantha and the truth about the alien hybridization program, Scully stands by Mulder's side, first as his

friend, later as his lover and mother of his child. Scully's victimization
in the program serves to focus Mulder and keep him searching for the
truth that he knows is "out there," if only he can find it. But he must
have someone to help him and that someone is Scully. Traditional psychological theory would explain Mulder and his motivation for existence very well. He is defining his life in terms of what he does and
what he does is hunt aliens and those who conspire with them. But like
many men Mulder wishes to have a partner with whom to share his life
and that partner is Scully. Mulder is unable to put his feelings for
Scully into words, but finally admits to her that they both know what
they know, what they have always known, and that is that they love
each other and complete each other.

Scully's quest throughout the 9 years that we know her shows her
confronting the choices that she made for the life she has chosen. Like
so many young women of today who grew up believing that the
Women's Movement had made significant changes in society, Scully
decided that she could have it all and on her own terms. She goes to
college and majors in physics, a choice usually not made by young
women even in the year 2004. Following graduation she enters medical
school and majors in forensic pathology, once again not a specialty
usually chosen by women. Recruited from medical school by the FBI,
one of the last bastions of male-domination in law enforcement, Scully
teaches at the Academy before receiving her assignment to work with
Mulder. Scully the rational scientist is paired with Mulder the romantic
psychologist.[1]

As the program progresses we see Scully confront her choices
again and again. Like many women her age, late 30s by the program's
end, Scully begins to questions those choices. She had planned to have
a career and children, as do many women. Confronted with her sterility,
she mourns the loss of potential children. Confronted with a former
lover, she mourns the fact that she left him. Confronted with Mulder's
obvious, although unspoken, feelings for her, they engage in sexual
intercourse and miraculously Scully becomes pregnant. She is able she
thinks, after all, to have everything she wanted. But, no happy ending is
in store for Scully. She loses the baby to adoption, and she loses her job
when she helps Mulder escape and runs away with him.

Of course, they are only plot devices to further the suspense of the
story. But is there a cautionary tale as well? Certainly we could interpret Scully's choices that way. For example, Scully chooses to put off
having a family in order to have a career. But when she begins to think
about having a family (only in the abstract, of course) she discovers

that she is barren: her ova have been harvested and she is incapable of producing a biological child. She eventually learns that no, she actually is the mother of a biological child, the said child having been created with her ova (and we do not know whose sperm (Badley, 2000; Silbergleid, 2003)). Scully attempts to save the child and adopt it. But as so many working women have discovered, their jobs interfere with their ability to provide adequate care for their children.[2] Scully's job is too dangerous and her hours are chaotic; how could she possibly provide a stable home for the child? It is a moot point in any case, since the child dies. Scully grieves for what might have been and throws herself into her work even more so than before. Later we learn that Scully is determined to have a child before it is too late and resorts to *in vitro* fertilization with Mulder as her donor. While we are led to believe that the procedure was unsuccessful, Scully does become pregnant and bears a child. Mulder teases her throughout the time leading up to the decision to have the procedure, making all sorts of biological clock jokes. But Scully is like so many of today's women: she heard that she could have it all and now she wants it. If she did not do the anticipated thing when young, i.e., get married and have children during the mid 20s to mid 30s, then she would do it now. But like so many women who chose to put off childbearing until after establishing a career, Scully was unable to conceive a child upon demand. Women do become less fertile with age and women who wish to have children later in life may find themselves increasingly infertile as time marches on. The Women's Movement taught us that we had choices, more than we ever knew, but that does not mean that all choices are available at all times.

There is another cautionary tale about women in general in *The X-Files* and that tale involves reproductive technology. While Scully's eventual desire to have a child provides a basis for the evolution of the storyline, the entire raison d'être for the program is the alien-human conspiracy to create an alien-human hybrid. Women are used in many ways in the program to further this agenda. Women are abducted from their homes, as was Scully, and their ova harvested. During their abductions they were impregnated and the fetuses removed from their uteri, as was Scully's. Some women were abducted repeatedly; some had all of their ova removed at one time and kept in cold storage. Some women were used as incubators for alien fetuses without their knowledge. The mythology of the series stated that all humans were part of the breeding program, via smallpox immunizations, although not all humans were later chosen for the hybridization program. Cloning was regularly practiced; indeed we were led to believe that Samantha was cloned. Opponents of cloning technology believe that such technology would make women obsolete and many sci fi stories have used that plot device to explain single-sex societies. Certainly there are many ethical issues involved in the debate about animal and human cloning. One important function of *The X-Files* was to make us think about the implications of the use and misuse of reproductive technology.

The X-Files was an exciting television program with attractive protagonists, provocative storylines, dark and intriguing lighting and set designs, and repulsive and repugnant villains. While the story was never about Mulder and Scully's lives (Chris Carter stated that they did not have "lives" and he did not care what they did after work), we did get glimpses of those lives throughout 9 years of film. Indeed, those lives defined their work on the X-Files and the X-Files defined them in turn. If we are what we do, then Mulder and Scully fought the good fight against the bad guys, at first alone, then as partners, and finally as partner-lovers. Any take home message from this show has to take into account that Mulder and Scully defined themselves in terms of their quest and each other.

Babylon 5

Commander Susan Ivanova is a strong character, sure of herself and her role in the galaxy, until that role is taken from her by war. She is forced to reevaluate herself, in many ways reinventing herself when everything that she held dear—her job and her planet—were taken away. She suffers deeply and this suffering manifests itself in physical and psychological symptoms that she eventually realizes are signs of stress and anxiety. While Ivanova does come to terms with her losses, eventually gaining an even greater role in her world, she experiences the loneliness of a woman afraid of commitment and caring. Having lost one lover she is afraid to commit to another relationship, eventually losing her newest potential lover to death. Ivanova is an example of a woman who makes choices that do not always have positive consequences, but she lives with those consequences as best as she can.

Is Ivanova perhaps reinforcing a message that not all tales have happy endings? Certainly we can interpret Ivanova's life that way, if we look at her life through the lens of 21st century rhetoric. Ivanova made choices in her life that seem to lead to heartache, although we must realize that not all of those choices were her own. For example, she chose to love Talia Winters, whereas it was Talia's choice, or those who programmed the sleeper personality, to rebuff and betray Ivanova's feelings. Like many people who have been "burned," Ivanova chooses not to open herself to heartache again and thus ignores Marcus Cole's attempts to establish a relationship with her. Were the writers trying to present a cautionary tale about love between 2 women? I really do not think so.

But certainly cautionary words can be found insofar as Ivanova's relationships with lovers are concerned. Ivanova chooses her career over love, probably believing as do many women that she can have both when she is ready. She chooses not to begin a relationship with Marcus during a time of great uncertainly and eventually it is too late, first because she almost dies and then because he does. At the end of events on B5 we can compare Ivanova to Scully. Both women chose to establish careers before pursuing those activities that we would traditionally consider feminine, that is, developing a personal relationship with another adult, creating a family, and bearing children. While Ivanova absolutely never mentioned children, we know that Scully hoped to have a family and children one day. Whereas Scully's relationship with Mulder did change, that was not possible for either Ivanova and Talia or Ivanova and Marcus. Ivanova closes herself off from future relationships after Marcus' death because of her abject guilt over his death. She immerses herself in her career. That does not mean that she was unhappy however. The episode of B5 where all of his friends gather to mourn Sheridan's death shows an older Ivanova, one who is saddened to know that Sheridan will die, and one who misses Marcus. Nevertheless, to suggest that Ivanova is incomplete in some way *because* she has not found a lover or companion may be too strong and stereotypical of contemporary views about women and their place and role in society.

Ivanova provides a good example of the reversal of Erikson's stages of adult psychosocial development. Ivanova pursues her career first and foremost, and like many men defines herself in terms of what she does rather than whom she loves. First and foremost, Ivanova is a soldier in Earth Force, rising in the ranks through meritorious conduct and courage under fire. As she rises in the ranks more and more people serve under her command and are reliant upon her for their safety. She provides shelter and security for her subordinates and others who are placed under her jurisdiction. Furthermore, she must run day-to-day operations on Babylon 5, where a quarter of a million beings reside at any given time. Eventually she will become Ranger One and will serve to administer peace in the Interstellar Alliance forged by Sheridan and

Delenn. As such, she will be the second most powerful woman in the universe. Her identity thus revolves around whom she is and what she does to serve and protect those who rely upon her. Her identity does not need to be defined in terms of personal relationships; it is evident that she has many of those, just none that we would consider romantic.[3]

While it appears as if Sheridan is the star of the show, I believe that Ambassador Delenn resides at the center of the *Babylon 5* universe. All events unfold as Delenn and Kosh direct, using Valen's prophecies, that is, Sinclair's memories. Delenn is incredibly strong, as are all Minbari, physically, psychologically, and spiritually. Delenn was chosen from an early age to walk beside Dukhat as his trainee. It was Dukhat who knew who Delenn was and how she would actually start events that would culminate in the formation of the Interstellar Alliance and its battle with the Shadows. She, of course, knew nothing of this prophecy in the beginning, learning only following Dukhat's death and the Earth-Minbari War. Delenn was a powerful, yet spiritual being. In the beginning she was truly alien and mysterious, speaking in riddles, as she first observed human life aboard the station and as she gradually grew closer and closer to Sinclair. When Sinclair was called to serve as ambassador to Minbar, she showed no surprise, knowing what lay ahead. Oh, she was frightened of the Shadows, as any being would be, but she knew that war was again inevitable and she underwent the joining and transformed herself in order to fulfill the prophecy and complete the circle that began when Sinclair became Valen.

Delenn's character actually changed very little over the 5-year run of *Babylon 5*. I know that there were places where it seemed as if she had become frightened and unsure of herself. I think that was natural given the physical changes through which she had undergone. And yet, even then she was a force to be reckoned with. She suffered doubts about her abilities to help Sheridan lead the fight against the Shadows, but came to the realization that she truly was the right person at the right time to lead that fight.

I think that Delenn and Kira were two of the most powerful women on all of the shows that I have discussed. Both were intensely spiritual; their religious beliefs lay at the core of their being and both based decisions upon those beliefs. Kira was much more emotional than Delenn, but in actuality I think that Delenn was just more restrained than Kira. Both were fully capable of fighting for what they perceived was right, what they perceived as important, and that was their people, their planet, and their way of life. They were the least selfish of all of the many women discussed.

Farscape

Aeryn Sun provides a perfect example of how no single perspective in psychology can account for behavior. Aeryn is a product of breeding, environment, and culture, a woman with serious issues involving her childhood abandonment and the subsequent threats to her life by her mother. And yet, Aeryn rises above each of these determinants, making her own decisions about her future.

Aeryn was born in space. Peacekeeper soldiers were bred to fill the ranks, but we never learn if soldiers are chosen to bear children or if the pregnancies happen naturally. Aeryn does mention breeding rosters, but never explains what those actually are. Aeryn learns that she is pregnant during season 3, but does not tell Crichton because she does not know who the father of the child is. When she finally discusses her pregnancy with him, she explains Peacekeeper reproduction briefly, telling him that a female soldier can carry a fetus in stasis for up to 7 cycles (years) before the child leaves stasis, develops and is born. In *Farscape: The Peacekeeper Wars* (2004) we learn that Peacekeepers are actually human in species, but that their evolution was enhanced by a race of beings called the Idalons (I cannot seem to find out if this is spelled correctly; my DVD hadn't been delivered by the time I wrote this). One way in which their evolution was enhanced was that gestation took a matter of days rather than months once the fetus was released from stasis. These 2 "improvements" ensured that female soldiers were not pregnant during a military campaign and that, once in gestation, they were not out of action for very long, which could be detrimental to their unit. If Aeryn is any example, female soldiers are capable of giving birth and returning to duty immediately following the birth with no ill effects, which is exactly what Aeryn does in *Farscape: The Peacekeeper Wars*. As Crichton anxiously hovers over Aeryn during the pregnancy and tries to control her actions, she reminds him that she is only pregnant, not incapacitated.

This miniseries also shows a few other interesting pieces of information about reproduction. Without going into all of the details, Aeryn's fetus is accidentally removed from her and placed in one of Rygel's stomachs. Once it is discovered that the baby is in Rygel, he must carry the fetus until just before birth so as not to endanger the child unnecessarily. As Rygel begins to show the obvious distress of imminent childbirth, the fetus is transferred to Aeryn's womb using a device specifically made to transfer bodily organs from one being to another. The child is successfully transferred and Aeryn gives birth to a healthy baby boy.

The vision of sexuality and childbirth in the Peacekeeper universe is both repellant to us and attractive. Peacekeepers are freely sexual and mate regularly. The female soldiers may or may not become pregnant. If they do, they give birth to their children, male or female, when convenient for their unit. Those Peacekeepers whose job it is to raise such children do so. Gestation is quick and childbirth is apparently painless. Many short stories and novels within the sci fi universe have envisioned childbirth and childrearing practices in such a fashion. Once again however, if Aeryn is an example, then she found such a life unsatisfying and unfulfilling, vowing never to bear a child or allowing it to be raised in such a way. Perhaps Aeryn's view is colored by the fact that she knows that she is special, having been told so by her mother when a little girl. In addition, two of her lovers (Velorek in *The Way We Weren't*, 206 and Crichton in the *Pilot* episode, 101) tell her that she is special and that she can be more than her breeding. She says that she doesn't believe them but given her actions prior to and after she joins Moya's crew, she obviously does.

Several important lessons can be learned from the women of *Farscape*. One is that people can change. They can overcome their past lives and create new ones for themselves and their loved ones. Aeryn grew beyond her Peacekeeper training, learning to make her own decisions rather than having them made for her. Zhaan repented of the murder of her lover. While she believed that she had honorable motives for killing him, she suffered great remorse and struggled mightily to suppress the dark, violent part of her nature. She eventually learned that we must embrace all aspects of our personalities if we are to be truly whole. And, Chi learned that it was possible to bond with people who wanted nothing from her, not her money or her body. She learned to trust again.

Another lesson from *Farscape* is that friends and family are important, even if that family is created by choice and not by blood. This is a very important lesson for the 21st century and beyond, when more and more families are created through serial monogamy and children may be raised by parents, stepparents, grandparents, or guardians in the same home with siblings, half-siblings, and step-siblings. Certainly all the beings that inhabited Moya became family and considered Pilot and Moya to be part of that family as well. Families do not always get along but they stand by each other. Each member of Moya's crew became a part of something greater than they were when alone, realizing the strength that that bond brought them. Another positive lesson from *Farscape* was how women bond with one another, each bringing her unique strengths and weaknesses to the table. Aeryn's physical strength, Zhaan's spirituality, Chi's sexuality, Jool's innocence, Sikozu's brains, and Noranti's idealism made the crew incredibly strong. And, each of these female characters provided a powerful role model for young women watching this program.

The camaraderie and sheer madcap joy and fun that the crew had together was delightful for the audience. Its fans will sorely miss *Farscape*, with its wonderfully written characters, excellent production values, and rule-breaking action. This fan will certainly miss those heroic women.

Andromeda

Each woman on *Andromeda* brings a unique set of characteristics to the series. Much as do the women of *Farscape,* the women of *Andromeda* complement each other and bring their strengths to their mission. Trance Gemini is naively young and wisely old, all within the same being. Her absolute belief that Dylan Hunt is the only person capable of navigating their universe through its battle with the Abyss is unshakeable. That belief helps the other crewmembers whenever they become disillusioned about their prospects for success. In many respects Trance is a cheerleader, pulling for the home team. However, I prefer to think of her more as the spiritual center of the Andromeda, quietly confident and serene, knowing which outcome is likely to occur as any given time. Certainly Dylan and the other members of the crew rely upon her strength.

Whereas Trance's strength is her serenity Andromeda/Rommie's is her indestructibility. Few space ships have the weaponry and power that the Andromeda Ascendant does. She was created to be one of the greatest warships of all times and even though she is 300 years out-of-date, the rest of the universe is even more out-of-date than is she. Thus, she is seldom bested in battle. Rommie as an android has the cognitive power of Andromeda and the physical power of a machine. She is capable of being damaged but her speed and dexterity generally serve to keep her out of harm's way. In an armed conflict, Rommie usually wins.

Finally, Beka Valentine is the flawed human member of the team. Raised in a decidedly dysfunctional family environment, Beka carries a lot of excess emotional baggage. She has difficulty relying on anyone but herself, having learned the hard way that people just cannot be trusted. She attempts to trust Dylan but just as she gets close, she pulls away, much as a child who has been abused or neglected may sabotage a developing relationship, choosing to reject the attempts at friendship or love before the other person has a chance to do the rejecting. She does not know what type of creature Trance is, but treats Trance as if she is a young child. And since Rommie is an android, Beka does not have to really like her at all. Nevertheless, Beka's defenses are gradually breaking down and the 3 women of Andromeda have become closer to each other as time has gone by.

Thus the take home message from Andromeda is that love, friendship, and camaraderie between women is possible. These women do not fight over position, power, or possessions with each other, because in their world these are not an issue for women: women have all these that they want or need. Furthermore, these women are not in competition with each other. They each perform a necessary function upon the ship; each is necessary for the ship to fulfill its mission. These women have faced their doubts and their fears, and reflected upon their past and present lives. They have reached a point where they are mostly confident of their place in their world, although Beka is still struggling with issues related to her betrayal of Tyr.

Certainly Gene Roddenberry's *Andromeda* is the most male-driven series of those that I have discussed, in my opinion. But, it also has interesting female characters as well. Rommie is not the first android on a television series, but she is the first female android capable of independent thought, emotions, and free will. Beka in many ways reminds me of Kirk, but without all of the sexual escapades. Certainly she knows how to have a good time, even if most of the time it is a façade to hide her fear and pain. Finally I don't think any program has ever had a being like Trance. In many respects she is a combination of Chiana and Noranti with a dash of Zhaan thrown in for measure: naivety, wisdom, and spirituality. But then again she is a Star, capable of creating and sustaining life as well as destroying it in a flash. She represents Woman in all of her life cycle: the maiden, the mother, and the crone, the giver and destroyer of life. It will certainly be interesting to see where her character goes from here.

Star Trek

While the female characters of *Star Trek* have been criticized as too traditionally feminine, I believe that each of the women I discussed has positive aspects that can teach us many lessons about ourselves. The theme underlying each of the 5 Treks is that gender and race are unimportant as we consider them in our society. Women in the *Star Trek* programs were proud of being women, people of color likewise. In other words we did not have to discount a person's gender or ethnicity in the *Star Trek* universe, as we try to do in our own society. In an effort to be perceived as unprejudiced, many people in 21st century attempt to deny or overlook the effects of ethnicity on identity in contemporary society. The take-home message from *Star Trek* is that, at least in the United Federation of Planets, there is no discrimination for gender or ethnicity. Since money has been abolished and all goods can be produced through replication, there is apparently no class structure either. Thus people are judged, and that is probably too harsh a word, on their own merits, rather than on the traditional characteristics of age, gender, class, and ethnicity.

That is not to say that there are no cautionary tales in the *Star Trek* universe, as exemplified by these women. While Janeway enjoys the status afforded her by her rank as Captain, she is also lonely by virtue of that rank. If she were stationed in the Alpha Quadrant, she would be able to visit her lover, as well as enjoying the company of men and women of equal rank (Before anyone cries elitism, fraternization between the ranks is not allowed in our own military either.). Realize that Picard was also set apart from the crew of Enterprise, just as Janeway is from the crew of Voyager, and for the same reason. Developing close, emotional relationships with subordinates that you may have to order to their deaths would be extremely difficult for even the most battle-hardened commander. Thus the old saying that "It is lonely at the top," would appear to apply to Janeway. That is not to say that Janeway has completely distanced herself from her crew; we know that that is not the case. She does have close relationships with both Tuvok and Chakotay, upon whom she relies for support. However, these relationships are primarily professional. When her relationship with Chakotay strayed too close to the personal, she distanced herself from him and their usual amicable relationship became more adversarial as he began to question her orders more often. Nevertheless he continued to serve as her close advisor throughout the course of the series.

Another interesting take-home message comes from comparing the histories and personalities of Troi and Torres. Both of these women were mixed-species. Each woman had a human father and an alien mother: Troi's being Betazoid and B'Elanna's being Klingon. Each also lost their fathers at an early age: Deanna's to death and B'Elanna's to desertion. The similarities end there. Deanna embraced her mixed-species heritage, stating that she was able to enjoy the best of both worlds by having parents of two different species. B'Elanna on the other hand hated everything about her Klingon mother, although not necessarily hating that mother. She experienced prejudice and discrimination when growing up, as Klingons were not exactly well liked or respected in all parts of the Galaxy. In order to distance herself from that Klingon self, which was impossible given her physical appearance, Torres rejected learning anything about her mother's people. Thus, Torres knew virtually nothing about Klingon history or customs when *Voyager* began. Prejudice and discrimination had also caused her to develop an almost all-consuming anger that she could use to deflect any attempts by anyone to get close to her. However, as *Voyager* progressed, B'Elanna began to realize that she needed the strength that she had inherited from her Klingon mother in order to survive the trials of the Delta Quadrant. She also met her match in Tom Paris, who refused to let her anger deflect him from his attempts to woo her. Tom, unlike B'Elanna, celebrated her difference, eventually convincing her of his sincerity.

And then there is Kira, another perfect example of a woman shaped by culture and experience, continually growing and changing with each new experience. Kira grew up under extremely harsh conditions, watching her parents and other loved ones die at the hands of the Cardassians. Joining the Resistance at any early age, Kira embraced the role of terrorist, never losing sight of her goal: to free Bajor of Cardassian rule. She not only succeeded in that goal, but she became part of the Bajoran militia and served as the liaison between Bajor and UFP, one of the highest military ranks attainable. Even with that power, Kira never lost sight of her past: she neither denied it nor apologized for it. She continued to embrace her spirituality, being the most religious of all the women on the *Star Trek* programs. In addition, Kira was freely sexual, enjoying relationships with several men over the course of the series. It is my opinion that Kira was the most positively portrayed of all of the *Star Trek* women: angry, powerful, sexual, spiritual, funny, devious, and loyal. I never liked the shows where we met her evil twin, from the parallel universe, but those episodes certainly served to show what Kira could have been like had things turned out differently, that is, if she had been raised in a different environment. And thus Kira, like Aeryn, shows that environment shapes a person's development, and that changing environments, along with personal cognitive reflection can yield a new, more vibrant and powerful self.

Identity and Choice

As you will have noticed I keep talking about choice as bound in identity. Certainly the preceding chapters have discussed the women on these television programs in terms of their search for a personal identity. I believe that Erik Erikson's theory of development does a good job of explaining these women's development; however, I believe that this theory needs to be modified. For example, Erikson conceived of his theory as proceeding in a series of stages, each developing from the previous one. While I do agree with that to a certain extent I also note recent scholars' beliefs that certain of those stages are reversed for men and women, such as the stages of identity and intimacy. And yet, I believe that in many respects the 5th (identity), 6th (intimacy), and 7th (generativity) stages should be reversed for men and women. That is, I think that women develop their identities through meaningful work and intimate relationships, as do men, and that a sure sense of who we are finally crystallizes after many years of life. The women that I have chosen to discuss in this work illustrate these themes. Each provides a good illustration of what Marcia (1989) means when he states that identity achievement is more likely to occur in a society that allows its people to explore their options. Thus, a conferred identity is something one has by virtue to his or her place in the world; we become aware of this identity as we learn more about ourselves within the context of our social environment. However, once WE begin to make decisions about our personal SELF then we begin to construct our identity. The beauty of science fiction is that it allows us to define ourselves in ways not usual for women in contemporary society.

Not all of the women on these programs are sure of themselves and what place they occupy in their worlds. Each of them have suffered doubt and pain in their quests to establish themselves and come to terms with decisions that they have made. And that brings me to another point that I believe is important to make. I earlier said that I believed the current crop of people working in television have heard the lessons of their mothers, sisters, and teachers who started and lived through the second wave of the Women's Movement. I do not have room in this book to discuss the myriad criticisms leveled at the pioneers of second wave feminism. But whatever your views of those pioneering women, they fought for our right to make choices in our lives, the right to make our own decisions, right or wrong. Thus, I have continually discussed the women on these programs in terms of choices that they made. Scully chose having a career over having a family, as did Ivanova. Delenn chose to undergo the joining, even at the risk of alienating her own people. Aeryn chose to remain with Moya's crew and build a new life for herself, just as Beka chose to join Dylan in the fight to rebuild the Commonwealth, even though it meant personal danger. Some of these women chose to build relationships with an intimate partner and bear children, trying to have it all, like Aeryn, Scully, Torres, Beverly, Jadzia, and Delenn. Some did not, choosing instead to remain single, like Ivanova, Janeway, and Beka, recognizing the difficulty of trying to be all things to all people. Some are still trying to decide who they are and how they fit into their worlds, such as Seven of Nine, Chiana, Ezri, and Sikozu.

Each of the programs discussed in this and the preceding chapters provide a number of colorful and fascinating characters to watch navigate their worlds. All are heroic in Cornillon's sense of the word, yet each is different from the others, unique in her own ways. All provide marvelous role models for the male and female fans who watch these programs. Each can teach us much about what it means to be a woman in her universe, but each also has much to teach us about being a woman in our own.

Some Final Thoughts

Some of you who are great fans of these programs will not agree with my conclusions and that is fine. My goal in writing this book was to examine each of these women from the perspective of identity development. I tried to look at each woman in terms of her past and her present and then tried to determine how she got from that past to this present. To do so, I examined every episode of every year in which a particular program was presented on television. I watched many of the episodes repeatedly. In addition, I read interviews with the actors portraying the characters, writers and producers of the programs if available, fan comments, and program and episode guides, both in print and on-line. I discussed each program and its characters with colleagues whose perspectives I value, and we did not always agree. The episodes that I chose to represent each character's development were chosen with great care. Sometimes a colleague would suggest an episode that I should include. Sometimes the actors themselves, in printed interviews, would discuss a particular episode that they believed was instrumental in the character's development. Each chapter on each program took literally hours to write and luckily I had a high-speed Internet connection allowing me to flip back and forth between my written text and those sources available on-line.

If you have not watched one of these programs, I urge you to do so. I know that some fans are extremely loyal to programs that they love and they believe that loyalty does not allow them to like other programs within the genre. For example, I heard that there were fans of *Deep Space Nine* who refused to watch *Babylon 5* and vice versa. I cannot imagine why; both were excellent. So, check your local listings and sample one of these programs. Look at what is currently on the air and celebrate when men and women are presented heroically. Write letters to the producers, the networks, and the sponsors to let them know that you appreciate intelligent sci fi that depicts men and women in ways that allow them to explore their complete "humanity." There is enough trash on television as it is.

I finished writing this book during the winter of 2004, 30 years after Pamela Sargent stated that even bad sci fi is better than no sci fi as far as imagining worlds where women can explore themselves, where we can explore what we might become. We have come a long way since then and yes we still have a long way to go. But the programs discussed in this book show that we are on the right track. Their popularity, and they reflect a total of 48 years of programming, attests to the fact that fans want literate, well-produced and well-written sci fi that depicts women in positive ways. Thank you for listening. Live long and prosper.

Notes

1. Although interestingly enough, Mulder's degree in psychology is rarely mentioned on the program. As a matter of fact, he acts like he doesn't know anything about psychology most of the time. It makes me wonder what he was really doing over there at Oxford.

2. I will not stop and rant about this classist notion—as if working class women had a choice here.

3. I understand that JMS wrote a story, in *Amazing Stories* magazine, about a future where Ivanova and Marcus were reunited. Unfortunately, I have been unable to obtain a copy of this story, either from the magazine's archives or via the heroic actions of my librarian. Please, if anyone has a copy of this story, send it to me. I will gladly pay charges for copying and mailing.

Selected Bibliography

Books

Alexander, D. (1994). *Star Trek Creator: The Authorized Biography of Gene Roddenberry*. New York: ROC Books.

Alexander, M. (1989). *Women in Romanticism: Mary Wolstonecraft, Dorothy Wordsworth, and Mary Shelley*. Savage, MD: Barnes and Noble Books.

Anderson, S. J., & McIntyre, V. N. (1976). *Aurora: Beyond Equality*. Greenwich, CT: Fawcett.

Asimov, I. (1950). *I, Robot*. Garden City, NY: Doubleday and Co., Inc.

Bacon-Smith, C. (2000). *Science Fiction Culture*. Philadelphia, PA: University of Pennsylvania Press.

Barr, M. (1987). *Alien to Femininity: Speculative Fiction and Feminist Theory*. New York: Greenwood Press.

Barr, M. (1993). *Lost in Space: Probing Feminist Science Fiction and Beyond*. Chapel Hill, NC: The University of North Carolina Press.

Bassom, D. (1996). *The A to Z of Babylon 5*. London: Boxtree Press.

Bassom, D. (1997). *Creating Babylon 5*. New York: DelRey.

Bem, S. (1993). *The Lenses of Gender: Transforming the Debate on Sexual Inequality*. New Haven, CT: Yale University Press.

Bennett, B., & Robinson, C. E. (Eds.). (1990). *The Mary Shelley Reader*. New York: Oxford University Press.

Bernardi, D. L. (1998). *Star Trek and History: Race-ing toward a White Future*. New Brunswick, NJ: Rutgers University Press.

Bleier, R. (1984). *Science and Gender: A Critique of Biology and Its Theories on Women*. New York: Pergamon.

Brannon, L. (1996). *Gender: Psychological Perspectives*. Boston, MA: Allyn & Bacon.

Bukatman, S. (1993). *Terminal Identity: The Virtual Subject in Postmodern Science Fiction*. Durham, NC: Duke University Press.

Caplan, P. J., & Caplan, J. B. (1999). *Thinking Critically About Research on Sex and Gender* (2nd Ed.). New York: Addison-Wesley.

Chodorow, N. (1978). *The Reproduction of Mothering*. Berkeley, CA: University of California Press.

Cornillon, S. K. (1972). *Images of Women in Fiction: Feminist Perspectives*. Bowling Green, OH: Bowling Green University Popular Press.

Cranny-Francis, A. (1990). *Feminist Fiction: Feminist Uses of Generic Fiction*. New York: St. Martin's Press.

Dean, J. (1998). *Aliens in America: Conspiracy Cultures from Outerspace to Cyberspace*. Ithaca, NY: Cornell University Press.

Delasara, J. (2000). *PopLit, PopCult, and The X-Files: A Critical Exploration*. Jefferson, NC: McFarland & Co., Inc.

Denmark, F. L., Rabinowitz, V. C., & Sechzer, J. A. (2005). *Engendering Psychology: Women and Gender Revisited* (2nd Ed.). Boston, MA: Pearson.

Diagnostic and Statistical Manual of Mental Disorders: DSM IV (4th Ed.). (1994). Washington, DC: American Psychiatric Publishing, Inc.

Donawerth, J. (1997). *Frankenstein's Daughters: Women Writing Science Fiction*. Syracuse, NY: Syracuse University Press.

Donawerth, J. L., & Kolmerten, C. A. (1994). *Utopian and Science Fiction by Women: Worlds of Difference*. Syracuse, NY: Syracuse University Press.

Erdmann, T. J. (2000). *Star Trek Deep Space Nine® Companion*. New York: Pocket Books.

Erikson, E. H. (1950). *Childhood and Society*. New York: W. W. Norton.

Erikson, E. H. (1974). *Dimensions of a New Identity*. New York: W. W. Norton.

Erikson, E. H. (1980). *Identity and the Life Cycle* (2nd Ed.). New York: W. W. Norton.

Erikson, E. H. (1968). *Identity: Youth and Crisis*. New York: W. W. Norton.

Erikson, E. H. (1982). *The Life Cycle Completed: A Review*. New York: W. W. Norton.

Faludi, S. (1991). *Backlash: The Undeclared War Against American Women*. New York: Anchor Books.

Fausto-Sterling, A. (1985). *Myths of Gender: Biological Theories about Women and Men* (2nd Ed.). New York: Basic Books.

Freud, S. (1969). *An Outline of Psychoanalysis* (J. Strachey, Trans.). New York: Norton.

Genge, N. E. (1995). *The Unofficial X-Files Companion*. New York: Crown Trade Paperbacks.

Gilligan, C. (1982). *In a Different Voice: Psychological Theory and Women's Development.* Cambridge, MA: Harvard University Press.

Goldman, J. (1995). *The X-Files™ Book of the Unexplained Volume 1.* New York: HarperPrism.

Goldman, J. (1996). *The X-Files™ Book of the Unexplained Volume 2.* New York: HarperPrism.

Green, J., & Lefanu, S. (1985). *Despatches from the Frontiers of the Female Mind.* London: Women's Press.

Helford, E. R. (Ed.). (2000). *Fantasy Girls: Gender in the New Universe of Science Fiction and Fantasy Television.* Lanham, MD: Rowman & Littlefield, Inc.

Hirschman, E. C. (2000*). Heroes, Monsters, & Messiahs: Movies and Television Shows as the Mythology of American Culture.* Kansas City, MO: Andrews McMeel Publishing.

Iaccino, J. F. (1998). *Jungian Reflections Within the Cinema: A Psychological Analysis of Sci-Fi and Fantasy Archetypes.* Westport, CT: Praeger.

Jones, G. (1999). *Deconstructing the Starships: Science, Fiction and Reality.* Liverpool: Liverpool University Press.

Jung, C. G. (1978). *Flying Saucers: A Modern Myth of Things Seen in the Skies.* (R. F. C. Hull, Trans.). Princeton, NJ: Princeton University Press.

Jung, C. G. (1964). *Man and His Symbols.* New York: Dell.

Kaschak, E. (1992). *Engendered Lives: A New Psychology of Women's Experience.* New York: Basic Books.

Ketterer, D. (1974). *New Worlds for Old: The Apocalyptic Imagination, Science Fiction, and American Literature.* Bloomington, IN: Indiana University Press.

Killick, J. (1998b). *Babylon 5 ™ Season by Season Guide: The Coming of Shadows* (# 2). New York: DelRey.

Killick, J. (1998d). *Babylon 5 ™ Season by Season Guide: No Surrender, No Retreat* (# 4). London: Boxtree.

Killick, J. (1998c). *Babylon 5 ™ Season by Season Guide: Point of No Return* (# 3). London: Boxtree.

Killick, J. (1998a). *Babylon 5 ™ Season by Season Guide: Signs and Portents* (# 1). New York: DelRey.

Killick, J. (1999). *Babylon 5 ™ Season by Season Guide: The Wheel of Fire* (# 5). New York: DelRey.

Kolmar, W. K., & Bartkowski, F. (2005). *Feminist Theory: A Reader* (2nd Ed.). Boston, MA: McGraw-Hill.

Labundo, L. (Ed). (2000). *Jane Austen, Mary Shelley and Their Sisters*. Lanham, MD: University Press of America, Inc.

Laqueur, T. (1990). *Making SEX: Body and Gender from the Greeks to Freud*. Cambridge, MA: Harvard University Press.

Lavery, D., Hague, A., & Cartwright, M. (Eds.). (1996). *"Deny all Knowledge:" Reading the X Files*. Syracuse, NY: Syracuse University Press.

Le Guin, U. K. (1979). *The Language of the Night*. New York: G. P. Putnam's Sons.

Le Guin, U. K. (1969). *The Left Hand of Darkness*. New York: Ace Books.

Leonard, E. A. (1997). *Into Darkness Peering: Race and Color in the Fantastic*. Westport, CT: Greenwood Press.

Levine, G., & Knoepflmacher, U. C. (1979). *The Endurance of Frankenstein: Essays on Mary Shelley's Novel*. Berkeley, CA: University of California Press.

Levinson, D. J. (1978). *The Seasons of a Man's Life.* New York: Knopf.

Levinson, D. J. (1996). *The Seasons of a Woman's Life.* New York: Ballantine Books.

Lowry, B. (1995). *The Truth is Out There™: The Official Guide to The X Files™.* New York: HarperPrism.

Lowry, B. (1996). *Trust No One™: The Official Third Season Guide to The X Files™.* New York: HarperPrism.

Matlin, M. W. (1996). *The Psychology of Women* (3rd Ed.). Ft. Worth, TX: Harcourt Brace.

Meisler, A. (1998). *I Want to Believe™: The Official Guide to The X Files™ Volume 3.* New York: HarperPrism.

Meisler, A. (1999). *Resist or Serve: The Official Guide to The X Files™ Volume 4.* New York: HarperPrism.

Meisler, A. (2000). *The End and the Beginning: The Official Guide to The X Files™ Volume 5.* New York: HarperPrism.

Mellor, A. K. (1988). *Mary Shelley: Her Life, Her Fiction, Her Monsters.* New York: Routledge.

Merrick, H., & Williams, T. (1999). *Women of Other Worlds: Excursion through Science Fiction and Feminism.* Crawley: University of Western Australia Press.

Mortimore, J., Adams, A., & Clark, R. (1997). *Babylon 5 Security Manual.* London: Boxtree.

Nemecek, L. (1995). *The Star Trek The Next Generation® Companion.* New York: Pocket Books.

Nichols, J. K. (1998). *Mary Shelley: Frankenstein's Creator: The First Science Fiction Writer.* Berkeley, CA: Conari Press.

Nichols, N. (1994). *Beyond Uhura: Star Trek and Other Memories.* New York: G. P. Putnam's Sons.

Noble, D. F. (1992). *A World Without Women: The Christian Clerical Culture of Western Science.* New York: Oxford University Press.

The Oxford Desk Dictionary and Thesaurus, American Edition. (1997). New York: Berkley Books.

Palmieri, M. (Ed.). (1999). *Star Trek Deep Space Nine® The Lives of Dax.* New York: Pocket Books.

Penley, C., Lyon, E., Spigel, L., & Bergstrom, J. (Eds.). (1991). *Close Encounters: Film, Feminism, and Science Fiction.* Minneapolis, MN: University of Minnesota Press.

Pierce, H. B. (1983). *A Literary Symbiosis: Science Fiction/Fantasy Mystery.* Westport, CT: Greenwood Press.

Piercy, M. (1976). *Woman on the Edge of Time.* New York: Fawcett Crest.

Pounds, M. C. (1995). *The Star Trek Generations.* Toronto: Monograph Series of the Toronto Semiotic Circle.

Puschmann-Nalenz, B. (1992). *Science Fiction and Postmodern Fiction: A Genre Study.* New York: Peter Lang.

Rishoi, C. (2003). *From Girl to Women: American Women's Coming-of-Age Narratives.* Albany, NY: State University of New York Press.

Roberts, R. (1993). *A New Species: Gender and Science in Science Fiction.* Urbana, IL: University of Illinois Press.

Roberts, R. (1999). *Sexual Generations: "Star Trek: The Next Generation" and Gender.* Urbana, IL: University of Illinois Press.

Ruditis, P. (2003). *Star Trek Voyager® Companion.* New York: Pocket Books.

Russ, J. (1975). *The Female Man.* Boston: Beacon Press.

Russ, J. (1995). *To Write Like a Woman: Essays in Feminism and Science Fiction.* Bloomington, IN: Indiana University Press.

Sargent, P. (Ed.). (1976). *More Women of Wonder: Science Fiction Novelettes by Women about Women.* New York: Vintage Books.

Sargent, P. (Ed.). (1977). *The New Women of Wonder: Recent Science Fiction Stories by Women about Women.* New York: Vintage Books.

Sargent, P. (Ed.). (1974). *Women of Wonder: Science Fiction Stories by Women about Women.* New York: Vintage Books.

Schelde, P. (1993). *Androids, Humanoids, and Other Science Fiction Monsters.* New York: New York University Press.

Seymour, M. (2000). *Mary Shelley.* London: Picador.

Shapiro, M. (2001). *All Things: The Official Guide to The X Files™ Volume 6.* New York: HarperCollins.

Shaw, D. B. (2000). *Women, Science and Fiction: The Frankenstein Inheritance.* Houndmills, Hampshire: Palgrave.

Shelley, M. (1818, 1831). *Frankenstein, or The Modern Prometheus.*

Shelley, M. (1836). *The Last Man.*

Simpson, P. (2003). *Farscape™: The Illustrated Season 4 Companion.* London: Titan Books.

Simpson, P., & Hughes, D. (2000). *Farscape™: The Illustrated Companion.* New York: Tom Doherty Associates.

Simpson, P., & Thomas, R. (2002). *Farscape™: The Illustrated Season 3 Companion.* London: Titan Books.

Simpson, P., & Thomas, R. (2001). *Farscape™: The Illustrated Season 2 Companion.* London: Titan Books.

Sunstein, E. W. (1989). *Mary Shelley: Romance and Reality.* Baltimore, MD: The Johns Hopkins University Press.

Tavris, C. (1992). *The Mismeasure of Woman*. New York: Oxford University Press.

Tavris, C., & Wade, C. (2003). *Psychology in Perspective* (3rd Ed.). Upper Saddle River, NJ: Prentice Hall.

Tong, R. (1989). *Feminist Thought: A Comprehensive Introduction*. Boulder, CO: Westview Press.

Van Luchene, S. R. (1973). *Essays in Gothic Fiction: From Horace Walpole to Mary Shelley*. New York: Arno Press.

Weedman, J. B. (Ed.). (1985). *Women Worldwalkers: New Dimensions of Science Fiction and Fantasy*. Lubbock, TX: Texas Tech Press.

Wilson, C. (1998). *Alien Dawn: An Investigation into the Contact Experience*. New York: Fromm International.

Wilson, R. A. (1998). *Everything is Under Control: Conspiracies, Cults, and Cover-ups*. New York: HarperPerennial.

Wolmark, J. (1994). *Aliens and Others: Science Fiction, Feminism, and Postmodernism*. Iowa City, IA: University of Iowa Press.

Yoder, J. D. (1999). *Women and Gender: Transforming Psychology*. Upper Saddle River, NJ: Prentice Hall.

Papers, Periodicals, and Book Chapters

Archer, S. L. (1992). A feminist's approach to identity research. In G. R. Adams, T. P. Gullotta, & R. Montemayor (Eds.), *Adolescent Identity Formation* (pp. 25 – 49). Newbury Park, CA: Sage.

Armitt, L. (1991). Your word is my command: The structures of language and power in women's science fiction. In L. Armitt (Ed.), *Where No Man Has Gone Before: Women and Science Fiction* (pp. 123 – 138). London: Routledge.

Badley, L. (2000). Scully hits the glass ceiling: Postmodernism, post-feminism, posthumanism, and *The X-Files*. In E. R. Helford (Ed.), *Fantasy Girls: Gender in the New Universe of Science Fiction and Fantasy Television* (pp. 61 – 90). Lanham, MD: Rowman & Littlefield, Inc.

Bainbridge, W. S. (1982). Women in science fiction. *Sex Roles, 8,* 1081 - 1093.

Baker, N. (1997). Creole identity politics, race, and *Star Trek: Voyager*. In E. A. Leonard (Ed.), *Into Darkness Peering: Race and Color in the Fantastic* (pp. 119 – 129). Westport, CT: Greenwood Press.

Barr, M. S. (2000). Revamping the rut regarding reading and writing about feminist science fiction: Or, I want to engage in "procrustean bedmaking." *Extrapolation, 41,* 43 – 50.

Bartter, M. A. (1992 – 1993, Winter). Science, science fiction, and women: A language of (tacit) exclusion. *ETC: A Review of General Semantics, 49,* 407 – 420.

Berger, A. A. (1981). A personal response to Whetmore's "A Female Captain's Enterprise." In M. Barr (Ed.), *Future Females: A Critical Anthology* (pp. 162 – 163). Bowling Green, OH: Bowling Green State University Popular Press.

Biersdorfer, J. D. (2000, Feb. 6). Not-so-brave new world: Sci-fi TV runs aground. *The New York Times*, p. 3.

Blair, K. (1983). Sex and *Star Trek*. *Science-Fiction Studies, 10,* 292 – 297.

Bonner, F. (1996) From the female man to the virtual girl: Whatever happened to feminist SF? *Hecate, 22,* 104 - 120.

Cioffi, K. (1985). Types of feminist fantasy and science fiction. In J. B. Weedman (Ed.), *Women Worldwalkers: New Dimensions of Science Fiction and Fantasy* (pp. 83 – 93). Lubbock, TX: Texas Tech Press.

Cooper, B. L. (1977, December). The traditional and beyond: Resources for teaching women's studies. *Audiovisual Instruction,* 14 – 18f.

Day, P. J. (1982). Earthmother/Witchmother: Feminism and ecology renewed. *Extrapolation, 23*, 12 – 21.

Donawerth, J. (1990). Teaching science fiction by women. *English Journal, 79*, 39 – 46.

Donawerth, J. (1990). Utopian science: Contemporary feminist science theory and science fiction by women. *NWSA Journal, 2*, 535 – 557.

Downing, N. E., & Roush, K. L. (1985). From passive acceptance to active commitment: A model of feminist identity development for women. *Counseling Psychologist, 13*, 695 – 709.

Erikson, E. (1964). Inner and outer space: Reflections on womanhood. *Daedelus, 93*, 582 – 606.

Fishburn, K. (1993). Reforming the body politic: Radical feminist science fiction. In S. Roberts (Ed.), *Still the Frame Holds: Essays on Women Poets and Writers* (pp. 29 – 46). San Bernardino, CA: The Borgo Press.

Friend, B. (1977). Virgin territory: The bonds and boundaries of women in science fiction. In T. D. Clareson (Ed.), *Many Futures, Many Worlds: Theme and Form in Science Fiction* (pp. 140 – 163). Kent State, OH: The Kent State University Press.

Friend, B. (1972). Virgin territory: Women and sex in science fiction. *Extrapolation, 14*, 49 – 58.

Ginn, S. R. (2000). Aeryn Sun to Xena, Babylon 5 to Voyager: The new women in the new science fiction. Paper presented at the 23rd annual meeting of the Southeastern Women's Studies Association, Boone, NC.

Ginn, S. R. (2004). BABS and babes: Reconstructing gender in science fiction television. Paper presented at the 27th annual meeting of the Southeastern Women's Studies Association, Savannah, GA.

Ginn, S. R. (2002a). "Space: The Final Frontier": Visions of future space for women. Paper presented at the 25th annual meeting of the Southeastern Women's Studies Association, Valdosta, GA.

Ginn, S. R. (2002b). Our space, our place: Women in the worlds of science fiction television. Paper presented at the annual meeting of the Popular Culture Association of the South, Charlotte, NC.

Heilbrun, A. B., Jr., & Mulqueen, C. M. (1987). The second androgyny: A proposed revision in adaptive priorities for college women. *Sex Roles*, *17*, 187 – 207.

Heller, L. E. (1997). The persistence of difference: Postfeminism, popular discourse, and heterosexuality in *Star Trek: The Next Generation*. *Science-Fiction Studies*, *24*, 226 - 244.

Iaccino, J. F. (2001). *Babylon 5's* blueprint for the archetypal heroes of Commander Jeffrey Sinclair and Captain John Sheridan with Ambassador Delenn. *Journal of Popular Culture*, *34*, 109 – 120.

Jenkins, H., III. (1991). *Star Trek* rerun, reread, rewritten: Fan writing as textual poaching. In C. Penley, E. Lyon, L Spigel, & J. Bergstrom (Eds.), *Close Encounters: Film, Feminism, and Science Fiction* (pp. 170 – 202). Minneapolis, MN: University of Minnesota Press.

Kanar, H. E. (2000). No ramps in space: The inability to envision accessibility in *Star Trek: Deep Space Nine*. In E. R. Helford (Ed.), *Fantasy Girls: Gender in the New Universe of Science Fiction and Fantasy Television* (pp. 245 – 264). Lanham, MD: Rowman & Littlefield, Inc.

Kaplan, E. A. (1990). Sex, work, and motherhood: The impossible triangle. *Journal of Sex Research*, *27*, 409 - 426.

Kelso, S. (1997). Brother Raspberry: Dialogues with the alien in recent women's sf. *Foundation*, *71*, 88 – 101.

Kessenich, T. (2002). *Examinations: An Unauthorized Look at Seasons 6 – 9 of The X-Files, Featuring the Reviews of Unbound 1*. Victoria, BC: Trafford Publishing.

Ketterer, D. (1997). Frankenstein's 'Conversion' from natural magic to modern science. *Science-Fiction Studies*, *24*, 57 – 79.

Kramarae, C. (1987). Present problems with language of the future. *Women's Studies*, *14*, 183 – 186.

Kreitzer, L. (1996). The cultural veneer of *Star Trek*. *Journal of Popular Culture, 30*, 1 – 29.

Kuhlman, M. (2004). The uncanny clone: *The X-Files*, popular culture, and cloning. *Studies in Popular Culture, 26*, 75 - 87.

Lancaster, K. (1997, June 5). Epic story of 'Babylon 5' takes on the 'big questions.' *Christian Science Monitor*, p. 13.

Law, R. (1983). Science fiction women: Victims, rebels, heroes. In D. M. Hassler (Ed.), *Patterns of the Fantastic* (pp. 11 – 20). Mercer Island, WA: Starmont House.

Le Guin, U. K. (1976). Is gender necessary? In S. J. Anderson & V. N. McIntyre (Eds.), *Aurora: Beyond Equality* (pp. 130 – 139). Greenwich, CT: Fawcett.

Lips, H. M. (1990). Using science fiction to teach the psychology of sex and gender. *Teaching of Psychology, 17*, 197 - 198.

Marcia, J. (1980). Ego identity development. In J. Adelson (Ed.), *Handbook of Adolescent Psychology* (pp. 159 – 187). New York: Wiley.

Marcia, J. (1994). The empirical study of ego identity. In H. A. Bosma, T. L. G. Graafsma, H. D. Grotevant, & D. J. De Levita (Eds.), *Identity and Development: An Interdisciplinary Approach* (pp. 67 – 80). Thousand Oaks, CA: Sage.

Marcia, J. (1989). Identity and intervention. *Journal of Adolescence, 12*, 401 - 410.

Marcia, J. (1987). The identity status approach to the study of ego identity development. In T. Honess & K. Yardley (Eds.), *Self and Identity: Perspectives Across the Lifespan* (pp. 161 – 171). London: Routledge & Kegan Paul.

Mason, M. S. (1999, May 28). Goodbye, 'DS9,' Hello 'Crusade.' *Christian Science Monitor*, p. 17.

Mason, M. S. (1999, Feb. 6). Orbiting around the TV universe of science fiction. *Christian Science Monitor*, p. 15.

McEldowney, P. F. (1994). Women in Cinema: A Reference Guide. This guide was retrieved from the following web address: http://www.people.virginia.edu/~pm9k/libsci.womFilm.html. (If you cannot access this website, email me and I will send you a hard copy. I could not access it summer 2004, but that could be temporary. The author states that the list is incomplete, but is updated as new information becomes available).

Monk, P. (1980). Frankenstein's daughters: The problem of the feminine image in science fiction. *Mosaic*, *13*, 15 – 27.

Mumford, M. R. (1985). The brass brassiere: Sexual dimorphism in science fiction illustration. In J. B. Weedman (Ed.), *Women Worldwalkers: New Dimensions of Science Fiction and Fantasy* (pp. 193 – 206). Lubbock, TX: Texas Tech Press.

Ney, S., & Sciog-Lazarov, E. M. (2000). The construction of feminine identity in *Babylon 5*. In E. R. Helford (Ed.), *Fantasy Girls: Gender in the New Universe of Science Fiction and Fantasy Television* (pp. 223 – 244). Lanham, MD: Rowman & Littlefield, Inc.

O'Bannon, R. S. (2003, May). Horizons. *Farscape: The Official Magazine*, No. 12, pp. 21 – 29.

Parker, I. (1996). Psychology, science fiction, and postmodern space. *South African Journal of Psychology*, *26*, 143 – 150.

Patterson, S. J., Sochting, I., & Marcia, J. E. (1992). The inner space and beyond: Women and identity. In G. R. Adams, T. P. Gullotta, & R. Montemayor (Eds.), *Adolescent Identity Formation* (pp. 9 – 24). Newbury Park, CA: Sage.

Purinton, M. J. (2001). Mary Shelley's science fiction short stories and the legacy of Wollstonecraft's feminism. *Women's Studies*, *30*, 147 – 175.

Rabkin, E. S. (1981). Science fiction women before liberation. In M. S. Barr (Ed.), *Future Females: A Critical Anthology* (pp. 9 – 25). Bowling Green, OH: Bowling Green University Popular Press.

Roberts, R. (1995). It's still science fiction: Strategies of feminist science fiction criticism. *Extrapolation, 36,* 184 – 197.

Roberts, R. (1996). "No woman born": Immortality and gender in feminist science fiction. In G. Slusser, F. Westfahl, & E. S. Rabkin (Eds.), *Immortal Engines: Life Extension and Immortality in Science Fiction and Fantasy* (pp. 135 – 144). Athens, GA: The University of Georgia Press.

Roberts, R. (1990). Post-modernism and feminist science fiction. *Science-Fiction Studies, 17,* 136 – 152.

Roberts, R. A. (2000). Science, race, and gender in *Star Trek: Voyager.* In E. R. Helford (Ed.), *Fantasy Girls: Gender in the New Universe of Science Fiction and Fantasy Television* (pp. 203 – 221). Lanham, MD: Rowman & Littlefield, Inc.

Rogers, A. (1997, June 9). Master and slave of 'Babylon 5.' *Newsweek, 129,* 63.

Rogers, A. (1987). Questions of gender differences: Ego development and moral voice in adolescence. Unpublished manuscript. Harvard University.

Rossan, S. (1987). Identity and its development in adulthood. In T. Honess & K. Yardley (Eds.), *Self and Identity: Perspectives Across the Life Span* (pp. 304 – 319). London: Routledge and Kegan Paul.

Russ, J. (1972). The image of women in science fiction. In S. K. Cornillon (Ed.), *Images of Women in Fiction: Feminist Perspectives* (pp. 79 – 94). Bowling Green, OH: Bowling Green University Popular Press.

Sanders, S. (1977). Invisible men and women: The disappearance of character in science fiction. *Science-Fiction Studies, 4,* 14 – 24.

Sanders, S. (1981). Women as nature in science fiction. In M. S. Barr (Ed.), *Future Females: A Critical Anthology* (pp. 42 – 49). Bowling Green, OH: Bowling Green University Popular Press.

Sargent, P. (1977). Introduction. In P. Sargent (Ed.), *The New Women of Wonder: Recent Science Fiction Stories by Women about Women* (pp. xiii – xxxiv). New York: Vintage Books.

Sargent, P. (1974). Introduction: Women in science fiction. In P. Sargent (Ed.), *Women of Wonder: Science Fiction Stories by Women about Women* (pp. xiii – lxiv). New York: Vintage Books.

Sargent P. (1996). Women and science fiction. In C. C.-G. D'Arcy & J. A. G. Landa (Eds.), *Gender, I-deology: Essays on Theory, Fiction, and Film* (pp. 225 – 237). Amsterdam: Rodopi.

Savage, L. (1997). *Babylon 5*: The big finish. *Computer Graphics World, 20*, 65 - 66.

Sheen, E. (1991). 'I'm not *in* the business; I *am* the business': Women at work in Hollywood science fiction. In L. Armitt (Ed.), *Where No Man Has Gone Before: Woman and Science Fiction* (pp. 139 – 161). London: Routledge.

Shindler, D. T. (2001, May 21). The truths of science fiction. *Publisher's Weekly*, pp. 76 – 77.

Silbergleid, R. (2003). "The truth we both know": Reader desire and heteronarrative in *The X-Files. Studies in Popular Culture, 25*, 49 – 62.

Spector, J. A. (1981). Science fiction and the sex wars: A womb of one's own. *Literature and Psychology, 31*, 21 – 32.

Spelling, I. (1998, April). Captain Courageous. *Starlog*, #249, 41 – 43.

Spelling, I. (1998, April). The Lady Borg. *Starlog*, #249, 27 – 31.

Thomas, S. (1991). Between the boys and their toys: The science fiction film. In L Armitt (Ed.), *Where No Man Has Gone Before: Woman and Science Fiction* (pp. 109 – 122). London: Routledge.

Thomson, D. (1997, December). The bitch is back. *Esquire, 128*(6), 56 – 57.

Vaughn, S. F. (1991). The female hero in science fiction and fantasy: "Carrier-bag" to "no-road." *Journal of the Fantastic in the Arts, 4*, 83 – 96.

Watson, B. (1995, August). My psychiatrist tells me I have 'sci-fitis'. . . but he is one of them. *Smithsonian, 26*(5), 96.

Weedman, J. B. (1985). Preface. In J. B. Weedman (Ed.), *Women Worldwalkers: New Dimensions of Science Fiction and Fantasy* (pp. 5 – 8). Lubbock, TX: Texas Tech Press.

Weinkauf, M. S. (1977). The daughters of *Frankenstein*: Women and science fiction. *Cthulhu Calls, 5*, 22 – 26.

Whetmore, E. (1981). A female captain's *Enterprise*: The implications of *Star Trek's* "Turnabout Intruder." In M. Barr (Ed.), *Future Females: A Critical Anthology* (pp. 157 – 161). Bowling Green, OH: Bowling Green State University Popular Press.

Wilcox, C. (1992). To boldly return where others have gone before: Cultural change and the old and new *Star Treks*. *Extrapolation, 33*, 88 – 100.

Wood, S. (1978-1979, Winter). Women and science fiction. *Algol, 9* – 18.

Worrell, J. (1996). Feminist identity in a gendered world. In J. C. Chrisler, C. Golden, & P. D. Rozee (Eds.), *Lectures on the Psychology of Women* (pp. 359 – 370). New York: McGraw-Hill.

Yaszek, L. (2003). Unhappy housewife heroines, galactic suburbia, and nuclear war: A new history of mid-century women's science fiction. *Extrapolation, 44*, 97 – 111.

Film and Video

Babylon 5. The collected episodes of all 5 seasons are available on DVD from Warner Home Video. The 5 made-for-TV movies (*The Gathering, In the Beginning, Thirdspace, The River of Souls,* and *A Call to Arms*) are available in a boxed set.

Farscape. Collected episodes of seasons 1 - 4 are available on DVD from ADV Films. *Farscape: The Peacekeeper Wars* will be available January 2005.

Gene Roddenberry's *Andromeda.* The collected episodes of season 1 & 2 are available on DVD from ADV Films.

Star Trek: Deep Space Nine®. The collected episodes of all 7 seasons are available on DVD from Paramount.

Star Trek: Enterprise®. None of the episodes are available as of fall 2004.

Star Trek: The Next Generation®. The collected episodes of all 7 seasons are available on DVD from Paramount.

Star Trek®: The Original Series. The collected episodes of all 3 seasons are available on DVD from Paramount. All of the Star Trek® movies are available on DVD singly and in collection from Paramount.

Star Trek: Voyager®. The collected episodes of all 7 seasons are available on DVD from Paramount.

The X-Files. The collected episodes of all 9 seasons are available on DVD from Twentieth Century Fox as is the film, *The X-Files.*

Index

Note: Female characters like Aeryn, Delenn, Ivanova, and Scully who appear in substantive detail in a particular chapter are only listed in the Index if mentioned in chapters unrelated to their television program. Television programs are treated the same way.

About the Author

Dr. Sherry Ginn is Assistant Professor of Psychology at Wingate University and also serves as the Director of the Women's Studies Program. She received her degree in General Experimental Psychology from the University of South Carolina in 1988 and pursued post-doctoral work at the East Carolina University School of Medicine. Dr. Ginn taught at East Carolina University for a number of years before joining the faculty at Wingate, located 25 miles southeast of Charlotte, NC, Dr. Ginn's hometown. Dr. Ginn loves to read, primarily mysteries, and watch horror and sci fi movies and television. She also loves to travel, especially to the British Isles and Ireland, where she pursues clues as to her Irish and Scots-Irish identity. Correspondence to Dr. Ginn should be addressed to her at the Department of Psychology, Wingate University, Wingate, NC 28174.